To Alex & Elise,

The answers are in here somewhere. Thank you for your support, my good friends. Love ya.

Gary Hill
1-24-06

The Real Lives of Dreamers

Jazz, Blues, Love, and Money

by
Barry Nix

authorHOUSE

1663 Liberty Drive, Suite 200
Bloomington, Indiana 47403
(800) 839-8640
www.AuthorHouse.com

© 2005 Barry Nix. All Rights Reserved.

No part of this book may be reproduced, stored in a retrieval system, or transmitted by any means without the written permission of the author.

First published by AuthorHouse 11/11/05

ISBN: 1-4208-5618-9 (sc)
ISBN: 1-4208-8582-0 (dj)

Library of Congress Control Number: 2005904571

Printed in the United States of America
Bloomington, Indiana

This book is printed on acid-free paper.

I have become a stranger to the world
Where once I used to waste a lot of time;
It has so long now heard nothing of me,
It may well think that I have died!

Indeed, I am not much concerned
Whether it believes me dead.
I cannot even contradict it,
For really, I am dead to the world.

I have renounced the worldly bustle
And live in peace in a quiet place.
I live alone in this, my heaven,
In my love, in my songs.

Friedrich Rűckert

1

Paul and Nicole
2002

Something was wrong. Correction, many things were wrong, many somethings. Paul Warner couldn't get up, but it was nothing physical. It was inertia. The inertia of a thousand things gone wrong at the same time. Defying probability. Straining the limits of plausibility. His perfect storm. So he lay there, on his self-created island of beauty, on his stacked, fluffy, allergen-resistant pillows, rustling sheets with stratospheric thread-counts and pushing aside a rich, fluffy comforter in his home of a thousand dreams, unable to rise.

His mind was active, alive with possibility and numbed by circumstances. His senses were enhanced, as they usually were. Birds sang to each other, attracted to his suburban Philadelphia sanctuary. Too many birds. They had come from everywhere. Like unlikely tourists unable to resist a free first-class ticket to a sunny beach in winter they had called everyone they knew, sent carrier pigeons far and wide to spread the news. Or so he supposed. Tens of species partied in four-part harmony and cooed to each other in loving tranquility. His nostrils took in the scents of late spring. A look out of his bedroom window revealed bursts of color: blue rhododendrons, purple irises, red, white, and pink peonies, white and yellow tulips, and several reddish Japanese Maples, all tastefully landscaped in a carefully cultivated two acres of weed- and clover-free Kentucky bluegrass. He was looking forward to the blooming of the Chinese grass and roses in the next several weeks.

He managed to reach over to a remote control. He pushed a button and the blues filled the beautiful, sun-drenched room; the blues of the hobo life lived on and off freight trains; the blues of men blowin' into towns in their Cadillacs with a pocketful of money and raisin' hell; the blues of broken-hearted men drinking whiskey; the blues of scared men running from chain gangs and followed by wild-eyed prison guards sloshing through swamps behind barking hound dogs; the blues of women who had endured enough slaps upside their heads and warned as much. He still couldn't move. The player switched to another CD. A tenor saxophonist improvised over a steady, bluesy bass line and a wicked drum pulse. That has to be Billy Hart or Jack DeJohnette on those skins, he thought, making that horn player sound better than he is, floating over the gospel-like chord changes laid down by the piano player. He turned up the volume as he became happy for no reason other than the music. Then the music stopped. His morning concert was over. Finally, he rose. Another day. What for?

He had excelled as a crisis manager, strolling into difficult situations with a level head and a virtual satchel full of electronic tools and leaving with a roomful of smiles behind him. And a fat check. He was an ex-athlete and an ex-soldier, a take-charge man. He rescued information technology projects from certain doom, put together teams of like-minded performers. He solved problems. He made the decisions that chicken-shit managers couldn't. He pushed people to perform. The incompetents, the deadwoods, hated him. The frustrated, the heretofore desperately quiet waiting it out, sacrificing their souls to keep an autistic child in a caring setting, or slogging through to provide everything for spoiled brats who really needed more of their time than their money, loved him. He had completed the first two chapters of a book detailing his philosophy and methods when the market for his services dried up faster than a grape in a Texas drought. He was still spinning a year later, wondering whether to ride it out or change his direction completely. He had been burning out a little and gaining weight, true, but he loved the action. He had fallen into the trap he warned everyone about. 'Make sure you have a life outside of work', he said. 'Don't define yourself by your job. Look at the Europeans.' How had it happened? Solve the problem.

Sitting in the garden by a small waterfall, a book of poetry Paul had given her by her side, Nicole was having her own problems coping with their new reality. She had become unfamiliar with adversity since their meteoric rise from nothing which, she told herself, was accomplished on the strength of their educations, their drives, and their strategy for upward mobility. She began to second-guess their investment decisions, their career decisions, and their friendships. True, they had dropped a bundle like everyone else, but Paul insisted on turning it into something else, some cosmic payback with dramatic repercussions. She paid all of the bills secretly from their other account, the one he refused to acknowledge existed. Although he claimed to be okay with it, he felt guilty for doing so well, for rising so far from his humble beginnings. They even had a name for it: Sudden Wealth Syndrome. Then the bottom fell out. The great Dot-Com Bust. Dreams of air. Thieves. Irrational exuberance. Recession.

Something would have to give soon. She couldn't keep up this charade much longer. He refused to listen to reason. She began to have trouble sleeping. Paul cut expenses to the bone. Good grief! She was running out of patience.

Paul, sensing her frustration, almost wished she would start drinking, feeling that it would somehow be easier to put up with than her constant parading about. They made each other miserable — his inertia, her haranguing — though neither thought of leaving, or so he thought. She understands, he told himself.

On top of all this, Paul thought, his body was letting him down. The decline of his physicality, aside from an accident or disease, was as devastating a loss as he could imagine. His body, in its musculature, its quick, cat-like movements, its strength, its welcoming reception to clothes, its pleasure-giving propensities, its generation of compliments, had guided the course of his life. Together they, his mind and his body, had traveled from the streets to sports fields and hard courts to the military in tens of states and several countries. He had climbed into and out of places designed to keep him out and in. He had engaged in impulsive sex and inspired, fulfilling love in unlikely settings and with unlikely women; but not now. He was not handling middle age well at all.

He cursed his body as his legs lost their spring, as the myriad minor injuries suddenly decided to tally themselves into an invoice he very suddenly seemed unable to pay, his hundred thousand mile surprise he called it. After years of requiring only minimal maintenance he now had to watch everything he ate, drank, and breathed. He swallowed medications for back pain and mold spores, stretched stiff muscles that cramped at every opportunity, gingerly rehabbed ankles that had gone under the knife; just as he had hit his career stride, too. A late bloomer? No. He was unlucky. The lucky ones were those who knew what they wanted to do with their lives by the time they were twelve. His good looks and beautiful body had imprisoned him in his own vanity; his love of freedom led him to live a fully improvised life, leaving him quite unprepared for a sedentary middle age that was normal, boring, and entirely unacceptable. At least he still had a full head of healthy hair, thank God. That would have put him over the edge.

In his recline, he often thought of sex, of the sluts he knew. Loose, throaty, and wide open sex. Yes, he had known some real sluts in his day, young, sensual women who didn't give a damn, confusing men with their pussies, always wet, always available, their bodies always pliable, responsive to every caress and every nibble. They weren't the most attractive women but they didn't have to be. Their availability made them more desirable than any made-up, dieting tease who chastised men for needing pleasure in their lives. Somehow, the sluts always found the sensitive ones, the ones who wanted to make a go of it, to turn off emotionally. The sex was free and usually the best that these young men would ever experience, certainly better than that offered by the good girls they would eventually marry; but they were stingy with their emotions, refusing to be possessed, except in bed. The sluts usually left town when they decided to seek respectability and leave their reputations behind them. If not, it didn't matter because responsible, frustrated men could smell freedom in their skirts and see their lost youth in their eyes, although they were often the same age. Yes, sluts performed a valuable service. Paul knew that and always appreciated them, held them in the highest regard. Sort of.

Sex. Hmmph. Not the same anymore. He had a gut now, not too bad but enough to get in the way. He moved slower, couldn't contort like he used to. Not enough sluts, anyway, certainly not in his age group and definitely not in his class. Then again, maybe he just couldn't see them anymore, like he couldn't see other signs of life, or clearly enough to risk Nicole's wrath, although he was sure she wouldn't mind a diversion here and there. She practically said as much. The truth was, he didn't want to be bothered. He hadn't met a woman who did anything for him in a long time. He wouldn't have minded needing a woman so badly that he would be ready to change direction, lose everything, dream of a future together, change his life, feel alive. Well, you have to get out of the house to meet 'em, right?

He remembered how much he loved burying his head between a pair of fleshy thighs and making them shake like dishes in a china cabinet during an earth tremor, rendering the owner of those thighs limp and having his way with her. The rest was really extra, right? Most women, he reasoned, could do with just a little pounding as long as they got a lot of licking, anyway. It may have been his looks that got him into their beds back in the day, but it was his rocking of the little man in the boat that kept him there.

So. On with life. Gradually, refusing to wallow in the mire of the self, he began to lose weight and read novels again. He became easier to get along with. The loud roar of everyday physical pain — the stiffness and tightness that had been made worse by hour upon hour of sedentary intellectual activity, teeth-grinding commutes, and daily workday stress, the body worn down from years of ceaseless athletic activity — had quieted somewhat to a steady hum which responded well to pain-killers, long walks, and extended stretching. His street-playing basketball days, though — flying through the air and eliciting ooohs and aahs from players and spectators alike, turning and twisting, jump shots and finger rolls, backboard blocks and area-clearing rebounds — were over.

He had been tough under the boards. You'd better not come in there with any okey-dokey stuff 'cause it would get slapped away. He was quick, too. His best shot, the one that got them going, was the turn-around, fade-away jump shot. It was a thing of beauty.

Then he felt absurd after months of depression, perhaps an indication of good, well, better, general emotional health. He no longer cried at the drop of a hat, at anything even remotely sad in the many art films he rented, with subtitles in several languages, or having even a tangential relationship to a vaguely-remembered situation that may or may not have occurred twenty years ago if, perhaps, the moon had been full and the brown/black/blonde-haired woman he was with felt as he did, if only for a short time. Sometimes, only a hit or two on a joint would unlock the details of those days, when he smoked daily and often. He had long ago given up trying to explain the magic of those days. It was more than the loss of, in many ways, an idyllic youth, for the loss was not merely within himself; the magic was gone. The world was too caught up in a new type of ruthless, savage capitalism, holding the magicians at bay with disdain, worshiping the sanctity of emerging markets and low interest rates. There *is* magic here today, he thought. Somehow, I've got to find it. Where do I begin? The simple questions, like the simple declarations borne of experience and a perception of the truth, always appealed to him, for they never changed. 'Life's a motherfucker!'

THE REAL LIVES OF DREAMERS

He was beginning to recover. Yes, only weeks before tears had simply needed to flow. Now there was room for hope. His emotions were out front again, leading the charge, dictating his actions and defying practicality like they hadn't in twenty years. He listened again to music of yearning and mysticism, conjured dreams of darkness and sensuality and dark-haired women with full mouths, lush breasts, and mysterious eyes dancing around a fire under a black, moonlit sky. Airy, tribal music by artists who, as far as he was concerned, didn't record enough, who inhabited many of his same places, the dwellings of the courageous. Dangerous places, full of the hyper-sensual, the hyper-emotional and often, the hyper-intelligent. A world of feeling where men, possibly considered failures in the material world, are often praised as heroes of another sort; where women need the smell and feel of many men, controlling them as they let themselves be worshipped, appreciated, and used; giving instead of bartering, receiving instead of resisting, reveling instead of tolerating. Celebrating men. So few did by the time they reached forty these days, in America, anyway. Yes, a different world, the sensual one, like the old days but farther away now; a world where the only purpose of material things is to enhance the sensual with speed and textures, colors and scents, tastes and sounds. It is a world from which workaholics seek refuge in the corporation, happy, if they're lucky, to find a family of colleagues united in a common, non-sensual goal, creating something viable from nothing or not much. These practical souls couldn't function for any length of time in the sensual world. Many were driven to the edge of sanity by lovers who thrived beyond their emotional capacities. They could not abide lives lived in poetic ecstasy, and were rendered incapable of coping with the teasing, testing, and crossing of their narrow emo-

BARRY NIX

tional and sensual boundaries. He, like so many others, had lived in both worlds, longing for one while prospering in the other.

Or, he considered, his recovery could stem from a peculiarly persistent, yet tragic, optimism — when reality dictated pessimism, a more self-destructive emotion which could lead him by an unsteady hand to the depths of depression for the remainder of his days — regardless of an assessment of the reasons not to, a cost-benefit analysis of the irrational. But there *were* no benefits. Ha, ha! He had been in that cold place before; many times, in fact. But, wait.

"It'll be alright."

"Put your faith in God."

"The Lord will provide."

"Good things come to those who wait."

"Don't worry."

He couldn't stomach naïve, idiotic, self-serving, unintelligent sentimentalism, especially not now, in the middle of his recession/depression. So what to do now? He wished he could go to a neighborhood bar or barbershop and find commiseration and laughter, feel like he belonged, drink a stiff drink and get a decent haircut. Such was his loss; the isolation of the social one.

And what did being black, oh, an African-American, mean today? Damned if he knew. He had always been a staunch integrationist. He remembered drying the dishes, back in '63 when he had a family life, and hearing news of the bombings of the Birmingham church. Three little girls? Such terrorism was beyond his comprehension, schooled as he was in the ways of the Catholic Catechism and taking it more to heart than most of the other children. It was a no-nonsense announcer who gave him the news on New York's WOR that morning. Somehow it reached Bucks County without an antenna. Negroes, for they were Negroes then, pursued a cause, as far as he could tell, with dignity and grace. Even then, he had a nose for who was telling the truth and who was trying to lead the gullible down the garden path.

He led a rich life, sharing cultural niceties and odd tastes with people from all over the world. He never hesitated to express his discomfort and suspicion of those who insisted on the superiority of their race, sex, religion, or musical sub-genre. Now, though, narrow minds seemed to prevail everywhere. An educated, well-traveled, relatively wealthy black man married to a white woman didn't stand a chance in such an environment. So, like so many others, he retreated.

He came of age in a political and cultural golden era, distancing himself from the hatred that the riots of the mid to late sixties and the Black Power Movement encouraged. He went out with women he liked, color or class be damned. Class, though came to matter much more than color ever would.

He had different heroes. Besides the obvious ones of the time, there had been the no-nonsense achievers like the Celtics' Bill Russell, the working men down the street, Sam Cooke, Otis Redding, and the shrewd congressman Adam Clayton Powell, Jr. For the thousandth time he asked himself what happened. He read everything he could get his hands on that offered some kind of plausible explanation. He was labeled a conservative because he believed in education, such a time-honored axiom of upward mobility as to be beyond question. He was labeled a conservative because he believed that a man worked at becoming the best man he could and that included working jobs you hated and not fathering a child until you were emotionally and financially ready. 'Too middle class', they said. 'Fuck you', he said. He refused to be questioned by functional illiterates hell-bent on retaining the mentality of slaves.

His acquaintances ran from him before they became friends.

"Too many of our people are full of excuses," he would continue. "For what? For profane, money-making machines we call culture while still sticking our hands out for free money, for reparations? All I want is opportunity and access to capital. The rest is up to us. You can't work a system you don't know, and you can't change a system you can't work."

The true artists and intellectuals, he argued, had been bullied underground, unorganized and isolated, by cursing thugs who served as cultural muscle for semi-literate nationalist and Afro-centric totalitarian thought police. They, the artists and intellectuals, had been thwarted in their goals by ignorance which intimidated, persisted, and prevailed. They were lost, rejected by the people they hoped to encourage, and accepted by white folks, 'the other camp', whether out of guilt or the recognition of genuine talent. They found a platform with an unintended audience and shook their heads in disbelief at their powerlessness compared to the lure of the quick buck, the unholy marriage of accounting and the debasing of a culture.

The cultural transmission, the passing down of survival tactics, had slowed to a trickle. Paul had experienced it. Many fathers vaporized, but many sons rejected the ones who stayed, who tried hard, and broke their hearts. There is no alternative value system, no cultural infrastructure. They are left with their own mistakes to make, to be paid for by everyone.

Sensible people found him insufferable, unable to enjoy himself in a nice social gathering. Un-sensible people ran from him. They called him crazy. 'Prove to me that I'm wrong,' he would plead, 'please!' Some tried. None did. He waited, hoping. The good, moral people he met invariably tried to lure him to their church to worship. Secular morality was unacceptable, the secular humanists vilified as bible-rejecting atheists. You want a social life with good people, you gotta listen to the preaching. Don't dwell on it. Don't drive yourself crazy. Do what you can.

He walked around the house and grounds again; truly beautiful, an oasis of the spirit. Such a peaceful place when it wasn't in turmoil. He never had a chance to enjoy it properly while working like a dog to get it, renovate it, and show it off. He was back to basics now. They had set aside a year's worth of expenses, a hundred grand, and it was almost gone. Their portfolio? Ha! Down by half a million, and there was nothing coming in. Un-fucking believable.

The grieving left him, returned, left again, returned. His depression sprang, not from some biological infirmity, but from environmental reductionism, the reduction of all things civil and good, the glorification of the inarticulate and increasingly illiterate, the in your face, mouthy shallowness of the purely materialistic. Here they come again, no, there they go; the whining, the drinking binges, the second-guessing, the hours sat staring at nothing, the days spent drunk and dreaming of exotic orgies on tropical islands, the complete isolation. The reading helped. There was a time….

He absorbed long-ignored, pristine volumes on his bookshelves, well-reviewed and purchased with good intentions, looked at longingly as he rushed to another of his endless appointments. Finally, as he re-entered the realm of the intellect, he prepared himself for erudite discourse, thought about acquiring more letters to put behind his name, picked up his torch and embarked on a search for the truth, a few honest people, and the perfect orgasm. He wanted to like himself again.

Once that was settled, his mission defined, he mapped out a strategy and a plan for execution. He designed a stress-reduction plan. He rarely went into Philly. He avoided personal contact with everyday people. He stayed away from teenagers and residential contractors. Small talk had lost its luster. He pooh-poohed anything to do with technology on more than a superficially informative level. Living within his own self-defined parameters, he felt the stress practically melt away from his mind and body. His palms no longer sweated, his breathing improved, the knots in his stomach unwound themselves, the muscles in his back loosened. He slept better than he had in years. Amazing. Even his complexion cleared up somewhat.

He followed the logic. He escaped to an even deeper interior world, long-since dormant, in which he found an almost hallucinatory cloud of pleasure, but not very conducive to the making of money and the sustaining of affluent living. So…. what to do now? Keep going.

He worked out harder and lost more weight. He was a more pleasant person. Some saw him as living proof of all those formulaic, syrupy messages of hope, a testament to the power of the Lord, a walking billboard for the power of positive thinking. Others looked at him questioningly, wondering how he could be so happy as his ship was so apparently sinking. He had no shame, they thought. 'Yes, we're looking for a change,' he would say, upsetting the delicate balance of the overworked slobs who, like himself, had been disappointed after achieving, or nearly achieving, the American Dream.

The reality was more complicated. It was The Mythologist who saved him, the anthropologist who searched and found cosmic life and mythology duplicated in disparate cultures, and spiritual meaning in mythological hopes and dreams. At times, Paul felt blinded by the wonderful sense of it all. He had wanted to know The

Mythologist, one of his many adopted fathers, and old Hollywood cowboys Robert Ryan, Lee Marvin and Woody Strode — the lone brother riding on the prairie in the John Ford Westerns — and Rod Steiger, who faced hard realities with a voice like thunder and never faltered. He wanted to know the writer Harold Robbins, whose characters grew up dirt poor and became rich, and all the other strong men in his books, his treasured books, and some old wise men he had searched out, if only once, and John Coltrane and Joe Henderson and the other musicians who may or may not have known how they affected a young brother from the inner city trying to get ahead in life, all of life. And Martin Luther King. Of course, Martin the Courageous. And Malcolm X, the late stage Malcolm, repenting and worshipping with the blue-eyed and the brown. You took whatever you could from whomever and wherever you could get it, anything to get you through this life. They didn't have to lead model lives. They only had to show him that they had some answers.

But how could a person know a man like the Mythologist, he asked himself, except through his books, disregarding the fact that he had left the physical world more than fifteen years before? He was, to Paul, a vast, unknowable spirit emanating light and dignity and knowledge. That was what Paul wanted for himself, but how would he get it? Somehow, he felt as though he had unwittingly embarked on his journey to the next level of his bliss, usually a conscious endeavor, as if nudged by the wet nose of a spirit-seeing dog.

Why don't more men want this? They do, he argued, but they don't feel free enough to express it with each other, except maybe the gay men, who were outside of his realm of intimate knowledge. Was there also a Jungian joining of the collective unconscious in homosexual pairings, a sharing of what homosexuals through history had known, the oppression to which they had been subjected?

BARRY NIX

He had once discussed this with a homosexual, a doctoral candidate in Sociology, who had dismissed the idea as absurd. Insisting on the correctness of his premise, Paul thought at the time that 'here is a man destined to be unhappy'.

His spirit rose from the underground, emerging scarred from the temples of commerce and strengthened by cultural immersion. Where to go? 'The divine is in yourself,' The Mythologist argued, 'but in the educated, aware self who reads and reflects.' Paul asked, 'Am I alone again? I need a partner.' But none came. He heard The Mythologist's voice, soothing but firm.

'She is not ready. You are the hunter. You must do this alone. Use your skills to bring back the nourishment your village needs. Prepare yourself for a new, higher, transcendent ecstasy. Consult the great texts for guidance. There are no limits.'

Paul had mentally enacted this scene with such clarity that he felt as if, by the sheer force of his desire for leadership, for companionship, that this mythological construct, anthropomorphized from his readings, was a vision hovering in a light blue mist just above his left shoulder. Immediately, without understanding that he had done so, he accepted the challenge.

He suddenly realized he was in his car, stopped at a traffic light, but everything seemed distant. There was some commotion around him. People seemed to be floating by, but he ignored them. He was tired. Too tired, too much thinking. Just relax. The dog, the spirit-seeing one, nudged him again. Despite himself, where was he now (?), he drifted away to pleasure, to the sound of distant Celtic bagpipes. He saw green Irish fields as if he were in an air balloon above them. He wondered about his next erotic encounter. Someone called his name. It was too late. Lush fields. Rich music. No limits. Gone.

THE REAL LIVES OF DREAMERS

Somewhere in Space

"Who started this conversation?" Paul asked

A refined voice, apparently of upper-class origins, replied. "I did. I am you and you are me and we are all together, but we are not the same. We argue too much. Let's just get along. Why can't you just listen to reason?"

"Reason to a corrupt man is an entirely different thing than reason to a natural man."

"So, I'm a naturally corrupt, reasonable man. A splendid mix of qualities in these times, don't you think? I mean, come on, old man."

"So I've adopted an English accent now?"

"Sorry, old boy…"

"Never call me boy!"

"Ooh, yes, sorry about that, cultural context and all that. So, where were we? Ah, yes, my personal qualities. What does any of that matter now, in this den of solipsism, this cave of the self, however many selves there are?"

"I'm tired."

"Yes, you're perpetually tired these days. Leave the running of affairs to the rest of us while you get your rest and dream your rich, multi-colored, surround-sound dreams."

"How else do I escape awareness and corruption, blown opportunities and lost love?"

"Oh, my my, you've got it bad and that ain't good. Maybe what you need is a sophisticated lady and some Prozac."

"And what exactly is a sophisticated lady in these harsh, post-modern, post-feminist times? I'm a throwback to another time. I thought sophistication meant graciousness and good manners. I thought money was discussed in the most general of terms. I thought languages and history and music mattered, and education was valued for its own sake. I thought discipline, for men and women, ladies and gentlemen, mattered. Leave me to my dreams."

"You have always been a dreamer. You have always lived in your books, your dreamy music, your surreal paintings, your film noirs, your staged representations. Don't you know that your authors, your artists, were creating worlds as vehicles for their own unreal ideas?"

"I've been to the mountaintop! In the real world!"

"It's only a summit! Martin knew that! Where the air is rare, and all of the people are as in a Garrison Keillor world, good-looking and above-average! Oh, and, yes, well-behaved and profound and well-read and well-spoken and full of love for each other, and lacking in jealousy and evil thoughts! Where no one is chemically imbalanced, no children are addicts, and all parents are very, very good parents! ……You are not an old man yet….You are too young for such thoughts. I, on the other hand…….I do love you, you know."

"I hope so. You are me….. You love me too much."

"We shall see, mein freund. We shall see. *Hast du gut geschlafen, mein selbe.* Sleep well, my self."

"Wake up."

"I am awake and asleep, floating and falling."

THE REAL LIVES OF DREAMERS

"Oh, will you give me a break?! Your soul-mates have been informed and they are on their way, seeing as you're in no position now to deny them their concern for you, you stubborn fool."

"I don't….oh, what's the use? Fine, bring them on. I don't need their help now, though, not like before."

"And who knew that? Did you give anyone the faintest clue, silent one? Oh, yes, keep it to yourself, strong and unshakeable. Play the hand you're dealt and all that, right?"

"Leave me. Just let me know when they arrive."

"And what about Nicole? Do you care how she feels, how she is taking all of this?"

"Just tell her that I am very, very tired."

"There's no room on the mountaintop, no salt in the ocean, only in the old wounds you are scratching. I think she's found someone else."

"How does he compare to me?"

"He doesn't compare to you, fool, but he's there, in mind and body, flesh and spirit, not gazing off into the stars and claiming to be there for her."

"She understands. When are they coming?"

"Soon. You have time for a few more good dreams, although I would have thought you'd have dreamt all there is to dream by now. Good Lord. Don't worry; I'll take care of all the niggling details."

"What did you say?"

"I said niggling, the small and bothersome details...oh, never mind. It's me! Do you worry about me?! Are you that paranoid?"

"Not paranoid. Ever diligent, always alert."

"Then tell yourself."

"I told you. For the hundredth time, you are me."
"Am I still?"

A pause. "Well, if you're going to linger, make yourself useful. How did I get here?"

"That's a long story, isn't it? Have you some time? Ha, ha. Of course you have. But it's not only your story that matters. Your soul-mates must be heard. There are one or two others, as well."

"Sigh, sigh. If you insist. I will behave contrary to my nature. I will be patient."

"Ah. Good show. Now we're getting somewhere. It's your nature that got us into this mess, isn't it, your refusal to just go along? Oh, never mind. Where shall we begin? How about 1967? And don't interrupt, please."

2

Paul
Philadelphia 1967

One summer night, when he was fourteen and on his way to becoming a man of his own design, young Paul Warner stepped into a semi-crowded subway car at Broad Street and Susquehanna Avenue in North Philadelphia, the inner city, the ghetto, Chocolate City, the 'hood, or whatever euphemism you please. Always observant, wary for signs of impending danger, he looked to his right and found a seat facing a girl about his age with smooth brown skin and searching round eyes. Across the aisle from each other, bathed in a yellowish light, they sat on plastic seats, rocking back and forth with the speeding train. She looked into his eyes and past them, asking questions for which he had no answers, offering gifts he was unable to accept or even understand, insistent. As innocent as he was, he returned her gaze and glimpsed his future, rumbling into the night in an anonymous, unspoken reverie.

Philadelphia 1971

His parents never respected him enough in those days, not to his face anyway. They didn't have to, though, in those days. They gave him food and shelter, didn't they? What else did he expect? He was the smart one, lacking in much common sense, they told him. Of course, there was no correlation made between this observation and the fact that they never taught him anything about common sense, or what it was, just that he was expected to have it. They never exposed him to those situations that would have lent themselves to the yielding of secrets of surviving in a hostile world. He would rarely encounter anything nearly as hostile as his own family, whether through action or neglect, inference or glare. His athleticism and creativity were ignored, taken for granted and indicative of how strange he was. They only knew that he was very smart, and very different. He was on his own.

He was a thinker and a dreamer, endlessly curious, easily bored, and rarely challenged. He did many things well, unbowed by even the slightest sense of inferiority which debilitated so many of his peers. His intelligence provoked fear, although the Catholic nuns in his elementary school never discouraged him. He sat in, by today's standards, unconscionably large classes and learned well but, to his detriment, lost interest easily, already a dreamer. He played baseball and tackle football and bottle caps and marbles, read books by the armload until, at the age of ten, he was in the adult section of the library, but only after having absorbed boyish adventure stories and tales of survival in all kinds of exotic locations. And the sports books! He read more sports biographies than Louisville had sluggers, more deep-in-the-trenches football stories than Wilson had leather.

Almost completely on his own — through observation or serendipitous exposure, but never, it seemed, through conscious adult instruction — he discovered jazz at four, the blues at eight, basketball at twelve, hard rock at sixteen, women at fifteen, weed at seventeen, depression at twenty-two, renewal at twenty-six.

1971. Before Watergate. Before Sam Erving woke up a generation and made us question where we were headed. When AIDS was a mis-spelling of people who assisted others, and crack was only a fissure. Still the sixties really, the first time he lived the song *Walking in the Rain* by Eddie Kendricks, the former Temptation, about a broken-hearted man hiding his tears in a storm. When he first heard the song he felt Eddie's sadness, but hadn't yet walked that particular walk. Not like now, letting the rain fall on his face, indistinguishable from his tears, as long as his brow didn't wrinkle up in pain, and as long as his mouth didn't distort itself into a sad frown. Tears and rainwater formed salty rivulets on either side of his face and gathered at his chin, inched their way down his neck and under his shirt, caressed his nipples and incited a shiver, added to the tightness in his chest, the shallow breathing, the sickening knot in his stomach, the physiological manifestations of the pain in his soul, in his young, broken heart.

He was nineteen and every love song now made sense; Isaac Hayes rendering soul to a Glenn Campbell hit, moaning for an entire album side of being repeatedly disrespected and wondering what the woman he loved, in spite of her despicable behavior, would be doing by the time he got to Phoenix; Otis Redding pleading to us all to try a little tenderness; Lou Rawls bemoaning his dead lover in *St. James Infirmary*; James Brown urging his baby to reconsider pleeease, pleeease, pleeease; and Ray Charles wailing 'I'm a Fool for You' after waking up and looking over to where his "baby used to lay". He was one of them now, a brother with a broken heart, a young man who understood some of the fundamental truths of life. Looking back over the years, he remembered that pain and how it had shaken him. He was only nineteen. He was lucky. His pain had let him know how alive he had been early in life. He had experienced unimagined joy, then fallen horribly, the first iteration of a madly recurring pattern. Again and again and again. Damn!

"You're getting ahead of ourselves. Go back to '68."

"Yes, you're right, for once."

1968 - 1973

During the summer of 1968, having gotten no further than that subway in his pre-romantic life, he played basketball almost all day of every weekday. He would never care for organized sports, for they imposed their own interpretation of his abilities, which he generally resented. His body baked by the sun, by July his really, really light-brother February pallor had achieved the patina that reminded Caroline of the crust of just-right cornbread. He was too thin, not a muscled man, but a sinewy and graceful man-child, still growing, gaining confidence in his game every day, strong and scrappy. He walked with the swagger of an athlete because he earned it, a contrast to his too-young, too-innocent face; a face that would not show its age or the wisdom its owner had searched for until several years after the fact, to the surprise of many suddenly-bedded women under the impression that they had been in charge of the proceedings with a fresh-faced kid.

BARRY NIX

Caroline, up from South Carolina for the summer and staying with a cousin, was fifteen and a virgin, not an easy feat given her looks, all hips and breasts, and a drop-dead smile set in a slightly round face. Her hair, black and straightened and never combed quite right, contributed to a look of wantonness that drove boys, obviously, and men, only somewhat less obviously, absolutely crazy, all the more so because she was very selective about whom she spoke to, and even more so about whom she spent time with on the playground. She brought her five-year-old cousin down the ten blocks or so to Berks Playground because those in her cousin's neighborhood, by the projects at Twenty-fifth and Diamond, were full of gang members and drunks who wouldn't leave her alone.

At first she just smiled and waved. After a few days of this, when it felt like the natural thing to do, he came over to talk. Up close, she was bigger than he thought, teetering on that border between what black men of that generation called 'stacked,' or built like a 'brick house', and overweight. She was curvy, soft and feminine, and when she opened her mouth to speak, when that slight drawl left her mouth and kissed his face, he thought he was gonna die. He hadn't wanted much to do with girls. They didn't play basketball, they weren't reading James Baldwin and Harold Robbins and Chester Himes, and they hadn't yet offered to solve the problem of 'the aching hardness' which distracted him in class and irritated him to no end. They spent pleasant afternoons talking. He had no money, nor the promise of any. He didn't need much, just his room, some food, a soda or two during the day, basketball, and a little book money. Taking a girl out seemed frivolous until that summer. He was learning to live, preparing a life, in large part dictated by Baldwin - the too-sensitive intellectual wanderer of the urban underside - and Robbins, the street-tough, uncompromising, knowledgeable man

THE REAL LIVES OF DREAMERS

of wealth and the world. Suddenly he felt poor. He was no longer Robbins's up-from-the-streets Danny Fisher. He was Paul, sweaty, skinny, and broke, his heart racing to this smart girl transcending her surroundings in the same ways he did, and quite naturally.

The first time he walked her home, after having kissed her madly and learning every inch of her face, her tongue, and the inside of her mouth, after having licked her neck, stuck his tongue in her ears, and nibbled on her shoulders in his parents' beautiful, inherited row home until he was wild with passion and tenderly pushed away, after he was able to compose himself, drink some water, and see things more clearly, the emotional release almost, but not quite, as satisfying as his dreams of firing liquid rockets into her deep space, he almost came home a bloody pulp.

The enormity of her request, for him to accompany her to the raging wilds of North Philly, far away from the main thoroughfare of Broad Street, where he later imagined the average tall, skinny, light-skinned suburban teenage transplant who spoke 'propah' English was looked upon with curiosity and asked questions *before* getting his ass kicked, seemed logical enough given his continually-engorged state. That request, drawl-delivered and smiling, obfuscated once again a mind that was too quick for his big-city public high school classes (although his underachievement was viewed as criminal by those with the eyes to see it), sure of itself in many questionable situations, yet lost in a new world of emotion and desire. It was the beginning of his doom, yet the first in a series of events that indicated to him that he was perhaps leading a charmed, doomed life.

He noticed the change as they crossed Twenty First Street. They had walked over to Diamond from 16th and Berks and turned west, crossing 19th and 20th Streets without a thought. They didn't say much, just basked in each other's glow, looking goofy and not caring. The terrain was coarser. There was more litter in the streets and more people on the stoops. It was louder. It became more crowded until they reached the 'Projects', several twenty-odd-story buildings of festering criminality, absent fathers, drunkenness, addiction, and hard-working poor people who, daily and constantly, fended off the pathological hordes. By the time they reached Caroline's cousins' building he just wanted to run away fast.

He counted thirteen ragheads, ranging in age from about nine to twenty, males shepherding their chemically-straightened hair, their 'processes', with 'do rags', shiny black and blue scarves wrapped around their heads and tied in back, different from those worn by a later generation. It seemed that they were all smoking cigarettes. They asked him for money. He gave them the fifty cents he had. They asked him for cigarettes. He had none. They looked at his lean, muscled basketball player's body, knowing he could move gracefully and quickly, sensing that maybe he held promise and was worthy of some respect, the currency held most dear in a market short on middle-class values and hard dollars.

They asked what he thought he was doing around there messing with one of their girls. He stood straight and looked them in their eyes as he paid them the tribute they craved. He told them he was walking her home and sought to explain further when Caroline stepped in and began hollering, telling them to leave him alone. She swung her big bag at the most aggressive raghead. They cleared a path for them to walk, through a gauntlet of sneers, testing his resolve, looking for any sign of weakness. The ragheads followed them to the walkway of the target building, a brick job with sheet metal doors and cinder block walls painted a half-pale, then halfway up a half-dark, green. They walked through dysfunctional hallways smelling of urine and barely lit, providing, not protection from hos-

THE REAL LIVES OF DREAMERS

tile elements, but predatory cover for the sacrificing of the weak, the come-uppance of the arrogant, and the destiny of the unlucky. They made it up to her cousin's apartment and had a rather nice visit, thank you very much.

Before his next visit, he invested in a pack of cigarettes, Kools, and approached the ragheads carefully. He spoke to Raghead Leader first, who returned his greeting, and offered him a cigarette. Raghead Leader smiled. As one by one they approached him, half his pack of twenty was gone and he was in like Flint. Several came to the apartment and requested smokes. He was oh, so glad to oblige. He barely had enough cigarettes to buy his way home.

The next day, he bid Caroline a fond adieu over the phone, and a good flight back to Columbia. He had had enough. She had rather suddenly become less appealing. He walked taller that day, glad that he was walking at all.

Reflecting on it later, he laughed at how easy it had been to win safe passage. There had been no ideological objection. The Ragheads had been bought off as easily as crooked border guards, their palms as greasy as building inspectors who suddenly saw compliance when two minutes earlier there had been ten pages of expensive-to-fix violations, smiling and slapping his back for understanding the rules of the game. No, he wasn't totally bereft of common sense.

Philadelphia was, and is today, not a city, but a town, not a teeming metropolis inhabited by busy worker-ant people, but a series of blocks of stuck-together houses which sometimes form neighborhoods, connected more by subways and buses than by either ethnic pride (separatism?), or civic responsibility (those privileged white people?). It seemed to be a happier place then, for black folks and white folks, discrimination notwithstanding. This was before other ethnic groups and gays mattered at all. The music playing in the streets and blasting from small record shops, leaking out of darkened corner bars and playing in the backs of buses by respectful reefer tokers — "Young man, would you please put that out on this bus?" "Yes, ma'am. I'm sorry. We weren't botherin' anybody, just tryin' to enjoy the music." "Hmm." — was so good that one sometimes wondered how it could get any better. But it did, for a short while, anyway.

    The best of the disc jockeys were legendary, mature, socially committed, and lacking in pretense, so different from today's self-righteous pseudo-sincere who would manipulate their mother's breast cancer to a maddeningly cloying piano soundtrack for ratings. There were Jocko Henderson, Larry Daly, and Jimmy Bishop of WDAS, Sonny Hopson and Perry Johnson of WHAT, the white hipsters Hy Lit on WIBG, Butterball, and Jerry Blavat - the geater with the heater, and the dean of Philadelphia radio, Georgie Woods, also of 'DAS. He loved them for the music they introduced him to. He loved them for their humor and their souls. These were men he admired, men who commanded respect, but who were unashamedly human.

    They were everywhere back then, men with more of a sense of themselves, men who made less, even in inflation-adjusted dollars, than much lesser men do today. These men read the paper, spoke proper English, and tried to observe most of the lessons of the Bible, a great moral document, but never mentioned it. They were more comfortable with women when, he believed, women were more comfortable with themselves as women, playing their game of being weaker, much more valuable to men's souls, much more responsive to good men, much more elegant, much more subtle, than so many who are freer, but so much rougher, so in-your-face, so little more than male imitators today.

It was a summer of James Brown, a year after Otis Redding was lost in a plane crash, and Motown which, with its talent school-trained artists who epitomized in many ways the upwardly-mobile American journey, ruled the popular culture of a country adjusting to Vietnam, hippies, and creeping integration. It was a time when black people had style, real style, and soul music could be felt by almost everyone; if not by everyone, then certainly by enough people to influence the popular dialogue and the collective memory of that time. Today, of course, there is so much good music that goes unnoticed by so many that there is no popular dialogue that matters. It was a world in which he existed, thrived in even, as long as he kept largely to himself and his basketball, his books, and his music.

High school was basketball so well coached it was no longer fun, revelatory learning, and a much-loved, charismatic principal, later killed by the Symbionese Liberation Army after effecting wonderful changes as a superintendent of schools on the west coast. The man who replaced him as principal, during Paul's senior year, went on to educate students in Cleveland and commit suicide when Paul had become a man. His adolescence was filled with death and destruction. He saw something better for himself.

Unlike so many in the Delaware Valley, the eight-county southeastern Pennsylvania and southern New Jersey metropolitan area of and surrounding Philadelphia, Paul never considered going to college locally. Of course, he knew only a few peers who planned on college at all, most being satisfied with no plan, a job, vocational school, dealing dope, or welfare, like their parents and most of their extended family.

He existed so much in his own world that he never stopped to question the uniqueness of his actions given his surroundings. They were the ones who were unaware, he thought, or chose to be, of the real possibilities brought about by exciting civil rights advances; unaware that, for the first time, black folks were given half a chance to train and compete. He was merely embarking on the life of an adventurer, making his way in the world, learning as he went, seeking romance and fortune. Given what he had been reading and listening to, while perhaps not the wisest, this was his most logical course of action.

That his initial foray into higher education (lasting almost two years) was a disaster was due to a combination of complex factors, but could be traced primarily to one, his lack of adult guidance. He was not sufficiently grounded, not sufficiently confident of his place in the world, though, in all fairness, what black teenager was in America in 1971? He hadn't explored enough of the world yet to be stuck in a carrel studying away the prime years of his youth. He had ants in his pants and he had to dance. He had fallen in love with marijuana, music, and sex. His dilemma was that his 'aching hardness' ached no more. He loved smart, sexy, free-thinking college girls and they loved him back. He wanted to be around them all the time. That is how he found himself walking in the rain on that day in 1971, a victim of his own energies. But he kept reading.

Maybe we spoke too quickly when we characterized this time as a disaster, for in fact it would shape much of the next several years. It was only a disaster in that he began to realize his powers. For the first time in his life he had sex every day, usually twice a day, and enjoyed a spike in his reputation when a macho passerby heard his girlfriend of the time grunting, moaning, screaming, and pleading through several closed doors. He was only employing techniques he had read about. As news of these sessions spread, other young ladies were naturally curious and trouble ensued. Oh, Paul was quite willing and free-thinking enough to accommodate these curious young women, but their boyfriends were not as receptive to the idea. Their ideas on sex weren't as, shall we say, *expansive* as his were. He wanted to *expand* his sexual universe in the most positive ways, but was occasionally stymied by the un-enlightened. He bristled at the thought of one person possessing another so completely as to limit their movements. And jealousy! When he felt the pangs of it he tried mightily to cleanse himself, to adhere to his not yet fully-formed philosophy of caring hedonism, caring but uncaring, or better, to remain gracious in his efforts to accept and to share. He was, to his surprise, largely successful. He found that women were more receptive to the idea, the hedonistic part that is, even initiated it, usually in secret, in the farthest and darkest corners of out of the way restaurants, away from those with whom they maintained a more traditional sexual outlook.

Until, usually unexpectedly and against their wishes, they fell in love with him. Unfortunately, he didn't return their love very often, not out of maliciousness, but because he just didn't feel it. Love changed them. They weren't fun anymore, whining and complaining that all he wanted to do was go to concerts and screw. Well, to Paul going to concerts and making love to intelligent, beautiful young women was hardly all there was, it was heaven on earth. Conversation, jazz, rock, and sex. And drugs, of course. Damn their agendas. Security, security. Let's live, he told them. Good girls they were, most of them, from good families and Catholic schools, unschooled in his brand of impetuous freedom. They left, unprepared to live, net-less, on his frightfully-high highwire for very long.

As time went on, he found himself looked upon as an intelligent fool, unwilling to accept the daily misery of life like everyone else. Had he found some people who really enjoyed their straight lives on a day-to-day basis, he might have listened, but he was usually too high to notice. Well-scrubbed and polite he was, but high, with that extra gleam in his eye, that half-charming, half-wicked smile that sent the unadventurous scurrying for any form of cover. His conversation was too wide-ranging, his mannerisms too androgynous at times, especially for a sportsman, and his actions too unpredictable. And only a few understood the music he listened to. Why, he only had one Earth, Wind, and Fire album. Don Cherry? He looked kinda funny. Joe Henderson? Is he a college professor? What kind of music could he make?

One day, the romance without finance thing got to him bad, sent him into a deep, meaningful depression, almost clinical in its depth and breadth, a call to action. No more schemes. His charm was wearing thin. What was happening to the country? The party atmosphere was changing. Fucking disco. The shallow response to real rock and roll and jazz. The blues, though, they just kept chuggin' along, ridin' the rails, pickin' up hobos and lawyers, the thrown-outs and the discontented, the alcoholics and the intellectuals, and the intellectual alcoholics.

Some would say that drugs had been his ruination and spoiled a prime capitalist contributor to society for years to come. But he had found his nature. It lay in the vision of a lone coal miner in the depths of a mine, surrounded by blackness, at first, anyway, and picking away, with a single lamp on his head for light, doomed to search for the untapped mother lode of the soul that was his destiny.

THE REAL LIVES OF DREAMERS

He was aware that he had options, that his life was dictated, to a large extent, by his choices and his nature. It was his nature that got in the way, his nature that dictated his choices in music and reading and women. He had to feed the miner, who proved difficult and insatiable because the mine itself took everything, yielding beautiful nuggets from time to time, always holding out the promise of a divine delivery. His delivery would not, he knew, lead him to the gold-paved streets rhapsodized in inner-city churches, fulfilled after abandoning the material world. Paul's carts of nuggets would only be granted after painful engagement with the real world, abstractions built upon his own empirical findings and long hours of study, and discussions with wise people, some real and many imagined. Yes, he was doomed.

He haunted libraries and playgrounds all over the east coast; played basketball with all kinds of people in all kinds of situations, in all kinds of light. He read treatises in philosophy, political science, and psychology. H studied painting and literature, photography and film. Kant, Rousseau, and Piaget, Baldwin, Richard Wright, Ralph Ellison Chester Himes, and John A. Williams, twentieth century Europeans, the literature of music, Picasso for years, the Impressionists, German Expressionists, the Surrealists, music heard through the audio and spiritual prisms of John Coltrane and Joe Henderson, Shakespeare and Moliere and Charles Fuller and Haki Madhubuti and Addison Gayle, Atget, Man Ray and Cartier-Bresson, Scorsese, Visconti, Ingmar Bergman, Bernardo Bertolucci, and Sam Fuller. Then he tried to relate to the common man. Didn't everybody? They said the sixties ended at Altamont, well definitely with Sam Ervin and the Watergate hearings, but he and a few million others kept on, convinced they could deliver on the promises of a fairy tale time. He paid a heavy price.

BARRY NIX

When he wasn't working one of his many mysterious deals, done to make enough money to avoid the straight nine-to-five world, he was back in Philly listening to jazz on Temple University's radio station and smoking a chunk of Columbia with Arthur, the mad young genius of the ghetto.

They first met in the spring of '67. Arthur had befriended Paul, who "spoke so propah," as Arthur put it, soon after he arrived in North Philly, following his family's financial downfall in late '66. They developed their basketball games together. Arthur was also a swimmer, with a swimmer's well-developed pectoral muscles, short, quick, and a hell of a passing guard. They had become friends, but Paul had always kept his distance, off in his own world. Arthur was going through his own particular hell, though Paul didn't find out until several years later. On the basketball court, the same one where Paul was to meet Caroline a year later, Arthur was a whirlwind of motion, racing up the sidelines and yelling, "Sling it!" to Paul as soon as he grabbed a defensive rebound. Paul slung it and Arthur was at the other end of the court on a fast break before the opposing team could even think about defending him. They usually won four or five games before being sidelined by a fresher team. It was Arthur who had encouraged Paul in his first and only fight, the fight he knew he had to fight to prove himself in the new neighborhood. It was a good fight, begun in moral indignation, executed in Ali-style mechanics, and ended in communal triumph.

THE REAL LIVES OF DREAMERS

Paul had been playing anyone who would play, addicted to the sun, the movement, and the game. One late July evening, a raghead from another neighborhood, a year or two older, was part of the opposing three-man team in a half-court game. As Paul easily dribbled past him, Raghead tripped him. Paul let it go with a "Hey, man." Later in the game, Paul grabbed a rebound and Raghead tripped him again, more deliberately and defiantly. Paul threw the basketball at him hard. It hit Raghead on his thigh. It hurt. Raghead threw up his hands in a boxing stance while backing up.

"Fair one," he stated. This was an invitation to Paul to fight with his hands. Paul stalled by muttering something about playing ball fairly. Raghead repeated his call.

"Kick his ass, Paul!" Arthur shouted.

Raghead was from Oxford Street, just a few blocks away but a different neighborhood. The rumblers from Paul's new neighborhood didn't like him. They wanted to like this new kid, Paul, but they weren't sure. Cat, in his early twenties and the neighborhood boss to the fatherless, good-looking and highly respected, tall and light-skinned like Paul, but heavier, more muscular, having observed the scene and wondered what Paul's response would be, urged him on with an encouraging nod. Paul put up his hands and the thing was on. By this time, a gaggle of onlookers had materialized, many of whom Paul knew. Paul was confident, for he had been intuitively shadowboxing in his basement, preparing for this moment. This was at the height of Muhammad Ali's popularity. Paul had practiced the Ali shuffle, moving around his imaginary opponent, dancing, feinting and jabbing.

Mrs. Parker, the recreation center director, a kindly, caramel-colored, gray-haired woman of fifty-five or so, after being assured that the fighters were not going to heed her pleadings not to fight, ordered them off the court, then off the adjoining baseball field, both of which were city property. By this time, the crowd had grown to about fifty people of all ages, hungry for excitement. They all marched to the alley next to the field and this time the thing was really on.

Paul, who was as right-dominant as anyone ever was, led according to the textbook, uncomfortably with his left hand, tossing ineffectual jabs, keeping the right ready for the hook. It wasn't working. Raghead bloodied his nose with two quick jabs. Paul, defying convention, switched his stance, leading off with his right. His weak left hand would be ineffectual to throw a hook, but that was the chance he took. That was all she wrote. He connected two hard jabs to Raghead's nose and drew blood, too. Instead of settling in for a long, protracted fight of attrition, Raghead pulled off his belt and started swinging it, buckle end out. The crowd, heavily in Paul's favor, moaned, but stayed away as Paul took off his belt, as well, wondering why events had taken this uncertain turn. Then, in a gesture of absurdity, a grown man, short and stocky, with a cast on his left forearm, jumped in and assumed a boxing stance as Raghead retreated. Paul's eyes widened, looking to the crowd for assistance. This time, they proclaimed the fight over. Cat, with his euphemistic green eyes, came in and smiled, hugged Paul and told him he did well as he hoisted him upon his shoulders. At that gesture, Paul felt a rush of pride, and great love for a man who had only spoken to him once or twice before. As Paul's long, skinny legs dangled in Cat's chest, they moved with the crowd, out of the alley and on to 16th Street. James Brown blasted out of someone's radio. The song was *I'm Black and I'm Proud*. There was a true sense of communal joy as everyone laughed and clapped and danced. Arthur chanted,

"Ali!, Ali!" Instantly, the crowd picked up the chant as Paul, lifted high, floated in the summer air under a clear blue sky, his ears ringing with praises from the neighborhood people, the people, more than any others, whose respect he craved. He never in his life fought again.

Arthur, though, never saw a joint, bottle, cigarette, white line, needle, or pipe he didn't like. Paul got high for pleasure. He got high, he experienced pleasure, and he stopped. He had gigantic but manageable appetites. Arthur wanted it all and would beg, borrow, steal, pawn, lie, trick, promise, screw, whine, and lick to get it. When it was all over, he had played horn with everybody who mattered and would generate a universal ain't-it-a-shame-about-Arthur head shake at the first mention of his name. His talent for self-destruction rivaled the famous flameouts of the time. Joplin. Hendrix. Morrison; and the model for too many mid-century artists, Charlie Parker. Well-loved and paranoid, charismatic and always late, a day late, for a gig, his notoriety fueled oil-slick fantasies of back-alley conspiracies against him, paling in comparison to the mad gushers of his own behavior, intense fires stubbornly uncapped despite caring friends and rehab, his destruction assured by the smoldering remains.

Arthur was Paul's soul mate, his teacher, his compatriot, another Harper's Magazine-reading, Lee Morgan-listening, athlete-in-residence. His race to self-destruction broke Paul's heart, especially after June Bug, in a Thunderbird wine-assisted, white people-hating, maniacal moment found himself staring down at his blood-soaked shirt as he listened to the rantings of a shotgun-toting Chinese store owner who had had enough. Much to his surprise, June Bug, at nineteen, left this world for Arthur and Paul to figure out, and Cat would soon be forever lost to heroin, a shadow of his former self at twenty-four.

During his ups and downs, Paul would always be able to retreat to his music and his weed. They remained unchanged. The beautiful, wild saxophone solo was, more or less, the same beautiful, wild saxophone solo ten years later, unchanged when everything and everybody else in his life were not, changing only with his escalating understanding of musical forms and patterns, the variants of expression and improvisation. The reefer only varied in potency and color and the number of seeds it contained. It did not treat him like people did, misunderstanding him at every turn. It did not attempt to belittle him in front of its friends. It did not try to convince him he was worthless. It did not ignore him when he asked for just a little attention. It did not betray his trust in it over and over again. It did not complain when he used it up. These, his music and his marijuana and his books, were the only constants in his life and would be for many years, the secure ports in his many storms, offering unconditional intellectual and emotional satisfaction, leaving him wanting only a woman's touch and orgasmic release.

To many black Americans, the ghetto, that area of big and not-so-big cities in which black people can feel free to be their true selves, or so many would have you believe, is home, despite its problems and its obstreperous psychological texture. This was truer before approximately 1969 than it is today, before integration occurred in suburban housing and in the workplace, and before doing well in school was equated with selling out. By 1973, the decline in desirable inner city housing stock, and desirable inner city morality, was well on its way. The flight of the black middle class, from areas with poor city services where they had been trapped for years, to areas with good services where they weren't wanted at all, had left many inner cities with a dearth of responsible fathers with good work ethics and good communications skills. Meanwhile, the Moynihan Report, in which a seemingly well-meaning former Harvard professor and current Irish-American senator had painted a somewhat accurate but uncomplimentary picture of black family life, was more vehemently ostracized than Muhammad Ali at a VFW meeting. Apparently, there were lies, statistics, and damn lies as the primary colors of emotional denials obscured the pastels of scholarly research and socio-cultural subtlety.

Paul, fresh from his readings, drug use, broken love affairs, and ever-deeper appreciation of rock and roll and hard bop, was confused by the burgeoning ubiquity of black victimhood when he was so hopeful for the future. Hope was dismissed with a sneer, optimism the province of the immature and unworldly. Addiction, poor hygiene, littered streets, and poor reading and writing skills were the lot of the ghetto, and no amount of proselytizing, smiling, willing-to-help young college kids was going to change that. Of course, these kids had their success stories, which often made the front pages, or at least the front page of the community section, but their successes were sellouts to be despised, for they were lacking an essential understanding of the new definition of black power. The new black power apparently resided not in books, grades, businesses, communities, art, and stable nuclear families, but in guns and threats, boycotts and intimidation. Later, of course, the modern minstrels appeared, ex-drug dealer/thugs celebrating their showcase of fantasy violence directed at males who longed for maleness in an increasingly unmale world. They were heralded as the new entrepreneurs, creating wealth and destroying much more as Americans

BARRY NIX

ran over each other to jump on the marketing-generated bandwagon. Black men, of course, were reduced again, no, reduced themselves, to Neanderthal stereotypes, fatherless boys who knew nothing of boxing, discipline, or other male-defining characteristics, playing at being tough. The white suburbanites engaged in their own fantasies, ghettoizing their music, films, and legal system. Here, the naïve and market-saturated proclaimed, is black culture, urged on by the older generation of black folks who should have known better. Until they, those who had fawned over the young because they were young and could still do things they couldn't, who had been too lazy to really parent instead of merely encouraging those with more opportunities than they could have imagined in their youth, who justified it all in the pursuit of money, really began to listen. Paul had been among those who listened early, who saw the signs years before, subsequently ridiculed like an Indian scout warning of a hurricane on a perfect July afternoon. He garnered no satisfaction in being right. Dry yourselves off, motherfuckers.

But that was later. Not yet. Continuing our story, when Paul had been kicked around enough, when he grew tired of futilely attempting to encourage those who saw despair as their birthright as much as others claimed entitlement to power; when he understood that the doors of progress were open only to a few men of color just then and he wasn't one of them before finishing his degree, which he wasn't ready to do just yet, he left. On his own, he merely observed economic life for a long time. He sat on the side. He worked but had no career, centered in culture and learning. He toiled at jobs — easily obtained because he was smart and a quick learner — without joy, released at five o'clock to read good literature and smoke good weed, to listen to good music and play good basketball and love good women. His life was, viewed from the outside, that of a rather

THE REAL LIVES OF DREAMERS

articulate, under-achieving young bum. From the inside, though, he was rich, a wealthy, interior man. He read, questioned, and studied well, learning much of the capitalist existence, alternately fascinated and repulsed. And one day, the time came to act more and observe less. The Vietnam War was over and the volunteer army had been born. Older and wiser, it was time for another adventure.

The Dentist's Office

"It's not so bad now, is it?" asked the big-breasted German dentist with the soprano voice. She leaned over, a big, cushy breast pressing to his shoulder. Paul finally had enough lidocaine and nitrous oxide to answer that no, it wasn't so bad now, a mere positive grunt from the back of his mouth, laden down as it was with plastic-gloved fingers and metal and plastic instruments. He pressed his shoulder into her breast. She did not adjust her position. He sailed away. She went to work.

He spent a few seconds trying to figure how he could feel her breasts pressing against him and hear the music fully, but not feel what she was doing to his mouth. He gave up and relaxed. A voice.

"All pleasure and no pain in the dentist's chair!"

"You again. That whirring sound is interfering with the music."

The dentist. *"Keep breathing through your nose. Don't forget!"*

The voice. "Yes, but you're only deferring the pain of the trauma to a later time."

"Pain deferred is not nearly as bad as pain in the present."

"It will manifest itself later, you'll see."

"Not all of it."

"You must face it now."

"I'm facing it just fine with lidocaine and nitrous oxide, thank you very much."

"You're avoiding reality."

"No, I'm in the chair. I'm doing what I need to do, but I'm in another place. I avoid the suffering, but I'll realize the benefits, healthy teeth."

"Suffering builds character."

"Breathe through your nose!"

"I've got enough character for you and me and the next ten patients."

"You cannot judge that."

"Shh. They're playing *Foreign Affair* by Tina Turner! …….I must be my own judge of character. Call it arrogance."

"I will."

"But I'm floating and you're living in pain."

"You are exhibiting the behavior of an addict. You are no better than a junkie whore who closes her eyes while being defiled."

"Some junkie whores enjoy their work."

"Yes, breathe through your nose."

"You are exasperating. You cannot run your whole life."

"You shouldn't live in the trenches for all of yours."

An angel posing as a dental hygienist asked, *"Is it better now?"*

"Yes, thank you, it just took a little time."

The voice again. "Yes, many things are better with time."

"And many things are better left forgotten, never to be awakened."

"You are a time bomb, unknowingly awaiting your detonation."

"I'm pleasantly defused. You can't comprehend that. I'm sorry for you, and many others."

THE REAL LIVES OF DREAMERS

"Life is pain."

"Breathe through your nose."

"I reject that."

"You cannot contribute to this world in your state."

"That's my dilemma, isn't it? This world is in no state to accept my contributions."

"Draw on your pain and teach."

"People don't want to be taught."

"You must find them. They are out there."

"They must find me. It is the seekers who find knowledge, not the lazy."

"Make yourself available. Do not die with a head and a heart full of unshared knowledge. It is a sin in all cultures, in all religions. There is no justification for it……You are silent."

"There is much that passes for knowledge today. How much of myself must I sacrifice to transmit this knowledge? ……..The angel says that it is time to finish. I'm still breathing through my nose. There's only pure oxygen now, pure…oxygen. "

"Go forth."

"My legs are wobbly."

"Your legs will straighten. Your mind will clear."

"Until next week then. You may want to take something as the lidocaine wears off," the tall, thin, brown-haired dentist from Missouri informed him.

Damn skippy about that, Paul said to himself. He blinked twice, saw her standing beside him, no German accent, no big, welcoming breasts, her eyes narrowed slightly in concern; another dream. She's a loving woman, undoubtedly a good mother, he thought. He wanted to hug her, to give her more strength, but didn't, as she barely managed a polite handshake.

"Yes, until next week. I think the pain will be bearable."

He walked unsteadily to his car and, feeling no pain, adjusted his eyes to the bright sunlight, looked up at an azure sky, took in the oak trees and Japanese maples, and basked in the late-morning, just-right warmth of a clear summer day.

He drove along an unfamiliar, strangely half-toned highway. Him again.

"We're not finished yet, not by a long shot. There is more to tell."

"Isn't there always?"

"You know nothing, still. I couldn't fill a thimble with what you know about Terry."

"Your favorite, eh?"

"Yes. Indeed. Sit back."

THE REAL LIVES OF DREAMERS

3

Terry's Early Years
1965-1968

Terry Blaisdell always wanted to look good and live well. His mother, Yvette, before she went insane, would always tell people about her five year-old who never met a mirror he didn't like, except those under hideous department store fluorescents; and she always made sure his clothes were well-coordinated.

He was the one with the neatest desk. He did well in school and couldn't understand why anyone wouldn't. It was simply a matter of paying attention. Why would anyone not? Later, he realized he had brought a little extra gray matter to the classroom. He was unusually focused and determined from an early age. He didn't know why, except that he loved his solidly middle-class neighborhood in Minneapolis, but wanted a luxurious house overlooking Lake Calhoun. He was one of two biracial children on his block and never understood why he was disliked by some of the darker children. As he got older, they always wanted him to choose, always questioned his allegiances and told him that he couldn't sit on the fence when the revolution came.

Irv, his Jewish father, a well-intentioned but weak man unable to handle the mostly self-inflicted psychological pummeling he took about his black wife and tan, curly-haired child, would look on in wonder, always joyful or depressed, never just around like other fathers. Terry always thought he was strange. Why couldn't he just have fun?

Irv had been disillusioned at an early age. It was never clear to anyone exactly how or why. He sought and found solace in the music of the blues, and comfort in the arms of black women. Yvette, unable to feel the joy of the blues and the subtlety of some of its messages, wouldn't allow him to listen to that music in her presence, feeling it was demeaning and spoke to the rural, illiterate past she was trying to escape. She was a librarian at the University of Minnesota, having graduated from Carleton College just after becoming pregnant with Terry.

Irv's parents, proud of their Jewish traditions, tried to understand their liaison, but didn't. "At least he's got an education," his mother, Sarah, would say.

"He's always in school," Hal, his father, would retort.

"He's a professional student! Maybe if he read the Torah more often he wouldn't be so confused!"

Irv was the rebel, though after a while he forgot if it was because he really believed in what he was espousing or because he thought it would be romantic to rebel against the tradition and honor that his father embodied. Hal blamed it on Sartre and Jack Kerouac and Allan Ginsburg. Irv didn't appreciate who his father, the man, was until it was too late, a sad but common occurrence. Nonetheless, Hal was a proud grandfather to Terry and spoiled him shamelessly, playing hide and seek at the dinner table in their home in St. Louis Park, which Terry had heard referred to as St. Jewish Park by jealous, uneducated people. Hal taught him life lessons that Sarah was sure Terry was too young to understand. Terry loved his grandfather more than love itself. At first, his grandmother was more of a shadowy figure in his memory, always cooking and doing something, never sitting down, always looking forward and never backward, never to the past.

Except for one bitterly cold, that is to say average, day in January. Terry was ten, so that would make it, what, 1965? He was sweating from playing football in the snow underneath a mound of clothes. He walked in to the great, big beautiful house, decorated in the formal German manner with big, heavy, beautifully inlaid wooden furniture and heavy, intricately designed fabrics. He poured himself a glass of ginger ale and saw Hal and Sarah sitting in the living room, listening to what he had learned to recognize as a Chopin etude. Sarah was ruminating about their son Irv, a disappointment, a brilliant disappointment.

"Depressed?! What's he got to be depressed about? What good does it do to think about the past?"

"He's a graduate student. He's getting a doctorate in history. What do you want, he should be a historian who ignores the past?"

"Why couldn't he be a doctor? We're Jewish! We don't need to study history. No wonder he's depressed all the time! I don't want to read any history books! I don't want to know any more!"

She fell into Hal's arms and wept. They had had this conversation before, but Hal, Terry's strong hero, who had endured so much, so much more than his confused son, took Sara in his arms, took off his glasses and wept with her as he lovingly stroked her hair.

THE REAL LIVES OF DREAMERS

Terry, still in his coat and sweaters and scarf and boots, waddled in. This was too much for him.

"Don't cry, oh-ma and oh-pa," he pleaded.

He stood there and began to cry for their sadness that he understood intuitively. Hal, upset at being caught by surprise, saw Terry's innocence on his face, despite his maturity beyond his years, and his heart cried out. Sarah felt guilty. She could never love this handsome boy the way her husband did, but now she hurt for him more than for herself. They reached for him. He ran into their arms and they all cried from way down. Sarah sobbed so hard that she scared Terry. Hal could only cry so much anymore and consoled the two of them with strokes to their necks and soft words of assurance. When they all finished, as the etude ended, they felt much better. They hugged once again and straightened themselves up. Then Hal smiled with an idea.

"How about hamburgers and strawberry sundaes?" he asked.

Instant smiles. Terry and Sara both thought that deciding to enjoy themselves just then was a fine idea. They went into Minneapolis and ate hamburgers and strawberry sundaes until they nearly burst. Hal made crazy, hideous faces at Terry and Sara. Sara chided him, looking around the diner for acquaintances before she made the most hideous face herself and Terry rocked with laughter in the booth next to Hal. They laughed all the way home. In bed later, as he heard them still laughing and talking excitedly, Terry wondered how often anyone could expect to know true happiness as the three of them did on that cathartic night.

BARRY NIX

The events of that day strengthened Terry and made him look at his parents differently. He began to see them as pathetic and weak, always drinking or whining and ignoring him and his need for them to be parents. Hal and Sarah always made more sense, seemed so much more alive, so much more mature, teaching, able to make decisions, like real adults.

Soon after, Irv, overwhelmed by his Jewishness and his interracial marriage and his poor academic performance, left for Europe. Just got up and left. Good riddance. Terry was left alone with his mother and her recently-discovered pride in her blackness. She began to read James Baldwin, imagined herself in Harlem and spat upon, refusing to see that she was in Minneapolis and rather well-liked, and looked at everyone around her differently. She stopped straightening her hair and wearing makeup. Being one of those women who looked fabulous with makeup and homely without it, she attributed the reaction to her new style, or un-style, to backwardness, a white standard of beauty, and a rejection of her true self, along with the accompanying claptrap that type of muddled thinking generated. As her hostility generated hostility, her existence became a self-fulfilling prophecy, full of self-hatred that masqueraded as self-love. Terry was totally confused, but refused to go along with his mother's whining. He had black friends and white friends and accepted anyone who accepted him.

Yvette began to bring very dark men with beards and dashikis to the house. Terry didn't care for some of them, especially the ones who wore sunglasses in the house all the time. He thought there was something wrong with them. They thought they were cool, and that it was alright to call James Baldwin an elitist faggot. They talked a strange language of revolution and oppression and read

THE REAL LIVES OF DREAMERS

poetry, most of it bad. Terry took them at face value and quickly learned who made sense and who didn't. He grew up fast, exposed to so much, possessing, even then, the ability to separate the genuine from the phony, the self-indulgent, and the insincere.

There were some nice parties with the scent of marijuana mixed with sandalwood and strawberry incense until the early hours of the morning, and meetings and pamphlets and women passed around, and talk of a history of oppression. The music almost made all of it worthwhile. He didn't understand some of that, either, but respected it for its emotional honesty. John Coltrane and Archie Shepp and Wayne Shorter and Grachan Moncur. James Brown and Curtis Mayfield he could understand. Get on up! We're a winner!

To his surprise, he found much of value in what they called the Black Arts Movement, proud, educated people determined to be accepted on their own terms. Occasionally, he was even able to hold conversations with some of these young nationalists, those who weren't overly condescending, parroting the party line at him as if he were a fool needing conversion instead of a smart kid. Once, one of them looked at him strangely and was particularly aloof until he finished the bottle of wine he had brought, until he was drunk enough to ask Terry about his lineage and, upon hearing his factual and unashamed description, uttered 'half-breed Jew' under his breath while giving him that pitiful look, that leper look. Terry was stunned, though he had long since learned to turn his heart off when around his mother. Yvette heard this exchange, but pretended she didn't, embarrassed by her son – who had ceased to become much more than a nuisance on her way to self-discovery – only because of what he looked like and what it said about her past thinking.

Yvette was furious that Terry continued to study the Torah, but not furious enough to forbid him to continue, thus forgoing the financial help she received from Hal. That was the only condition that Hal placed on his assistance, that Terry be given the option and the opportunity to continue his studies in Judaism. He had to help. He was no guilty fool, but shamed, nonetheless, by his son's abandonment of his family. Terry was now a year from his Bar Mitzvah and they had heard nothing from Irv.

Terry was fascinated by the planning and the organization required for his ritual entry into manhood. The ceremony was to be held at the synagogue they still trudged to on the north side of Minneapolis to attend, shaking their heads at the new residents, mostly uneducated, black, and poor, and mostly recent arrivals from Mississippi and Alabama. The congregation had begun to flee en masse to St. Louis Park, a south side suburb, and had broken ground on a new synagogue, but it wouldn't be ready for another few years. Their synagogue was a jewel in a rapidly fading neighborhood, built just three years after the war, in 1948, and at a cost of $230,000, a rather large sum in those days.

Yvette asked Terry, in her inimitable and increasingly hostile fashion ('You listen to me, boy!'), not to bring any of his white friends to the house when her friends were over, especially the girls, and then not to bring any 'white devils' to the house at all. It was around this time that she changed her name to Kashima, or Yorima, or some kind of -ima, he couldn't remember, claiming that she was freeing herself from her slave name. Terry thought that was really funny, since he at no time felt like a slave, except when hemmed in by the increasingly-brighter headlights of his mother's insanity as it rounded corners and began to occupy the whole road of his consciousness when he was in her presence.

His only peace was with Hal and Sarah, wonderfully old and wise and full of life. Terry worried because they had begun to move a little slower in the last couple of years. They needed help every now and then, in addition to their housekeeper's assistance. They received it from Terry and their tight-knit community of fellow Jewish émigrés.

Under Hal's tutelage, Terry helped prepare for his Big Day. Despite his aging, Hal was beside himself with excitement. He taught Terry the best phone manners and how to speak with polite authority to get things done. With Hal beside him, Terry handled the bookings and deposits for the florist and the photographer, and made sure the instructions to the caterer were followed to the letter.

Hal always had people over. He read widely and shared freely. He was a wonderful conversationalist, a good thinker, and a gregarious host. Music? Well, there was always music.

Every Tuesday evening Hal's friends would come and listen to a self-styled string quartet play their own sad, intriguing compositions, written many years before, or a Dvorak piano concerto performed by Otto, who had enjoyed some prominence in Berlin before leaving with Hal and Sarah.

Sarah was a bit of an introvert. She lived her life with, and through, Hal. He lived enough for both of them, she would tell anyone who asked. She had two good friends of her own, Franziska and Arabella, both refined, educated women, old friends from the beautiful port city of Lubeck in the German north. They would sometimes go to a very civilized café in downtown Minneapolis and listen to Chopin while sipping tea and eating pastries prepared in the German style, a little more delicate, a little less sweet. Her friends were of the same mind. They didn't talk much. They read about and observed the freedoms the college kids enjoyed as they came running into the café, breathless. They watched the young couples walking and hugging, hooking their fingers in the back pockets of each others' jeans. It made them feel young again. They thought of their parents and their own teen years, filled with so much promise, until...

Hal dragged Sarah, a beautiful philosophy student, out of Berlin, literally kicking and screaming, only weeks before the Nazis seized power in 1933. No one else listened, no one but Otto, who seemingly had the most reason to stay. Most of his other friends called Hal crazy. They all perished in the next several years, all but a few who found their way to him, the leader of the expatriates in St. Louis Park, after the war, with hollow eyes and paper-thin skin, screaming in their sleep, alive only a short time in America, cared for by the congregation, remembering how comfortable they were in telling Hal how foolish he was, never, ever dreaming that they would pay so heinously for a mistake in judgment, for their own arrogance, and the passive acceptance of each brutish Nazi legislative slight until it was too late. No, it was not easy to leave one's homeland, one's *heimat*. Yes, the war and the McCarthy hysteria had taken their toll on her. Then the assassination of that wonderful President Kennedy. And now Vietnam. This was some country they had emigrated to, Sarah thought, ignoring Jews being slaughtered until it suited them to get involved. And the way they treated the coloreds! Not so bad in Minnesota. This was where they all came to be treated better. Yes, everyone in their group was getting rich.

As his Bar Mitzvah approached, Terry moved into the room in the big house in which he'd already spent so much time. Hal gave Terry more books and encouraged him to read The New York Times and discuss the issues of the day. Through his actions and instruction he taught Terry the value of grace under pressure, imparted impeccable manners, directed him to the writers who mattered, and taught his willing pupil how to think logically. And, of course, there were his Jewish studies. Because he learned the art of thinking clearly at an early age, Terry handled his schoolwork easily. He was struck, from his unique vantage point, by the Jewish emphasis on learning, education, and accomplishment, that it was what one did on this earth that counted. The attainment of higher education was expected, as was community service. It was the most tightly-knit community Terry would ever experience.

Sarah was the stickler for table manners, and would accept nothing but grace and charm. She set a beautiful table. They ate on elegant Delft china which sat on wispy tablecloths of fine Belgian lace.

There were rumors, much to the chagrin of the classically-trained musicians and composers in Hal's circle, that they had hired a jazz band for Terry's Bar Mitzvah, a whole group of black men playing that strange music Hal would sometimes play on the exquisite stereo he built himself when he was ready for his guests to leave.

"Listen to this," he would say, "how far is this music from Jewish klezmer music?" While they scratched their heads and scrunched their faces at his analyses, he would close his eyes and listen to horns, too many horns for them, and then strange rhythms and absolutely unacceptable chords from someone who had the nerve to call himself Monk.

Hal won them over one day, though, as they were all searching for coats and preparing to leave, when the most unbelievable arrangement of "Over The Rainbow" came on the radio station from New York through Hal's special antenna. Terry would never forget the looks on their faces. Otto stopped in his tracks and dropped his umbrella, unable to speak, his face contorted in amazement at the horn arrangement that had seemingly found every possible harmonic nuance and demanded the most superior performances from the musicians. And the vocalist! Hal thought it was Billy Eckstein, but it wasn't, as the singer soared and dipped and took ownership of the whole house for a few beautiful, enchanting minutes. When the song ended Otto was in tears. Hans was shaking his head. No one said a word for a full minute before they all clapped as one and talked excitedly about their shared epiphany. Maybe this jazz music wasn't so bad, huh? There was the bridge. Late in their lives they had discovered a new joy that would provide them with endless hours of listening and comparisons and discussions. Hal's eminent status among them, as the former owner of a department store in Berlin and a sage among brilliant men, had been elevated even further, for they would never listen to music in quite the same way again. Hal had known all along that they would respond one day, for he had been subtly re-conditioning their ears, and when the time was right, and for whatever reason, bam! It was all in the context.

The next day, Otto came back and sat down, looking agitated.

"You know that record, Hal, that record?! The singer's name is Austin Cromer. It's from 1956. Nobody knows where he is now. And the arranger? My God, it's a woman! Her name is Melba Liston. And she's a trombonist, too! Oye Ve! She arranged it for Dizzy Gillespie's Big Band. I don't believe it! Who are these people, making music like this?! Don't buy it. I ordered copies for everybody."

A few days later Otto presented the recording to Hal, *Dizzy Gillespie's Big Band Live in Hi-Fi From Birdland.* Otto invited Terry to come with him as he drove around in his Cadillac delivering his gift of music to several of the others who were there that day. They ate and listened and laughed at each stop. Terry enjoyed the company of these adults infinitely more than the goofballs his own age. It was another afternoon to remember.

Otto became obsessed. At the ripe age of fifty-four he would go on to study jazz history and write serious jazz criticism, influencing the art form. At seventy, he assisted in the formation of the jazz studies programs at several small, but prestigious private schools. His wife, Johanna, helped Otto and wondered why it was European Jews who wrote about, promoted and recorded this music that native-born Gentiles pilloried as primitive jungle music and no more.

Hal placed his hopes and dreams in Terry now. After their 'Over the Rainbow' day, Terry began to spend all of his time at the house as Hal became increasingly hostile to Yvette. He refused to call her anything else. He read enough to know that there was most likely a strain of anti-Semitism in her new revolutionary fervor. He would not let her ruin Terry. Not that that was a real possibility. Terry had more sense than was good for him, as the saying went. He sometimes seemed much too old for his years.

Terry's Bar Mitzvah was a great event in the community. Hal stood straight and tall as he greeted guests. He thought he would faint from pride as Terry walked behind the Torah, then conducted the service as if he were born for it. The celebration afterward went as planned. Oh, when the jazz band came out, the room took a collective breath. Not to worry.

"They were so well-groomed and conducted themselves with such flair!" Franzisca said at their cafe the next day.

"I'll say!" Arabella chimed in, a little too enthusiastically. Sarah and Franzisca looked at her suspiciously.

"What?! I just had never seen, I mean, they were so...elegant, but so, so masculine. I've never seen Negro men like that before."

"Hal told me the bandleader used to play with that Ellington fellow, the one people go on about all day," Sarah piped in, happy to contribute.

Everyone who was invited, and Hal was sure it was everyone in St. Louis Park and a few neighboring suburbs as well, attended. What a time, he thought. They played all his favorites, *Take the A Train, Someone to Watch Over Me*, and a whole medley of Cole Porter tunes. What a crowd. They went nuts!, he thought, and the dancing! He hadn't seen many of the people in the room that happy in thirty-five years.

"They made those songs sound easy," he told the barber shop crowd of mostly musicians that had quieted down after greeting him with a standing ovation upon his arrival the following weekend, "but they weren't easy, I'm here to tell you!" That was the best haircut he ever had. Hal's life was almost complete.

Terry could not believe the average thirteen year-old walked away with as much money as he did. Between the envelopes he received that night and the trust fund that his grandparents started for him he would be set up enough to have choices, to take his time and decide what he wanted to do in life. He didn't yet know the costs of the daily living to which he had already become accustomed. He just made the deals. He liked it. Already, he had been dealing with sums larger than Yvette and Irv made in a year.

The next year was punctuated by periods of whirlwind activity and serene calm. That summer, for the first time, Terry accompanied Hal and Sarah on their annual vacation, a month at

THE REAL LIVES OF DREAMERS

the Concord Hotel in the Catskill mountains in upstate New York, the old Borscht Belt. In addition to the vaudeville-style reviews, the Yiddish spoken all around him, and the matzah ball soup (Jewish Penicillin), he saw many of the great Jewish comedians: Henny Youngman, Buddy Hackett, Myron Cohen, Woody Allen. In one summer! He never, ever laughed so much. Kids couldn't go in, but he didn't care. He and a couple of buddies and a girl or two would sit outside the log cabin clubhouse and listen, sometimes laughing louder than the adults inside. His sides would hurt from laughing so much. His stomach hurt. He was hoarse. He should have been on the stage, he suffered so much.

Hal stole jokes all the time. Weeks after returning, he would have the whole neighborhood rolling in laughter, telling a different joke to each person he encountered on his daily walks. One day at the barber shop, while in the chair and waiting for Sol, he told one he had saved up special.

"A nice Jewish girl brings home her fiancé to meet her parents. After dinner, her mother tells her father to find out about the young man. He invites the fiancé to his study for schnapps.

"So what are your plans?" the father asks the fiancé. "I am a Torah scholar," he replies.

"A Torah scholar." the father says. "Admirable, but what will you do to provide a nice house for my daughter to live in, as she's accustomed to?"

"I will study," the young man replies, "and God will provide for us."

"And how will you buy her a beautiful engagement ring, such as she deserves?" asks the father.

"I will concentrate on my studies," the young man replies, "God will provide for us."

"And children?" asks the father. "How will you support children?"

"Don't worry, sir, God will provide," replies the fiancé.

The conversation proceeds like this, and each time the father questions, the fiancé insists that God will provide.

Later, the mother asks, "So how did it go?"

The father answers, "He has no job and no plans, but the good news is that he thinks I'm God."

He shouldn't have told that joke while Sol had scissors in his hand. Hal wore a hat indoors for two weeks.

Krista, an attractive widow of forty-five, especially liked to hear him tell her Buddy Hackett's off-color jokes, their equivalent of a back-alley affair. After he "finished," she would blush a deep red, then run into her house, laughing guiltily and straightening her hair as Hal adjusted his pants' waistband.

One late afternoon in late October, as an orange sun set on orange and brown leaves, after Terry had come in from a long run and showered, Hal called to him from his huge library off the main hallway. Terry loved that room. There were thousands of books there. Hal had instructed him how to catalogue using the Dewey Decimal System, like the libraries in town, and Terry catalogued twice a week for several hours. He had his grandparents, his schoolwork, his Jewish studies, his track, and his music. Life was full.

Hal was deteriorating fast. Terry had accompanied him to his doctor's office twice that week. His voice was raspy. He spoke slowly. He asked Terry how he was doing. Unnecessary. Terry always told him everything, but Hal still had his secrets.

"I'm sick, Ter. So is Sarah. I'm sorry we won't be able to see you grow to become the man I know you will become. I think we did alright, though. I am as proud as a grandfather can be."

Terry cried. He wasn't ready. He cried when they didn't wake up the next morning. He cried as he tore his shirt over his heart to symbolize that they were his true parents and recited the blessing, the Mourner's Kaddish. He cried as he laid their bodies on the floor, covered them, and lit candles. He cried as he called the synagogue's chevra kaddisha, the holy society, to send shomerim, guards, to sit with the bodies. Strangely, they seemed to be waiting for his call. He cried as he grew up, faster still, and made all the burial preparations, hired a detective agency to find Austin Cromer, flew him in from Florida to sing *Over The Rainbow*, and paid him handsomely.

Their friends' grief was immense. The synagogue held a huge service for the two of them and buried them side by side. Terry cried uncontrollably at the funeral, again, for himself. Hal and Sarah had found peace. No more haunting memories. No more stiffness and tired joints. No more medicine. He had lost the last people who really loved him and was now without the emotional support that only family, he thought, could give. Someone with numbers tattooed below his wrist, an old man with sad, knowing eyes, put smelling salts under his nose and he jerked up, grateful and suddenly aware of the sympathetic faces around him. He cried straight through the fifth day of Shiva, thankful that, in the Jewish tradition, all the mirrors were covered. He cried, not for Hal and Sarah, for they were ready, but for himself, for the loss of a life that would be left behind and never regained. On the sixth and seventh days, he silently read the Torah's wisdom, dry-eyed, concerning mourning and grief, on a box in the middle of the ten people who made up his minyan, his prayer group, including Otto and Arabella, Franziska and Sol and Krista.

Terry didn't know how their deaths could be determined to be from natural causes, but knew that they were not self-inflicted. They were just ready. Enough suffering. No one cared how or why, not even the insurance company. They paid without an investigation, without a question. Terry wondered. His parents weren't there. He didn't know who he was.

Hal left instructions for Terry to be taken care of. The elders of the synagogue saw to it that they were followed to the letter. He didn't want to go back home to Yvette and her misery. Hal had planned for that, too.

It rained and thundered hard the seventh night of Shiva. As Terry slept in Hal and Sarah's bed, still not ready to let go, Yvette/Kashima/whatever her name was received a visit from three very wet, no-nonsense-looking men who proffered a bulging envelope and very few words. She signed some papers. She was on the next thing smokin' and Terry never heard from her again. Deep, parental love, a new experience for him, now lay in the ground, but would inform his every action. And for the time being, hatred, introduced to him by his mother and her ilk, was gone as well.

1979

Terry sat in the partially-renovated living room of a partially-renovated house in a partially-renovated neighborhood in North Minneapolis. He was upset, bone tired, and feeling alone. He had been on his own since his appointed guardian, Arabella, Sarah's friend and fellow pastry lover, had died the week before his high school graduation in '73. Otto was in New York. He had been the youngest of Hal's circle. All of the others, those from the Old World, were gone now, led by Hal to the other side, falling like obedient dominoes. The remaining members of his very extended Jewish family were from another generation and had grown up in America; well-meaning but obviously uncomfortable with Terry, the Black Jew of St. Louis Park. He continued to read the Torah, but stopped attending synagogue. By then it didn't really matter. He had already lost too many relatives and friends. He was ready to tackle the world on his own. He had been loved, nurtured, and encouraged. Money for his education was sitting in the bank. He harbored no animosity, encouraged feelings of guilt from no one. And he could always go to the synagogue.

After high school, he tried to read everything he could, especially biographies of accomplished men from all corners of the planet, ancient Greek history, whatever interested him, whatever felt right, wherever his readings led him. This summer it was biographies of jazz musicians, though there weren't that many.

He wanted to help the downtrodden, but his commitment to restoring the community to its former glory was waning. He was a person, wasn't he? He seemed perpetually unable to satisfy anyone. Everyone had their expectations, as if he belonged to everyone else, to them. He was too cerebral to ignore the tugging that he felt in his heart, a yearning for something more to replace his flagging commitment to community organizations. Follow the formula or risk being ostracized and shut out. He had tried two years at the University of Minnesota, the U of M. They had been fine, but enough, for now. He had too much energy. There was too much to do. Besides, his inheritance and Bar Mitzvah money were dwindling, spent, not frivolously, but differently than a typical U of M accounting major. Of this he was certain. He had to put the remaining money to work.

He had to face the fact that he was a failure at real estate, and disturbed by the selfishness and greed that sizable government grants engendered in people whose motives he had trusted only a little while before. It was time to move on to something else. Some would call him a quitter, seeing virtue in his attempting to finish something for which he displayed no aptitude and from which he received no pleasure.

He wanted adventure. He needed to meet new people. He needed to travel more. He had let his academic and artistic friends talk him out of joining the new volunteer military. They insisted he would be out of his element, that he would be miserable in an authoritarian environment. He relented. Now he wondered. His street friends thought he was crazy to even consider it. He didn't know any veterans. Vietnam and acid had soured people on the military. His running buddies, though, the high school and college runners who met at the U of M track every Sunday morning, thought he would thrive. Given his sampling of these diverse opinions, he realized he could have been three completely different people.

But to the black upper middle class of Minneapolis, those he identified with on some level, the military was unthinkable outside of one of the academies. He was hardly a West Pointer. They looked askance at anything less than a professional or graduate degree, and expected a bright one like him to have his doctorate by his thirtieth, or at least his thirty-fifth, birthday. Tough crowd. He fished in his pocket and found a joint.

Maybe this is why they don't like you much, he laughed to himself. He had his academic friends, who thought he was wasting his potential, and his street friends, with whom he got high and played ball and chased women, except, of course, the academic women. He had to do that by himself, and once they, the academic women, realized that, no matter how hard they tried, they could not reconcile his passion for order and achievement with his love of drugs and music and women of all colors, they joined the ranks of the could-a-been-maybe-ifs.

He drifted in and out of camps easily. He groomed and dressed well, and exuded charm in both his manners and conversation. But he was always asking logistical questions, 'How does this work, what makes that happen, who controls this section of town', and was considered someone to avoid if at all possible by people happy to just get through the day.

Today, it had been the same damn thing again. He needed to keep his few black women friends away from his more abundant white women friends. There always seemed to be problems; uncertainty, jealousy, assumptions. Not everyone shared his New Age-everybody-together spirit.

He often wondered how good people could remain friends with bigots, then realized that was exactly what he had been doing. He had to make choices. His choices were for humanity, he finally told his friends, for people who respected other people. Less enlightened souls thought he was naively idealistic and didn't hesitate to tell him so. He was doomed to a life of pain, they said. He was trying to figure things out. He wasn't self-destructive. He was a calculating lover of life, attempting to live every moment, and hatred wasn't part of his life plan.

Consistency, he told himself, and the inner strength to handle whatever came your way was what he needed. People told him he lived in a fantasy world. He told them they were horribly resigned to lives of soulless boredom in intellectual purgatory. They left him alone, shaking their heads on the way out. He smoked some hash and picked up his reading where he left off, Hampton Hawes' *Raise Up Off Me*. He missed his grandfather terribly.

One humid night in August, he was pondering his life while swigging beers and listening to a funky, singing guitarist working the circuit and establishing a name for herself. She was pretty damn good, this Bonnie Raitt, he thought. The place was a converted barn or railroad car or something, aptly named The Cabooze. It was bright, loud, and raucous. He loved it.

He sat at the bar with the alcoholics and druggies, men engaging in abbreviated, stoned conversations consisting mostly of gestures and smiles, and young women, twenty to twenty-three, in their happy, carefree, slutty phases, with painted faces, flimsy tops, and tight jeans, kissing and rubbing against a dozen men, staggeringly drunk and never paying for a thing.

It was eleven o'clock and the place was packed. There must have been five hundred people there. It smelled of beer and cigarettes, perfume and the occasional joint. As with almost everywhere he went in Minneapolis, his was one of only a half dozen or so tan or brown faces. To his right, a rare bar stool became available and was instantly swooped on by a young man who convinced Terry he was looking in a mirror, except the visitor was about five inches taller than Terry's five-eleven, with a gentler face that contained more immediate, more probing eyes. Each did a double take when they faced each other. The drunk that Terry had spoken to a moment ago spoke up. "Damn, bro, you got a twin, man. Don't fuck me up like that."

Rather than deny it and explain, Terry responded, "Sorry, man, what can I tell you?"

"Okay, man, but promise to warn me before your triplet comes, okay?" he laughed.

Terry laughed back. "Yeah, man, no problem."

He turned away to face the stranger. "Hey, man, hiya doin'? What's your name?"

His more handsome double responded in a slightly high, accented voice. "Anthony. What's yours?"

"Terry. Where're you from, Anthony? Want a beer?"

"Yes. Thank you. I'm from Holland."

Terry signaled to the barmaid with his index finger and a smile. "Damn, that's great. What brought you here, vacation? How long have you been here? Why do you look like me? C'mon, man, I need answers."

Anthony laughed and nodded to the barmaid who put his beer down from a row that had just been poured. She gave him a lingering smile that Terry had never seen her give anyone else in the six months he had been coming to the place. Hmm, he thought. He's got it. Anthony, though, didn't respond to her. Upset at having extended herself and being ignored, she spent the next twenty minutes vainly trying to get his attention, until the bar manager gave her a why-don't-you-give-it-up look. He must be gay, she thought. He'll do fine on Hennepin Avenue.

"I'm thinking about doing graduate work in cultural anthropology at the U of M. I'm very interested in your blues music. I came to Minneapolis because a friend told me that what you call 'race relations' are thought to be fairly good here. This music is quite good. I haven't seen too many white Americans play blues. John Mayall, from England, is quite good."

Terry was fascinated. He hadn't paid enough attention to the blues since Irv left, but did enjoy it.

"Muddy Waters came through a few months ago. He had 'em goin! He had folks jumpin' on tables and wiggling like they were afflicted with somethin'."

It occurred to him that he was now very drunk. Afflicted with somethin'?

"Have you heard *Mannish Boy*?"

"Oh, yes," Anthony replied thoughtfully, "It is a classic already. Wonderful."

Terry liked Anthony immediately. His English syntax was interesting, too. They talked and listened to the music, with Anthony citing influences and guitar styles — declaring Bonnie Raitt to be enamored of the bluesman Son House, who was so good he was spoken of in whispers — until the place closed. Terry forgot he had been depressed.

The next night he took Anthony to a hole-in-the-wall in North Minneapolis that most whites didn't know about, and most likely wouldn't have patronized if they had. Anthony ate barbecued ribs and chicken, potato salad, corn bread, candied yams, and collard greens until he couldn't move. He became so excited at hearing live blues in a traditional element — with black folks from Chicago and Mississippi and Alabama, seeing wide-brimmed hats and long cigars and big-hipped women and mean-looking men — that he became agitated and talked about that night for weeks afterward. He wanted to go back, but Terry discouraged it. He didn't like the looks they had gotten there, looks that said, 'We know you're slummin' now, and we'll let you get away with it this time, but don't come back here no more.' He hadn't really known what to wear, so they looked slightly out of place in their more expensive club clothes. It was hard to explain this intra-racial cultural anomaly to Anthony at first, who assumed that racial unity in America ignored class lines, until he accustomed himself to his surroundings somewhat, assisted by Terry's running narrative.

Terry quit the real estate business and looked around for something to do. Anything but a job, he told himself, but that unpleasantness was looming larger as his savings continued to dwindle. Anthony always paid for everything wherever they went, from a seemingly inexhaustible supply of money. As luck would have it, he sublet or bought, it was never clear which, one of Terry's dream homes by Lake Calhoun, but Terry couldn't envy him, as gracious and unassuming and maddeningly likable as he was. Anthony lived well as naturally as he breathed. His high voice and accent caught people off guard and they deferred to him. His polite manner and exquisite taste won him friends quickly. His only downside, as the buzz in certain South Minneapolis and suburban circles went, was his association with Terry, the notorious partier. Oh, he was much more grounded than Terry, though, they said. It was fortunate they hadn't heard the stories that Terry heard, the ones told over a joint and, increasingly, accompanied by gram bags of cocaine.

"We're only young once," Anthony told him. Terry sometimes wondered if he'd live to grow old, and if it was worth it anyway. He could die soon from his fast living and still leave a good-looking corpse.

He grew to love Anthony and sometimes wished he were a woman. He knew that it could have been sexual with hardly a thought, but they didn't want that — Terry found the mechanics quite unappealing— though Anthony was in what he called his 'Gay Period'.

"Who are you, the Picasso of sex?!" Terry asked.

The next year was a haze of music and drugs and, for Terry, women of a certain kind who seemed to have radar for cocaine and were willing to do anything for it. Terry eventually found out that Anthony had earned an undergraduate degree in structural engineering from a school in Holland that Terry could never hope to pronounce correctly. Anthony took one graduate course per semester, enough to keep him honest, but not too much to get in the way. At Anthony's insistence, Terry gave up his apartment and moved into his own wing of the house. He read biographies of wealthy people and began to form a plan for his own ascent. Despite their difference in sexual preferences they were perfect roommates and, after partying until there was no more partying left to do, arrived at the same conclusion only hours apart. It was time to stop and move on to...something.

More than once, he had to help Anthony out of a scrape. He was so gentle and always expecting the best in people. Then there was that talk of the bath house orgy in San Francisco in which Anthony was apparently the center of attraction. Devastatingly handsome at twenty-six, he had been just plain beautiful at nineteen. Some guy in a club on Hennepin Avenue had recognized the memorable mulatto with the accent and high voice. Anthony paid him some money, five thousand dollars Terry found out, to keep quiet. The guy called again and demanded more. Anthony laughed and said sure. Then he very calmly made a call to Holland and spoke Dutch. He shook his head and got off the phone smiling.

"What?," Terry asked.

"That was my father. That guy won't be coming around again."

Well, the talking stopped when the guy was found stuffed in a trash can one morning by the canoes they kept at Lake Calhoun. Ruling out coincidence, Terry figured there were some things Anthony didn't tolerate well. He was never even questioned. Terry shivered at the thought of knowing someone with that much power. After debating with himself for several hours, he decided to mention it to Anthony.

"He must have pushed someone too hard. No big loss for humanity, right? Let's eat." And that was the end of that.

It was around this time, in August of 1980, that they became halfway serious. Anthony found some Jamaicans at the U of M and played soccer regularly. Terry began to run more regularly, extending his easy two miles to four and sometimes six, three times a week.

On the Wednesday before Labor Day, they were driving down Lake Street after eating yet another soul food lunch when Anthony asked Terry to turn the 280Z around and park. Amazed, Terry followed him into an Army recruiting office.

Well, Sergeant White wondered what he had done to deserve what happened to him that day. These two high-powered guys walk in, talk to him awhile and argue before leaving. He musta done a good job, talkin' about the travel and experience and it makin' real men outta them 'cause the next day, after he had given up on them, they come smilin' into his office and sign some papers. They needed a couple of months to clean themselves up and take care of some loose ends, the older-looking one with the funny voice winked, but they would find something decent to do and ship out at the end of October. They breezed through the tests, scoring so high that Special Forces and Offficer Candidate School reps took note. This was the same test that Sergeant White had so much trouble getting recruits to even pass lately. And he exceeded his quota and made his bonus. Damned if he wasn't happy. That funny-talkin' one was going to intelligence school and the other one lucked up and got a photography slot. He knew there weren't no damn photography slots open. Who did that so-and-so know? Sheeit. Sometimes even black brains count, he guessed. He scratched his head. It don't matter now, he thought. They got theirs and I got mine.

That night they celebrated, smoking and snorting and drinking for the last time. Anthony was giddy. A man's life had to mean something, he said. His father was so happy that Terry could hear him hooping and hollering around the room on the phone. Terry enjoyed talking to Anthony's father, Jimmy. They laughed and laughed. Jimmy was from Alabama, full of stories and down-home humor told in a still-present southern accent. Jimmy insisted that his memories were still too vivid to ever step foot on American soil again. Terry promised to visit him in Eindhoven. After they hung up, Anthony called and invited some women friends to join them, but they couldn't make it at the last minute. He reported that one's mother had taken sick and the other one needed to study. Anthony didn't seem to mind at all.

Undeterred, they saw an unbelievable Eubie Blake concert at the Walker Art Center, an old-fashioned review from the Vaudeville days. He was in his nineties. Anthony made a point of seeing the old guys, the ones in the musical history books, at least once before they died. The show reminded Terry of his month in the Catskills.

Life was suddenly full of promise and unknown adventures. After drinks, some coke, a joint and a scary ride home with a cab driver who had one hand on the steering wheel and another on a joint that Anthony gave him, Anthony hugged Terry in pure joy and stumbled off to bed.

The next morning Terry awoke feeling spectacular. He wondered why, beyond the obvious reasons: the sun streaming into his window, the pleasant hangover, the music drifting up from downstairs. He felt emptied out, as if he had had a night of very fulfilling sex. But he couldn't remember anything. After Anthony went to bed, he sat up for awhile, listening to music on the veranda. It had been a warm October Day and a cool breeze blew in from the lake. He listened to Leigh Kammond, the elegant-sounding Minneapolis jazz announcer, then played Bob Marley, McCoy Tyner and Dizzy's *Over the Rainbow* for the first time in years. Somehow he had managed to wind up in bed, dreaming of Hal and Sarah and wondering what was to become of his life.

He showered and dressed and went down to the kitchen. Chaka Khan's voice drifted through the built-in speakers. Anthony was dancing, spinning, and singing along. Terry was about to share his thoughts with his party animal partner when something in Anthony's smile, his bounce, his exaggerated motions as he talked to himself made Terry stop before he entered the room. Anthony had prepared a feast. There was something different about him. He stood taller. At breakfast, while spreading cherry jelly from Holland on a croissant, he announced, to his own tabletop drum roll, that his Gay Period was officially over. Terry knew then that he had been the final, unknowing arbiter of this momentous decision. He stopped trying to remember.

Exactly one month later, Anthony told Terry the story of his life so far on the plane ride to Atlanta, on their way to connecting flights before they went their separate ways for a while to take basic training in Arizona and Alabama. He began with the story of his father, Jimmy.

#

4

Jimmy
1936-1944

Jimmy was born in 1918. He grew up in rural Alabama, black and cursed with brilliance, in the wrong place at the wrong time. He was just outspoken enough to stay alive, but he was the cause of a lot of worry and head-shaking among the church elders. He graduated from his segregated high school early, the mores of the South slowly suffocating him as surely as a boa constrictor wrapped around his chest. He read the weekly copies of The Chicago Defender that were smuggled into town and passed around. The stories painted pictures of a city that had work and was fairer to blacks. The Defender was the black newspaper that had so much influence it could eventually claim some responsibility for the Great Migration of blacks from the South to the North. Jimmy knew he had some decisions to make.

After a particularly nasty encounter with some ignorant white locals, it was a sympathetic white police officer who put him on a bus to Chicago and suggested that it would be safer for him to go to school up north before an Alabaman killed him for asserting his right to be who he was, for refusing to apologize for just being alive and literate. Dark and tall, he was teased about his skin color unmercifully as he grew up, and was always very sensitive to it, especially when that was all that people, black and white, seemed to see. They couldn't see the soulful reader of poems and the listener of jazz when he could find it, and the delta blues when he couldn't, a hoper of hope in a circumscribed existence in a circumscribed world, for he insisted on being somewhat common-sensical in the midst of absurdity. Such were the times.

Jimmy got on the bus, and then took a detour to Kansas City, Missouri to be around jazz musicians. He would wait tables because he thought living in Kansas City at that time was more important than any other plans he might have had, or almost had. He was right. He took accounting and music theory classes at night, money and jazz, and chased women on the weekends, charming them with his deep southern drawl and old-fashioned manners, and amazing them with his growing music collection and his obsession with the music and the men who made it. He lost most of them with his ramblings, but Ruby appreciated his memorizing Coleman Hawkins' *Body and Soul* solo, scatting it like Louis Armstrong while she sat up in bed eating her favorite vanilla ice cream with cherries, sharing his excitement the night he got it right, all of it, the intonations, the phrasing, the dips, the highs. He would run to the Walgreen's down at the corner of the next block from where he lived, run back, climb the three flights of stairs, past the other roomers in the respectable boarding house, and back to his room before she had even touched earth after their lovemaking. She woke up to cherry kisses all over her beautiful brown face, then laid back as he spilled freezing cold ice cream on her breasts and licked it off. He wouldn't let her touch the ground yet.

She knew that most of the dark men wanted those high-yalla gals, some almost light enough to be white, but Jimmy didn't care about color. He was happy to be accepted, dark skin and grits, too. Ruby, whose real name was Rowena, found the young men paraded in front of her by her preacher father boring, but didn't really like many of the hipsters, either. Jimmy was different alright. He was just passin' through, she knew, on his way to somewhere, damned if he knew where. He wasn't marrying material, not yet. She was on a mission to leave her father's house, but to live in the manner to which she had been accustomed almost since she was born. She sighed as he entered her again, relishing the feeling, trying to freeze it, knowing that she would have to go soon. She was on a mission.

Jimmy cried for one full day after Ruby left him the following month, then forgot about her. He was close to getting on as a Pullman porter, an elite job for black men in those days, after petitioning Mack Johnson for months. Mack always showed up with money in his pockets after the New York run, cussin' about peckerwoods and how they expected him to bow and scrape. He had been warned by some of the older porters. They had seen a lot like him come and go, they said, and more than one in a pine box. Jimmy was pressed quickly into service one day, found by an old-timer with a look of urgency about him.

"You the one been beggin' Mack to come on the Pullman?"

" I don't beg anyone."

The old-timer was impressed by Jimmy's use of the word *anyone*, instead of the near-universal phrase *no one*, but worried about his uppity airs.

THE REAL LIVES OF DREAMERS

"You a proud one, ain't ya? Watch yo'self, young buck. Ah got property in Kansas City, New York, and New Jersey from kissin' the white man's ass. Been doin' it for twenty years. You have to know who you are as a man. Then it don't matter what you do for appearances. You stand up too tall you'll be swingin' from a rope. I've seen it. Ah might see it again soon."

His eyes glazed over as he looked at the ground in front of him, remembering things that shouldn't have been remembered, that should never have been seen. Finally, he asked a question. "Are you as full of fire as that fool Mack? You seen him?"

"Yes, and no," Jimmy said. "What happened?"

"Don't you worry 'bout that. He tells me he taught you a lot already."

"Yes, sir, he did."

That's better, the old-timer thought. He sized Jimmy up again.

"Come on, son. We need some help on the New York run."

Jimmy was awe-struck. His reading and listening seemed to be paying off. He would miss a couple of classes, but his instructors weren't worried. He was doing extremely well, they said. Besides, they could use the break from their favorite student, so full of questions all the time. As he climbed the steps to the train at the station, although he had arrived fifteen minutes prior to the old-timer's announced time, he saw very well-groomed colored men in black pants, white jackets, and small caps moving industriously to and fro, at the beck and call of the old timer. He felt he was prepared. He knew how white folks could be, always wantin' to be superior. He had sat in his room until late, going over different situations and how he would respond to them, keeping in mind the old man's advice.

"Your name is boy, George, or whatever those fuckin' peckerwoods decide it's goin' to be, and their name is sir or boss. Some of 'em ain't too bad, and the sooner you learn to read 'em, the better off you'll be. Why, some of 'em from New York will try to treat you like you're as good as they are, especially the Jews. But always be careful. There's two types you gotta watch out for, them's that's from the South, cause they're ignorant and they like bein' ignorant, and any white man with a woman. He's generally gonna wanna show off for her, keep you in your place."

"Always keep your distance, and for God's sake, Jimmy, don't even think about lookin' at a white woman. She may be Greta fuckin' Garbo in heels, you better keep your eyes down and do your job."

As he entered the train, the men looked up.

"Hey there, youngster. Oldtime is back this way."

"Thank you."

On his way to the back of the train, he passed several men getting ready, preening in a mirror, buffing black shoes that he felt couldn't possibly shine any brighter, pulling white jackets out of plastic bags and appraising them, affixing folded hand towels over their left forearm just so. They mostly spoke to him in relaxed voices. Oldtime gave him more instructions, quizzed him for a full thirty minutes, and declared him ready, conditionally. The other men were visibly relieved as they all retired to the dining car for their meals, one hour before passengers would begin embarking.

Jimmy marveled at these men. They were all educated, well-spoken, and proud of it. There was a teacher from New York, a writer from Chicago, an opera buff from Tulsa, and a cook, a chef really,

THE REAL LIVES OF DREAMERS

from Philadelphia. These were the jobs they could get in a hostile world. And the money was better than anything they could make in their chosen professions, for now, anyway. Jimmy had a meal like he had never had before; prime roast beef au jus, the freshest mashed potatoes he'd ever tasted, green beans, again so fresh they melted in his mouth, and buttery, steaming hot rolls that were oh-so-soft, with some exotic flavor mixed in. He had had good food before, just not this good. It was hard for him to believe that these colored men ate this good all the time. He liked it and didn't want it to be a novelty he told his grandkids about, but a habit. The banter among them was relaxed, with less of the jive that he heard with his musician friends, and dignified. These men had a great deal of pride, he told himself, and he would do his best to emulate them.

He learned that Mack had been identified as the man who robbed and beat a customer. The customer was actually from New York. Mack had read him wrong and received a scathing tongue-lashing for being too familiar. Mack had disappeared. The men debated whether or not he was guilty, and how this incident would affect their employment.

Unfortunately, Jimmy wasn't as prepared for the run as they thought he was. He smiled and looked his charges in the eyes, before one of them, dumbfounded, complained to Oldtime. A few of the dignified men with whom he enjoyed dinner changed drastically once the run began. They shuffled and scraped, bowed and slurred their words, and received the biggest smiles and the best tips. They were almost as bad as Steppin' Fetchit in 39 Hours to Kill, a portrayal so disgusting to Jimmy that he and his Kansas City hipster friends walked out of the theater in an uproar and were almost arrested. It was these men who were assigned the southerners. The others provided outstanding service in elegant, clipped English, befitting the best English butlers Jimmy had seen in mystery movies. Jimmy followed their leads and received the same rudimentary tips as they did. It was another lesson in pride versus commerce.

Oldtime noticed the look on Jimmy's face during certain portions of the trip. Was that disgust? That would never do. Was he even aware of it? He could take no chances now. At the end of the run, he pulled Jimmy aside and told him that he could make the run back to Kansas City and that would be that.

"Thank you very much and no hard feelings, young buck, but you've got a fire in you, and this ain't the place to put it out. I know things are changin', but not here and not now."

Jimmy thought it was time for a change. He left Alabama to be around music, but hadn't really gotten to know Kansas City first hand yet. Back in town, he headed straight for the jazz clubs and, after paying some dues, became known as the best host in town. Because of his reputation, as a host, a friend of the musicians, and a clothes horse, he switched jobs at the different clubs at will, depending on who was in town or who the house band happened to be. He started at the Harlem Nightclub on East 15th Street and saw Benny Moten's band perform.

The stories he'd heard about Kansas City didn't do it justice, thanks to Big Tom Pendergast and his roughhouse political machine that controlled the city.

The liquor flowed, the women danced, the hoodlums ruled, and the musicians worked and created more music. He was in the clubs all the time, working or not. Jimmy Slim, reputed to be a member of mobster Lucky Luciano's inner circle, first visited the Hey-Hay Club, at Fourth and Cherry Streets, to see Charlie Parker

THE REAL LIVES OF DREAMERS

and George E. Lee. He was a cold man, as calculating as any Jimmy would ever know. He gave Jimmy a hundred-dollar tip for his service. That was a whole lot of money in those days. Jimmy Slim and his cronies would sit in the back and stay late. He was impressed that Jimmy didn't make rumbling noises under his breath, and was as sharp at two AM as he had been six hours earlier. They talked about business and Sicily, fascism and the persecution of Jews in Germany, Churchill in England and Mussolini in Italy. They were making preparations for war, opportunists facing down the inevitable and planning to walk away with a couple of bucks. Ambitious as he was, Jimmy wanted to get close enough to Slim's fire to feel its warmth, but not get singed or, if he was really unlucky, thrown into it head first. He listened, but kept his distance, filing away bits and pieces of information. It was that night that Jimmy Slim, notorious for his ruthlessness and unbeknownst to Jimmy, decided to become Jimmy Turner's godfather, to look after him wherever he was.

Jimmy enjoyed a stature he dared not dream of in Alabama. He was making a very good living, thirty dollars a night with tips on average, but he only cared about the music. Even he couldn't possibly hear of and see all the talented musicians that came through.

Once, he managed to get on with a club in the Ozarks, in Eldon, Missouri. Charlie Parker, the brilliant raggedy man who would mysteriously disappear and then re-appear, was playing with the Tommy Douglas septet. Jimmy was knocked out, enthralled, swept away, and busted up. He couldn't believe this music. The musicians who played it were more sure of themselves than any colored men he had ever known. He began to absorb their confidence and ways of looking at the world. They were all gravitating to Charlie Parker, Bird, already a legend. When he wasn't all-consumed with Bird, Jimmy managed to see Mary Lou Williams, Count Basie, Lester

BARRY NIX

Young, Duke Ellington, Hot Lips Page, Coleman Hawkins, Chu Berry, Ben Webster, Jo Jones, Tadd Dameron, and so many others it didn't make any sense. To be in this environment was a life-force for Jimmy, though he was one of the few Negroes who understood and appreciated what was happening right in their midst. This confounded him to no end. The musicians had given him his legs, the ability to stand up as a man, not some loudmouth declaring who he was, but a dignified man of the world who carried himself with integrity. It was much more than he had hoped for. Then reform hit Kansas City. Big Tom Pendergast was on his way out and Jimmy didn't like the noises he heard. He left Kansas City in '39, soon after Bird pawned his horn and jumped a freight train to Chicago. Pendergast would be jailed later that year and dead by '45, the clubs would close, and that rich period of American creativity would come to an end. And Jimmy Slim would always know where Jimmy was.

1945-1949

Jimmy had to get to Europe and fight a real war. He found himself fighting a different war in Fort Sill, Oklahoma, a war for his dignity again, over and over like an ocean wave, at times a roar, at times a whimper, but always there. There were several GI's, all colored in the segregated units of the second World War, who bothered him every day. They had gotten together and decided they didn't like him and that was that. He was too dark. He was too short. He read too much. Deciding on a plan, he challenged the biggest one and whupped up on him something terrible. After that day they left him alone. He was no longer teased, chided, or set upon for being different. There were no more fights within the group. They were ready to fight a different enemy, but they had been training for a mission for which orders had not yet come. Their taut nerves and lean bodies were poised to spring at any second, but their commanding officers, all white and all from the south, refused to believe in their heads the truth that their guts told them repeatedly. They didn't care about the stories they heard about the 'Fightin' 332nd', the cream of the colored troops trained to be pilots at Tuskegee Institute in Alabama. These officers were fighting their own, very intense war, driven by their expensively-nurtured value system. They were doomed, they thought, to dream of combat every night as they cursed their rotten luck for being assigned to lead the colored troops.

The colored troops, of course, were poor, middle-class, brave, cowardly, sullen, loud, fearless, and fearful, just like the white troops, but in different ways. They were dictated by suppression, whiskey dreams, the blues, the good girls they might marry back home, and the bad girls, real bad girls, who made them holler in the night and promise to live at least one more day. Colored folks didn't commit suicide much, but Jimmy Allen Turner had considered it often, though not since his Kansas City days, because he knew he was a liability to himself in America. That was before he decided that after the war he was going to Europe, where a black man was an exoticism and treated like a man, like Sidney Bechet was.

Although Jimmy didn't carry a soprano saxophone from which he could coax sweet melodies and racial harmony as Bechet did, he felt that, in Europe, there was a chance for him to achieve some sort of freedom and express outwardly the dignity which he insisted upon inwardly. He had seen too many smart black men eaten alive, resorting to the same behavior as the ignorant farmhands and illiterate coons who basked in their belief of their own inferiority to anyone with paler skin. But he refused. He was lucky, he felt, to have had the self-control not to have exploded before now. If he continued in the United States, he knew, he would be lynched, beaten first by a gang of ignorant tobacco-chewing crackers determined to teach all niggers a lesson about their place in life. Beaten, then cut, castrated and hauled up, a noose around his neck, still hollering from the unbearable pain, black folks hiding in trees off the clearing, crying and praying to Jesus as the horse galloped away, his neck snapped, the crackers doing a jig, someone lighting a match to his bloody body, and everyone posing for pictures next to the still-swinging corpse. Not me, Jimmy said. I just have to survive this war.

He survived. They had finally been sent to fight. The officers, mediocre tacticians, ignored the advice of their battle-hardened NCOs and were dispatched with handily by German troops that Jimmy imagined had a good laugh at their stupidity. The unfortunate reconnaissance men and drivers who had followed orders and suffered a similar fate were mourned. But Jimmy had seen something.

As Lieutenant Gilmore lay dying and waiting to be evacuated, his large intestine clearly visible, Jimmy, the medic, took his time as he prepared a morphine injection. The left side of a once-handsome face was a mass of pulp. The night sky was frighteningly beautiful, lit by flares and explosions, rockets and small arms fire, but Jimmy was peaceful, smiling, for revenge was living, to be alive, as this pompous son of a bitch lay dying beside him.

Eventually, finally relenting to Gilmore's pleading, cursing and whining, allowing for the slightest tug at his humanity despite his hatred, he injected the morphine into Gilmore's leg. Gilmore responded almost immediately, his long exhaled sigh and glazed-over eyes reminding Jimmy of the junkie jazz musicians he had known in Kansas City, all trying to capture the magic that was Bird.

THE REAL LIVES OF DREAMERS

Staff Sergeant Jim 'Jimbo' Johnson appeared, also smiling. He was a big man, black as coal and wise beyond his years, although at 35 he was the oldest of the troops in the Company. As was typical in these situations, he was enormously respected by the men under him while also expected to bow and scrape to white idiots of higher rank. Johnson had told Jimmy of one very fine white officer, who had taught him plenty and befriended him and who, of course, was sent packing within three months of his arrival. Jimbo hated Gilmore more than Jimmy did, and had seen two fellow NCOs succumb to his racist pathology.

Jimbo knelt close to Gilmore.

"Feel better?" he asked.

Gilmore was able to nod weakly.

"I called, but they said they can't come for you. They're too busy taking care of some fine black soldiers who were led to their destruction by stupid peckerwoods like you."

Gilmore registered, despite his wounds, a look of shock. Jimbo reached over and gingerly unholstered Gilmore's officers'-only, standard-issue .45.

"I was gonna kill you, but I'm just gonna leave you to die. I'm just sorry I got here too late to stop Turner from giving you that injection."

Jimmy froze, not knowing what to do.

"Now," Jimbo continued, "I'm gonna hurt you, make sure you die soon and can't be fixed up. As you die, I want you to think about your life. Think about what your pitiful ass sacrificed because you needed to feel superior to hard-workin' folks who wanted to do the right thing and serve their racist-ass country. Think about the life I'll live. I'm gettin' a college degree, maybe two or three, and motherfuckers like you will sho' nuff wish I died in the war.

And I'm gonna carry your face with me everywhere I go, you stupid fuckin' peckerwood."

Before Gilmore could react, there was a pop. The morphine had shut off his pain receptors, but he could feel that something else was wrong. There was liquid coursing through him, but not the way it should, he thought. Everything was so hazy. What was that crazy nigger saying? He felt his body stiffen involuntarily.

Jimmy watched as more blood oozed out of Gilmore's right side. He was struck by no particular moral imperative, for he had been living with a vicious knot in his stomach that he hadn't been able to get rid of. Observing his lieutenant, prone, powerless, young and afraid of death, Jimmy neither objected nor cheered. He was saddened, not by Gilmore's impending demise, but by the price of hatred to everyone concerned, how it sucked the compassion out of men, how it made everyone question the value of others in malicious ways, and how it had already damaged his young soul. He decided then and there that he would find freedom somehow, that he would live his life free of the kind of hatred he had witnessed, somehow, in some way.

Gilmore stayed like that for four more hours, in wonderment, scared, alone, and hated, questioning his life and his approaching death through an opiate-induced haze. The noise, the rat-a-tats, the booms, the screams of surprise and pain, had subsided. The rainbow-streaked sky had turned grey. He was finally given some water out of a black soldier's canteen, a gesture he ordinarily would have refused with a sneer. For the first time, he started to question his upbringing and how he had proudly upheld that baleful tradition of hate. Sorrowful, but unable to evoke pity from the group of GIs who gathered around him to witness his last minutes; humiliated, but unable to stand and revive a modicum of decorum; hypnotized, but unable to snap his fingers and regain his senses, he lay dying. "This is no way to die," he thought. But he did.

Eventually, Jimmy found himself in Amsterdam in 1945, just several weeks before the end of the war, after his time in the supply depots of Italy had made him a rich, confident man, oblivious to the white officers and NCO's who suddenly seemed afraid to ask him where he had been patrolling, much less tell him what to do. They looked at him as if he were a ghost or a Voodoo priest, so atypical were his proud bearing and his mysterious influence. He had dangerous friends who even had some say about things in the Army. One day, while on patrol, he saw a pale young woman huddled in a corner of Dam Square. She reached out to him for help with bony hands, looked at him with hollow, horror-filled eyes, and asked for food in a raspy, but tender voice. He married her.

Helga never fully recovered from her wartime trials with the Nazis. Jimmy had never been so gentle with another woman. He agonized over her frequent sicknesses, but discovered much about himself that he liked when taking care of her. His wartime epiphany, like that of so many others, had been that, although his assignments in Europe had at times been harrowing and violent, he had experienced a number of profound and tender moments. Tenderness in a soldier, he thought, until overseas deployment, had been an unaffordable luxury, a danger to survival, a compromise, a personal possession to be held in the strictest confidence and brought out only on special occasions, in the comfort of one's own soul. He decided that, despite the aggression of others, and despite the fact that Americans had just fought and won a good and noble war, the problem, as far as his life was concerned, was America, and he would never go back.

He didn't have to. He had a trunk full of money, American dollars, stashed away, a perk of being in the right place at the right time, and a good head for numbers and other details during wartime.

One perfect spring night they had dinner in a jazz club that had been opened by a friend of his after settling in Amsterdam, like Jimmy, after the war. Helga had felt particularly strong and surmised that she was on her way to becoming fully healthy. Her doctor agreed. Jimmy felt wonderful. They laughed, heard some good music, ate and drank well, and made love with fervor. It was all smoke and mirrors, one night's high point before a permanent decline. He had five years of utter happiness, more than he ever thought of requesting from a God who had severely tested his faith since he was old enough to know better, a non-believer despite the Alabama Baptist hollers and shouts he had been subjected to as a child, decrying this world and planning elaborate escapes to the next.

After the funeral, Heinz, Helga's brother-in-law and an attorney, pulled Jimmy aside, took him for a drink and changed his life again.

They commiserated over several pils before Heinz was able to get to the point. Jimmy let Heinz do most of the talking, reveling in his elegantly-accented English, Dutch by birth and British by training. Heinz took a deep breath and satisfied himself with the explanation that Jimmy needed one crisis to replace another, that of mending his broken heart.

"Jimmy, I…I know someone who is in a very difficult situation and I need your advice."

Jimmy straightened up in his chair, suddenly alert. "Of course, Heinz. Anything."

THE REAL LIVES OF DREAMERS

Heinz looked at Jimmy before he spoke. He was neither attractive nor unattractive in a strict sense, but if he were a woman who needed protection, Jimmy would be her first choice. His jaw was set hard, his eyes liquid, and red now, the cheekbones clearly evident, the body firm, the nose somehow strangely acquiline for a black American, though Heinz rarely thought in those terms with Jimmy, the hair relatively straight from pomade and one hundred daily strokes with a mohair brush.

"A woman I knew in Germany became pregnant by one of your soldiers, a Negro, in the First Armored Division. He was on holiday, coming to see her when, well, something happened, a horrible traffic accident."

Jimmy felt that Heinz was lying about the last part, the accident. He had a feeling it was something more horrible than a traffic accident, something from a distinctly American horror show. Nevertheless, in the interest of friendship, he accepted Heinz's explanation.

"This circumstance was made much worse. She gave birth to her second child, a boy, the first was a girl two years ago, and then she died. The Germans are screaming about these two half-Negro babies and your government is moving very slowly to rectify the situation. They hadn't married because she would not without her father's permission, and he would not give it. Those rotten German bastards."

The Dutch held for the Germans a particularly ugly place in their otherwise peaceful hearts in the days and years after the war. He took a sip of pils.

"Of course, the hope was that once the grandparents saw the children they would relent and cry and welcome them into their loving arms. Well, the bastards wouldn't even see their own grand-

BARRY NIX

children, refused to come near them. Can you suggest some way in which we might help these two innocent children, Jimmy? Do you know someone who could put in a good word, maybe a family to take them in, something? I am too old for such a thing."

Jimmy straightened up completely now, all business. No, at sixty and a confirmed bachelor, Heinz would not do, no matter how well-intentioned.

"Where are they now?"

"At my house, in Eindhoven."

Jimmy straightened his tie. "Do they have papers?"

"The daughter was born in America, in Harlem. She is an American citizen. The boy is ten days old. He is Dutch."

Jimmy spoke slowly. "Yes….I know some people."

Jimmy excused himself and went to the bar. He laid out fifty U.S. dollars and asked the bartender to place a call to Kansas City and, five minutes later, another one to Palermo, Sicily. Ten minutes went by and the bartender signaled for Jimmy to take the second call. Heinz observed him smiling broadly and gesturing. Once, he raised his voice and Heinz could hear Jimmy speaking what sounded like Italian for a moment. He hung up and gave the bartender another bill, walked back to the table and sat down.

"Let's drive to Eindhoven and see what we can do for them."

As Jimmy followed Heinz into his well-appointed townhouse on a little street in Eindhoven, both weary from the day and the drive in spite of the fact that Jimmy had hired an off-duty GI to get them there in one piece, these two drunk mourners imbued with a renewed sense of purpose, he was full of sadness, apprehension and curiosity. Right away, with a sense of urgency, as if a wind would blow out of the west and carry Jimmy away from the orphans' safe

THE REAL LIVES OF DREAMERS

haven, Heinz led him to an upstairs bedroom where an old woman in a shawl sat, a gas lamp at her shoulder casting an orange glow over the room, singing Dutch lullabies to a light-colored baby who had long ago succumbed to her hypnotic melodies. Her voice was that of an angel. Her singing seemed to evoke long-lost memories. Jimmy thought it to be one of the most beautiful sights he had ever seen, until he saw the one year-old girl in a hastily-purchased crib in the corner. She was a caramel color, with mostly sandy-colored curls, some even blonde, and full, pinkish lips. Jimmy had never seen an innocent mulatto baby, only adults with varying degrees of guilt, self-hatred, fear of being found to pass for white, and superior airs.

"Their parents must have been beautiful."

"No. They were quite ordinary-looking. A strange way of biology, I think, ordinary-looking people producing extraordinary-looking children."

This child was gorgeous and victimized all who looked upon her. He saw freedom in her green eyes, his and hers and her brother's and, contrary to the elaborate plan he had improvised, partly over the phone, partly during the near-breathless ride from Amsterdam, scooped the children up and claimed them for his own, and was whisked from Eindhoven in a fast black car in the cool early morning just before dawn, his ears only hearing in shadows, his eyes seeing mere echoes, of Heinz running after them and proclaiming himself the children's godfather, and the old woman sing-songing wishes for happiness and love.

5

Anthony
1957

Anthony had been sexual for almost as long as he could remember. Too sexual, even for the liberated climate of the Netherlands in the fifties. At eight he was known as "little Henry Miller" for his eagerness to romp naked and encourage cute little single-braided-haired girls to do likewise. He loved his aunts, as all the adult neighbor women were known to him, oh so much, particularly the buxom Aunt Belinda, who lived just across the fertile green pasture in their village outside of Eindhoven, four hours from Amsterdam.

One day, on the pretense of going to see her teenage son, Jan, his defacto big brother, he walked around the back of their little cottage and spotted Belinda toweling herself after bathing, a scene straight out of one of the art books his father kept on the top shelf of one of the living room bookcases. As he watched her heavy breasts seem to pull her down as she bent over to dry between her legs, something, he didn't know what, came over him, this innocent with the libido of a young man. He felt a funny tingling in his stomach and then, as if by some curse visited upon him by the sorcery of women, felt an unbearable pressure. The bulge in his pants scared him. He wanted the stiffness to go away. He wanted to be that towel. As she straightened up and dried her back, he became dizzy. Her stomach was ample, but not obese, her hips big and fleshy, her thighs firm but lonely tree trunks yearning to be hugged. In a daze, after leaving his shoes by the window, he crept around and into the house as stealthily as an Apache brave stalking a buffalo. Eyes closed, he had his thin arms locked tightly around a fragrant thigh before she even saw him. She screamed from fright. He screamed from fright, opened his eyes and was greeted by the plumpest, most well-proportioned rump he had seen until that day during his short-lived career of neighborhood window-spying. She attempted to shake him loose and screamed again. This motion served to twist Anthony around so that he was face to face with an only slightly hairy bush, trimmed to her husband's specifications. Well, this was just too much. Weakened by this unexpected vision of up-close femaleness, Anthony felt himself loosening his grip. He fell to the floor and hit his head, not hard, but hard enough to make him even more dizzy.

Poor Belinda was beside herself now, a regular Dutch housewife taking a quiet afternoon bath before commencing the evening's chores of dinner, cleanup, and preparations for bed. Now, she was nude and wet with an almost unconscious eight year-old sex fiend. Anthony's bump on the head served to bring out her nurturing side, overruling her indignant side for the time being. She teetered for a minute and scooped him up to her full breasts, carried him into her bedroom and placed him gently on the bed. Anthony was not so unconscious as to be unaware of his enviable position, not so dizzy as to be extremely upset when he landed on the bed, no longer squished in her breasts and stomach and hips. Belinda rushed over to her closet and put on a robe and pulled it tight, not knowing what to do next, wishing Anthony were ten years older. She sat up on the bed with him and rocked him in her bosom until he fell into the best sleep he'd had since the anonymous womb he had joyfully inhabited some years before. When he awoke, they agreed to keep this rather difficult to explain episode a secret. As he left, she called him 'my little prankster'.

 During the next several years, Belinda served as Anthony's not quite surrogate mother, for he was always trailing her and touching her. She gave him countless playful slaps on the wrist, but to no avail. Sometimes, he was little more than a pest and other times her personal student of life, until he was fourteen. She taught him how to appreciate good food, how to listen to Classical music, how to look at art, and, later, finally, how to make love. Since their "shower day," as they called it, they needed to be near each other, just to breathe each other's air, finding common ground in their un-intentioned conspiracy of secrecy and innocent love. Belinda suggested that Anthony help her with her garden. They worked long hours, toiling in the warm sun to burn off energy that would one day insist on expelling itself in its most natural form. Anthony amazed her with his powers of concentration and his passion for learning. In three years they had a magnificent garden that was the talk of the countryside, along with a few ancillary, but harmless, comments about the source of this gardening energy. On spring evenings, he would lie with his head in her lap on a stone bench surrounded by red and yellow and white tulips and assorted maples and imported bonsais winding along a dirt trail, and feel just the right blend of satisfaction with the present and wonder about the future.

 In winter, Anthony was a voracious reader and wrote down accounts of the most interesting of the stories told by the old men in the village, true or not. He excelled in mathematics and logic, fortunately mediated by an uncommon sensitivity and compassion, and, fortunately or unfortunately, accompanied by a ruthlessness towards those who would approach him or anyone he cared about with less-than-enlightened intentions. He was particularly fascinated by twentieth century European artists; Picasso, Braque, Kandinski, Man Ray, and, of course, Degas and his bathing women; Cartier-Bresson; Debussy, Stravinsky, Mahler and Darrius Millaud, and, later, D. H. Lawrence, Anais Nin, Camus and Malreaux.

When Anthony was thirteen, and Jan had gone off to study at the London School of Economics, Belinda rid herself of her husband, Pim, a cool man to answer to such a frivolous-sounding name, asking only for the house, an adequate allowance, and a small percentage of one of his growing stable of businesses. He was neither malicious nor pious, as exciting as a piece of tree bark and as caring as a scratchy wool blanket, but a good provider — when being provided for had mattered more than anything else to Belinda — to a young woman who had survived by her wits during the war.

By Anthony's sixteenth birthday — the day Belinda relented, worn down by years of almost-surreptitious ogling, stroking, kissing, nibbling, biting, pawing, whining, and outright begging — he was tall and strong, already a promising soccer player, with the shapely, muscular thighs to prove it. It was worth the wait. When he finally entered her for the first time it was almost, but not quite, anti-climactic. Naturally, he took to sex like sand to a beach. At Belinda's knee, he became as good a young lover as there ever was, uninformed by heartbreak and the experiences of the moodiness of multiple lovers. Almost effortlessly, he gave her her first orgasm at forty-one, a fact he found sad, horrible even, but joyous because he had taken her places no one else had. She had never had bouts of sex — full-bodied, aromatic tests of passion, endurance, emotion, and internal plumbing — with such an athletic performer, finally lying back in a limp, sweaty heap on twisted, sweaty sheets. She told him he had the tongue of a wizard. He loved her deeply, and always would.

J immy knew of Anthony's love for Belinda almost from the beginning. He talked to them both separately, shook his head and walked away. He didn't understand it, but saw nothing inherently wrong with them spending time together.

He had provided several governesses in succession to lighten his burden when the children were younger. As teens, they both appeared remarkably self-sufficient, each engulfed in their own world, but also enjoyed the time they spent together as a family. Realizing what he gained from his time in the military, he was somewhat of a disciplinarian, more in regard to academics and good manners than anything else. It was more than he had a right to expect, the children and a life full of jazz and travel. He was a rich, free black man in Europe. From what he knew of the world, he could not conceive of a better existence.

From the time Anthony was five years old and, later, when Jimmy could wrest him from Belinda's increasingly tenuous clutches, or lure him from one of the soccer fields in town, he took him to hear jazz in Amsterdam and Paris, especially the American expatriates and the touring musicians from the states. Anthony was always the youngest patron of the various clubs and was subsequently doted on by the barmaids, club owners, and musicians. He handed Louis Armstrong a handkerchief backstage, ate chicken with Art Blakey, drank orange juice with John Coltrane, and sat on the piano bench with Carmen McRae. He also met Bud Powell, Randy Weston, Art

THE REAL LIVES OF DREAMERS

Taylor, and Duke Ellington. He knew them as extraordinary people who were treated like gods in Europe and, with the exception of Ellington, as pariahs at home, by white and black folks. Many of them complained of racism in the States, but couldn't see moving to Europe, while many others could and did, like Johnny Griffin and Dexter Gordon had, and prospered. He also knew the answers were complicated ones, and didn't pretend to understand them, although he tried. How could the pull of home be that strong, he wondered? Of course, the music came from America, he reasoned, and began the endless debate, with himself and others, on the merits of suffering as a matter of course in the creation of great art. Early on, he felt he knew the answer. Yes, artists must suffer, and there were myriad ways in which the artists themselves, or others, could enact that suffering. Run-of-the-mill creations could be fashioned in middle-class environs, but he decided that great art required true suffering, by artists and those around them.

Many of the older musicians blamed Charlie Parker, Thelonious Monk, and Dizzy Gillespie for chasing average people away from jazz with what Satchmo, Louis Armstrong, called 'that Chinese music', and Elvis Presley and Little Richard for replacing their music as the popular music of America. Billy Eckstein told the story of Bird's not being right ever again after his first tour in the south. Anthony always remembered that story, along with his father's mixed bag of tales. All he knew was that one day, maybe when folks could get along better over there, he was going to see and feel and smell the south, and stand at the crossroads, 'cause that was where the blues were born, his blues of sharecroppers and hunting dogs and hobos, of good whiskey and bad, big-legged women, of crying and loving. He already had the blues, the happy Dutch blues. He had Belinda, her Anais Nin to his Henry Milller.

BARRY NIX

Naturally, Jimmy wanted Anthony to learn piano and exposed him to the best; too early, one would think. The players so enraptured Anthony that he felt that, for him, playing music was useless. Their prodigious technical skills and unique personalities, although electrifying and enthralling, were more than intimidating, they were completely off-putting. Who could pick up a tenor sax after drifting to sleep to Coleman Hawkins? Who would practice chords after being floored by Art Tatum, who even the other musicians talked about in awe? And hadn't a horn player, a talented saxophonist, thrown his horn off a New York bridge after he heard Bird play? 'No, thank you,' Anthony said. Jimmy was left with the sorrow and uncertainty that resulted from his enthusiasm to share this earth-shaking music with his son, only to scare him off. So many things came so easily to Anthony that he wanted no part of those that didn't. He was a gloriously happy listener. Oh, he could read music and discuss scales and flatted fifths and triplets, minor pentatonic scales and trading fours, and be happy to leave it at that. Besides, he appreciated the blues more than hard bop. He didn't mind plucking a simple, Monk-influenced, sexually charged blues tune on the piano every once in a while, but that was all, certainly no competition to Thelonious. He was becoming more and more curious about America, more so than Jimmy ever would be, and about the changes that had taken place there. Jimmy would never step foot in his country again and that was his choice. Misery found you soon enough without your having to go look for it, he reasoned.

Agnietje, Anthony's stunningly beautiful sister, felt only slightly excluded when Anthony and her father went to the clubs, but she knew she was being protected from certain elements. She would discover alcohol and sex on her own, not with her father's help. She was perfectly happy to go into town with her girlfriends and watch the young men ogle and giggle, afraid to approach her.

Anthony and Agnietje didn't get along famously, but neither did they fight like other siblings did. For this Jimmy was extremely grateful. She never needed to ask for her brother's protection, for they were respected and perhaps a little feared. Anthony, the marvelous athlete with his good looks and his wise-appearing eyes, and always first in his class, as well. And the father, well no one really knew where he got his money. But he was a good man, so it could not have been anything evil, could it?

Anthony, not being a malicious sort, unfortunately wasn't aware of the effect he had on average people with average emotions, such as jealousy. It was only when it almost ended, his childhood of a thousand dreams, during his privileged entry into the larger world, that he truly understood the depth of his father's love for him. Only when he understood the enormity of his young-man decisions did he long for the sanctity of his ever-present extended familial mantle of protection. Only when change threatened his sense of himself did he understand the safety in continuity. And only when love was gone did he understand its loss.

By Anthony's seventeenth birthday, when they could enjoy a modicum of respectability because of Anthony's increasingly mature and sophisticated looks and Belinda's ever-more youthful appearance, they both knew that their days together were numbered. They had grown tired of covert actions, though they had many wonderful times together. They had perfected the art of appearances, masking their earthy intentions with the reassuring fragrance of a word-and gesture-perfect aloofness. They had lied, snuck around corners, communicated with elaborate signals and nearly indistinguishable eyebrow movements, created and disbanded alliances, bribed assorted service people, and hired sundry forms of transportation. As they engaged in their subterfuge, sometimes in fun and occasionally with great reluctance, but generally matter-of-factly, Anthony came to see that Belinda was anything but a "normal" woman, that she was flowering with him, and he with her, but, of necessity, for different purposes, and moving towards different destinies.

There were no arguments, not even petty bickering. Years later, a well-traveled soldier told him how women would start bickering over nothing, seeking to create distance, to negate their lover in their eyes, to make a parting of necessity more palatable, ruining for her lover, of course, much of what had come before.

And there were no great chasms of race (it never came up) or class. The difference was that Belinda, in the nurturing of her seedlet, from the awkward boy who first appeared in her bathroom to a sturdy tree-trunk of a young man with tragically good looks, a quick, incisive mind, and the techniques of a world-class cocksman, had accomplished a rather significant feat, given as she was the ideal raw materials, a feat in which she took great pride, and one which had quite obviously run its course. She was preparing for the other side of middle age, while he had everything ahead of him. She had given him all of her best, and he had healed her wounds from another life, renewed her lust for living, and shown her that there was no victory in settling for a boring life of privilege. He was an artist who had to lead an artist's life. She had to get away from him before he realized it and destroyed her.

She knew about artists, you see. For it was Anthony who made her remember, when enough time had passed since the traumas of the war, as he lifted her off her feet and spun her around, as she once again experienced the heady, giddy joys of a happy life moment by moment and the world blurred before her eyes. It was

THE REAL LIVES OF DREAMERS

Anthony who made her remember, yes, that she had been, in her youth, a promising dancer.

    Her departure was sadder than even she could have imagined. He sat beside her on a bench at the train station, silent almost until she moved towards the train. Her bag was light, but she moved like an old woman, the pep in her step lost for now. She boarded, assisted by a conductor with a more than casual interest in her well-being. Anthony wanted to scream. He wanted to kill him. He could barely stand as his stomach churned and his head pounded. She watched him, shoulders hunched, a wan smile, forced and unconvincing, his face becoming smaller and finally disappearing as she was swallowed up by the darkness of the tunnel ahead.

#

6

Nicole
2002

Nicole sat in a chair beside Paul's hospital bed. The noise outside the room rose to accommodate the energy of the morning shift as they arrived in pairs. She watched him and sobbed softly. He sure seemed to be moving around a lot, side to side, arms up, then down, hands gesturing as if trying to make a point, all while his eyes were closed and his consciousness removed from this world. He seemed to be in conflict. It was all too mysterious for her. She wasn't much for talking to people who couldn't respond, then thought that she had been doing a lot of that lately anyway, coma or not. Almost unconsciously, she began to speak, in spite of herself.

"Don't leave me, Paul. I know things have been rough, but we'll work it out. I'm sorry I haven't been there for you. Sometimes, most of the time I guess, I just didn't know what to do, or what to say. I feel so helpless, so helpless."

She felt that her pleading was foolish, that her feelings didn't weigh very heavily on whether he would come out of it or not. She cried some more and stopped, cried some more and stopped, until she cried the way she should have months ago, big, screaming sobs, pounding the bed sheets, standing and whirling herself around until she was dizzy, looking up to the heavens for answers, fighting the nurses who came in, gratefully feeling strong, masculine arms resisting her flailing, until she felt the prick in her arm as she celebrated feeling anything at all again, and falling limp in a strong man's arms, laughing one big laugh before darkness and pure, restful sleep overtook her. Paul always told her to respect the power of good drugs.

That afternoon, Nicole looked around the place. She had never liked to utter its name. The care, she was told, was among the best in an area known for the best. Thank God they had kept the medical insurance premiums current. The caregivers, another convenient euphemism in an age of euphemisms, were shockingly caring. This is what money and good manners and a little luck yielded, she mused. The man recognized her and approached. He had been all business, not as considerate as she would have liked, but far less gruff than others in some of the horror stories she had heard; the wrong insensitivity verbalized at precisely the wrong time, the retribution, the careers derailed by a lack of human kindness. So no, she would call him what he was, drop the veil just a bit, as reality gradually became a bit more acceptable, as she became a bit less fragile. He was a doctor, a highly-paid specialist, a neurosurgeon. She took a deep breath.

Dr. Wisniewski was an average-looking man of forty-five, except for his clear blue eyes that suggested that their possessor was someone with a passion for learning, who would research and find many disparate nuggets of information until they congealed into a uniform whole. His mouth was small and unsensual. His glasses were too big for his face. He felt lucky to still have a full head of hair, though it badly needed trimming. His only saving graces, externally speaking, were the custom-made shirt and beautifully-colored silk tie chosen for him by his personal shopper, a friend of his recently-deceased wife who had died of breast cancer the year before.

He approached the fragile woman slowly. Colleagues noted that his compassion with this woman was pleasantly out of character. His medical school professors had expressed surprise that he had lasted this long, given his ferocious competitiveness and take-no-prisoners attitude. They had strongly recommended that he spend his career in research and not at patients' bedsides. But the death of his wife, up close and personal this time, and the ravages of experience, had humanized him and lent an appealing sheen to the lackluster emotional complexion of a brilliant mind focused, in linear fashion, on success.

This woman was not just another patient's wife. She had conveyed to him the urgency of her appeals, not in the usual hysterics of women unaccustomed to coping with adversity, but in strikingly subtle ways. He had been surprised to learn of her emotional outburst that morning, and wondered if he could expect more of the same now.

Her intelligence and emotional maturity were fatal to him, and he had thought of no one else since their first consultation. She, with her quiet determination and matter-of-fact insistence on the highest standards of professionalism, had made him feel as though he were in the clutches of a bureaucratic quality control audit. She told him that she appreciated his methods and thoroughness, although his quest — and that's what it was, an adventure into the spirit world

— for answers had motivated him to consult the ancient texts in search of a logical explanation for her husband's condition. She was extremely feminine, in her body's curves and her tastefully-applied make-up, the elegance in her clothes and accessories. She exuded a womanly confidence that he didn't see often enough these days. He noted with alarm that he was probably in love. He was out of control. This Paul Warner was a lucky man. He would kill to have a woman like this. He just wanted to hold her, maybe feel her up a little. But first things first.

"Mrs. Warner. Good morning."

"Good morning, Dr. Wisniewski."

"Please, let's walk to my office and sit down."

"Fine."

They entered his office and he closed the door behind her while offering her a seat, momentarily losing his focus after being embraced by her perfume and hearing ocean waves crash upon rocks, wondering if, like a judge scheduled to hear his nephew's juvenile indiscretion, or a cabinet member with defense contractor holdings, he should recuse himself. He wanted her for himself, but he was entrusted to save the life of this woman's husband.

Her apprehension was barely noticeable, another trait deserving of his love, he thought. He didn't like overly-emotive women, which meant, to him, most women, but she presently exhibited very little feeling, although faced with the uncertain prospects for the man she undoubtedly loved. This was troublesome. He was shaking as he sat gingerly behind his desk, his crotch in a semi-engorged state. He wondered about the eroticism of this moment. He needed time to figure it out, but he had no time, and so became even more aggravated.

"Dr. Wisniewski." He was lost. What was he going to do? He cleared his throat and shifted in his chair, stalling. He felt like a doctoral candidate unable to defend a controversial thesis. Stick to the facts.

"Mrs. Warner, how are you holding up? Are you feeling better?"

Nicole was caught off guard. "What?"

"I mean, in light of the situation, this morni…of your husband's ilne.., I mean condition.., I mean, state." Unbelievable. Paul Warner's state could be of no concern to him now, unless it was California, on the other side of the country from him and his love.

"I…, thank you for asking. I'm alright, I suppose. I'm really alright."

"I know this is difficult, full of uncertainty." He was amazing himself.

"Yes. It is." She looked at him expectantly.

"Yes." Deep breath. Okay now.

"Well, Mrs. Warner, we ran the additional tests, as I said we would, and the results are inconclusive. The tests are all unremarkable. We simply don't know why, or how, your husband is in this semi-comatose state. There is no logical or medical explanation."

She didn't seem surprised. "None that is consistent with the current state of medical knowledge, anyway."

Now he was hard. Very hard. She is a smart one, he thought. An offensive response. Is she trying to bait me?

"Current knowledge. Yes, that's right, I suppose." Don't patronize her, fool. Well, of course, current knowledge! Don't nitpick!

"Yes, that's right." Stated with a certain finality.

He continued. "The accident was only a fender bender. He may even have been unconscious before the accident itself. He suffered barely a bump. There wasn't even a concussion. Neither was there any perceptible confluence of unfortunate medical events that could be determined to presage a freakish, er unusual, physiological response." He twisted his hands together and scratched the right side of his neck twice, the second scratch exactly as long as the first.

"Having said that, upon observation he seems to be quite happy. He smiles often. His expression changes. There is significant REM, uh, rapid eye movement. His vital signs are stable; blood pressure and heart rate are at ideal levels, at meditative levels. His general health is actually improving. His red cell count is up. Protein levels are optimal. The nurses exercise his legs. He does not move voluntarily, but there seems to be less stiffness in the joints. The lines under his eyes have vanished. The complexion is healthier. I could go on and on." He got up.

"In short, Mrs. Warner, Mr. Warner appears to be in an extended sleep, three days so far, from which he does not want to wake. He is almost grumpy when disturbed. He seems to be in a very nice place, an eery place of heightened awareness, on an extended vacation. It's the strangest thing I've ever seen in twenty years of practice."

She interrupted his thoughts. He had been pacing, as if lecturing a medical school class.

"A spiritual place," she said.

"Excuse me?"

"It is a spiritual place. Your description was accurate, but you seemed to dance around the term. My husband is a very spiritual man.......in an agnostic, secular humanist way."

Stephen Wisniewski was accustomed to the silk-like cocoon of his ego. It enveloped him in a cozy confidence. It was warm and friendly. Now, however, he was beginning to feel cold in his own office, elegantly-framed diplomas from Tufts and Johns Hopkins notwithstanding, sumptuously-plush, plum-colored carpeting be damned, mahogany bookshelf-lined walls to the contrary.

"Spiritual, yes. Spiritual." He was suddenly unable to flippantly deliver a verbal back-handed blow to someone else's sense of self; an inferior non-person, unworthy of conversing with someone of his intelligence and superior training, as he had been accustomed to doing, until fairly recently, on at least a daily basis. He began to panic as he realized that this woman was far beyond him, that for the first time in his life he was truly unable to deny that he was out of his league. No, he couldn't love this woman. It wouldn't have worked anyway. Dr. Stephen Wisniewski, M.D., Ph.D. was afraid, and no longer erect. There was another world out there, he thought, inhabited by people like her, alien life forms possessing a higher emotional awareness, acquired at greater cost than his gilded education. He had to get away from her.

He's behaving strangely, she thought. What an odd man. His behavior was doing nothing to deflect the stereotype of the brainy doctor/scientist, and she hated stereotypes. He should be in research. He's not equipped to handle these situations. She wondered when he last had a woman or, perhaps, a woman had him, bent over a table, plunging into his rear with one of those strap-ons, something only sold in disreputable stores. She looked in his eyes and suddenly, inexplicably, felt a surge of Amazonian power. She suddenly thought she could make him do anything she wanted, short of jeopardizing his career, no matter how humiliating. She boldly looked deeper into his eyes. Yes, there was fear. Unexplainably, this unsexy man had made her more excited than she'd been in a long, long time. He seemed to be granting her powers, as if she had pulled Excalibur out of the stone. Drunk with new-found possibilities, she lifted the sword skyward, twirled it around. Yes, she would rule him.

THE REAL LIVES OF DREAMERS

In a flash, she knew why Paul didn't turn her on anymore, this man that other women lusted after. He was too tough — he always knew what to do; too manly — he always had the right answer; too strong to be dominated — he was most effective in a crisis; too confident to succumb to the pure power of the pussy. She entered the world of the possessed.

The transformation complete, she locked his eyes with hers. He was pitiful. He looked like a sniveling weasel. She walked to his office door and locked it. He looked as if he wanted to yell for the police. He opened his mouth, but nothing came out. He couldn't take his eyes from hers. What a punk. A weak, pathetic excuse for a man. She let her gaze roam his body. A gut. No muscle tone. Probably a...never mind. Still standing, she hiked up her skirt, leaned over, and with both hands took off her panties and held them out in front of her. He looked positively apoplexic. She took a step, one long step, and she was breathing in his face. With her free hand, she grabbed his tie and yanked him to her. With the other, she rubbed the panties in his face, then grabbed his rock-hardness and stroked him hard.

His knees gave out. He was sweating profusely. He whimpered, then let out a yelp, like a dog whose tail had been stepped on. Her scent in his face drove him to the brink of release. She threw the panties across the room. He looked after them lovingly, but before a second whimper could escape his throat, he felt his neck being jerked violently by his tie. He was in a stupor, induced by powerlessness. Then she was sitting on the desk, legs raised and apart. She pushed his head down to her crotch. He had barely gotten his tongue out and taken two swipes at her love button when, from his depths arose a mighty roar, an unbearably pleasant itch, then a puffiness trailing its way into his urethra. His explosion was loud, but muffled, and messy. He fell back on the floor, out of breath, whimpering like

BARRY NIX

a beaten-down dog. Nicole was having none of this. She jumped off the desk and sat on his face, rocking back and forth, pushing her clitoris on his lips, searching for the best feeling. Not satisfied with this arrangement, she reached down and yanked his head up and rubbed his wimpy, limp upper lip on her sweet spot, back and forth, harder, then feverishly rocking until she knew it could happen. She saw the sun, the moon, and the stars and almost pulled his hair out, then let his miserable head fall to the floor with a thump, which sent another wave of desire through her. Arranging herself over his mouth again, she tried to push herself down his miserable throat as he tried to set a new oral land speed record with his tongue. Wave after wave after wave went through her. She came for five minutes, happy that she was a woman and could do that. She emptied herself on his miserable tailored shirt and changed forever. Before she heard sweet violins playing in a clear blue sky she was sure that Paul would be so proud of her for taking charge of her situation, and she came again.

The next day, she made him clean her bedroom in the nude, wearing only a lace apron during his lunch hour. He dusted her window sills as his erection poked through the flimsy lace. For his reward, she slapped his butt cheeks to a rosy red and rode him while stroking herself and putting her fingers, wet from her juices, in his mouth. She later wondered where they were going with this as she speculated as to which of them would suffer more if the other suddenly broke it off. In some ways, she felt more pitiful as the dominant one. She had entered the sensual world, the world of the possessed. She had never felt such confidence and power. Education and money had never done for her what those two days had. She shivered. She could almost feel Paul orchestrating it all as he smiled in his sleep.

THE REAL LIVES OF DREAMERS

She tried to laugh as she had only the night before, full and throaty, but she couldn't now. She was too afraid.

As Nicole drove home from the hospital two days later, she wondered about the unexplained events in her life, one of which had been partially explained the night before. She had shown up at Wisniewski's office late, surprising him as he was reading a medical journal and taking notes. She waited patiently in a chair in his office as he worked, drifting off to Mahler's First, remembering the Philadelphia Orchestra's magnificent performance under the leadership of a young European (Russian?) conductor the year before. Somehow he managed to finish his article. As he was gathering his papers, she got up and saw a printout of a spreadsheet of observations. One page was labeled Key Eye Examination Findings in Patients with Altered Levels of Consciousness. She read for a few minutes. After muddling through the medical terms, she came away with the understanding that there was a wealth of information in the eyes of the afflicted for those trained to see. It was in the eyes. What had she seen in Paul's eyes before the accident? It had been a while since she had looked.

She thought how fundamentally her life had changed in the last six months. The financial problems paled beside Paul's coma, and her sudden sexual flowering, at the age of forty-three, occupied her thoughts more consistently than did her love for him. At first she felt shame, then remembered something that he had said once, something that she had dismissed as another near-lunacy because it flew in the face of traditional ideas.

"Be brave, baby. Don't ever let anyone or anything prevent you from living your life to its fullest. Never make a vocation out of mourning. Grieve briefly and completely. Then get on with it."

His words had seemed cold when spoken, particularly in America, which had gotten in the habit of making media spectacles of its grieving. But she realized it hadn't been easy back in the old days, before things opened up more on the race front. He told her how he had had to let himself feel the pain and anger of the moment, then move on. That's why he looked young when other men his age were on restricted diets and dropping dead from heart disease. "They keep it all bottled up", he said. "Me, I'm not that cool. But I'm no fool, either."

But he *was* cool. He laughed at the bigots they occasionally encountered, black or white, male or female. Right in their faces. A deep, rich, belly laugh that would bend him over and pull him back up. He told her that experience had taught him that some people needed to feel superior to someone else, and when they fell short according to their particular yardsticks of success – education, money, zip code, season tickets, who they knew, whatever – they resorted to childish antics, some to name-calling still, in this day and age. That made him laugh even harder and louder. This thing that so enraged so many people just bounced off him like a tennis ball off a brownstone wall. He reasoned, for he always reasoned, that to let a stranger affect his sense of self was a sin against himself, committed, not by the stranger, but by himself. So, he argued, "since I love myself, I can't let a random act affect me. Now, if they criticize my character or my personality, apart from any media-conceived notions and contemporary social inaccuracies, and not because they could not fathom a black man possessing my particular personality, full of confidence and life, then I might listen to them, and question myself. Then you are talking about something real." Play your saxophone, baby.

THE REAL LIVES OF DREAMERS

They, the bigots, urgently longed to deny him his happiness, walked away with rage in their hearts when they realized that this black man had achieved simple peace of mind, that he possessed answers about his life that they had yet to find for their own, that were too hard for them to discern. He had no right to be this happy, they thought. Some of them wished, he surmised at one point, that they were in the South a hundred years ago and fantasized what they would do to this uppity Negro with his happy-go-lucky attitude.

Enough of that, she thought. She had things to consider now. Paul laid in a coma while she carried on with the most submissive of men, Wisniewski, *a highly-regarded neurologist.* She laughed as she plundered her past, looking for a clue to indicate the extreme pleasure she achieved from dominating her miserable, pathetic doctor. She could find none. Damn. It was there, somewhere. She was angry that it was locked away so deeply. Wait. It *had* to come from Paul somehow. She sat down. Why did she love him? She had initially been attracted to his strength. But he is an intolerant man. He cannot fathom weakness. He had chased friends away when confronted with their weaknesses.

She remembered Georgie. He was a comrade-in-jazz, about ten years older than Paul, articulate, flirtatious, and fun. Had she ever felt more appreciated than when around those two? They talked endlessly about the people they had seen and played songs for each other, put together compilation CDs, raved about the meals she prepared. There were some happy times.

One bright Saturday afternoon, Georgie had come over for a game of chess. He had returned from a visit to central Pennsylvania the previous day. Nicole had spent an extra minute or two in the mirror, looking forward to one of Georgie's generous hugs, close and warm, his hands on her back just above her ass. Paul never minded. He even encouraged these hugs, finding something to do in the meantime. He preferred a little demonstrative release to pent-up sexual energies that frustrated everyone concerned. And if Nicole really wanted to make love with Georgie, he thought that he would know it, and not forbid it.

"Georgie's a good man. Let me know if you feel you need to take it further. We'll work it out."

A need, he had said, not just a casual desire. Accommodations would have to be made. He would make them because, above all else, he wanted her to be happy. Of course, any desire, however simmering, was immediately cooled by Paul's admission that he, in all his sexiness, may not be the only man that Nicole would ever want, lagging sex drive or not. This concession infuriated her. She saw it as patronizing when it was not, resented Paul for his forethought when he felt only enlightened and well-intentioned. This was the type of good intention that ruined marriages, the subtleties conveniently disposed of when blatant accusations would do just fine.

She admitted to herself that her impulse to despise him was irrational, but hung onto it just the same, especially since he had blasted Georgie for feeling low because someone called him the 'N' word, this man of accomplishment. Paul lashed out. He told Georgie to ignore ignorant people when he could and to step on them if they tried to make their problems his problems. Georgie was ashamed. He had acted in the heat of the moment, confided a lingering sense of self-doubt and was punished for it. He swallowed hard and took Paul's words to heart. Nicole was surprised at the emotion behind Paul's words, and disappointed that he hurt his friend. She told him so later that night. His response was simple and, for him, surprisingly brief.

THE REAL LIVES OF DREAMERS

"I turned him around. Of course it hurt. Could have saved his life, his opinion of himself. He's a good man and it hurts me that he even spends time worrying about being called a name by some ignorant fool."

He had thought these things through to their logical conclusions, he told her, and hadn't heard or read anything to make him change his thinking on the matter. He was still thinking about it the next morning. That got him going on the race thing, how he had felt when he came back from Europe and the Army, how things were better and worse than he thought they would be, and how he was sick of black racism, black self-hatred, and black anti-intellectualism. All this before she had her coffee. What could she say? He apologized and went off to brood and listen to Thelonious Monk. She loved him. She despised him.

"There is power in a woman's irrationality", Luanne had told her years earlier. "You must nurture it, feed it, so that you're completely unpredictable and, therefore, desirable".

"That's absurd and old-fashioned," replied the younger Nicole, a promising mathematics and philosophy major.

"Our strength lies in our ability to be rational in difficult situations, to overcome the straitjacket our emotions put us in."

"You believe all that feminist claptrap if you want to. You talk to your boyfriends while I control mine."

"Control?! Is that what you want from a man?"

"Yeah, honey. Money and control, with a capital C. Men are children. They are all looking for their mothers."

"I categorically reject that attitude. I think it's shameful. Aren't you even going to give love a chance?"

"Love?! Ha!"

Nicole could only pity the men who had fallen victim to Luanne's predatory beauty. Paul and Nicole had been in St. Paul for the Ice Festival in '99 when into the Radisson walks Luanne, still single and still full of vitriol. After the first round of pleasantries in the lounge over hot tea, it was obvious that her attitude had not mellowed. She was now even more cynical, reminding Nicole of the know-it-all whorry woman in that all-the-rage television show, "Sex and the City".

She bragged about how she used men and again declared them useless. Nicole was horrified. She thought Paul would tear Luanne a new one. He looked in her eyes and told her that he found that kind of talk disrespectful to him as a man, and to please cease and desist. She replied with some drivel about precious male egos, the standard party line. Nicole started to get up to leave.

"No, baby, I'm going to the men's room. Talk over old times if you want."

He was entirely too calm. Nicole hadn't seen it, but she was sure he had taken his deep breath of control, the breath of reason that told him it would be better to get even than to get emotional with this dunce.

Nicole was torn. She was at the same time disgusted and fascinated. After composing herself, she discovered that Luanne was a successful corporate lawyer, feared and despised and up for partner. She probably intimidated the hell out of judges, Nicole thought. It was refreshing for Nicole, who lived a very nice life and worked with other underpaid people she admired and respected, to be reminded that there were many Luannes out there, dressed to the nines, catching planes with Luis Vuitton luggage, and unbelievably shallow. Any man who spent time with her probably deserved what he got, right?

In watching her interact with two men at the next table, it appeared that Luanne's patina of charm and seeming generosity had worn dangerously thin. They were nice, solid midwestern men who were looking to enjoy the moment and, although they hardly looked like men who could afford to refuse the possibility of a really good time when it was offered almost as an afterthought by a beautiful woman, they turned away from Luanne in practically the middle of one of her shallow, fabricated, self-aggrandizing sentences. Nicole, for the second time in five minutes, felt the need to dissociate herself from this walking, talking breath of foul air. As she was about to excuse herself (let Paul find her at the bar), a waiter walked behind Luanne and tripped, leaving a trail of strawberry sauce in her hair and down the middle of her pale yellow blouse, which was tucked into a gorgeous skirt of hip-draping tan microfiber, but which currently served as the repository for several very creamy desserts.

Nicole could not supress her urge to laugh. It felt so good! As she held her hands in front of her chest to feign restraint, Luanne's face glowered into a quite appropriate strawberry tint and she opened her mouth to say something as the waiter, a very apologetic and very muscular Hispanic man of about thirty, called for help and attempted to wipe clean an uncontroversial area on Luanne's sleeve. She, true to form, wrestled free with a look of pure venom, got up from her chair, and slipped on a fugitive banana slice. Now she was nearly in shock. Once the other diners were assured of her safety, several, then several more, began to laugh hysterically, because Luanne had somewhat loudly rendered her muddle-headed and viciously negative opinions of Walter Mondale, Neil Diamond, immigrants and anyone who made less than two hundred thousand dollars a year, alienating everyone in the room within minutes of her self-servingly officious arrival.

    The heretofore staid diners burst into spontaneous applause. Nicole even heard hooting and a rude comment or two. As the waiter whisked himself away towards the bar, Nicole turned and saw Paul smiling broadly, clapping even more enthusiastically than the Iowa couple beside him, before he slipped the waiter a twenty-dollar bill, then another. Observing this gesture, other patrons handed the waiter money and business cards, grabbed him and hugged him, then slapped each other's backs, suddenly feeling better about the day and themselves. An overly libidinous teenage girl from a wealthy Minneapolis suburb seized the opportunity to kiss him hard and rub herself against his hard body before being pulled away by her embarrassed mother.

    The waiter, Caesare, a hard-working recent Cuban immigrant struggling to adjust to ten below zero nights, thought he would be fired, but instead walked out of there with two months' rent and a healthy bulge in his pants, muttering and smiling to himself in Spanish about the Promised Land that was America.

#

7

Terry
1984

Let men tremble to win the hand of a woman,
Unless they win with it the utmost passion of her heart.

Nethaniel Hawthorne

Terry had been with Lena for three months already, about the usual time to go, when a GI's lover would realize that she was European and loving this American soldier would not lead to anything.

As he put a CD in Lena's beautiful-sounding stereo unit, Terry thought about why he had always liked older women. He liked substance with his sex, he told Paul and Anthony. Younger women could be tutored, treated well before their minds were poisoned by knuckleheaded men and bitter women who hadn't known any better themselves, but he got tired of that after a while.

Back in the States, most of the women he met that were his age had their own ideas, flexing their feminist muscles, feeling their way around in a brand new world, difficult. The older women, those who had good sense, felt just a little freer, a little more sure of themselves in the new sexual landscape, and they were willing to teach an eager young man a thing or two. Everything was different in Europe. Lena was ten years older and twenty years wiser. He felt freer than he ever had in the States.

Anthony, with his mysterious pull, had gotten them stationed in Frankfurt, in the middle of GI-weary Germany. Terry tried to fight the feeling but, despite his Jewishness, he thought he had died and gone to heaven. He was made for Germany. In the interest of preserving a healthy skepticism, his one rule was that, if he could help it, he would never have anything to do with a German born before 1940. You could never be sure.

It was their time, his and Anthony's, right now, despite the smart-assed teasing they received from undereducated soldiers, those of the economic draft who traveled from the ghettoes and trailers across America, always looking for the closest McDonald's, their idea of home and American superiority, determined to export their particular brand of under- and working-class ignorance rather than import anything of European substance.

Terry, Anthony, and Paul lived in barracks during the week and partied all weekend 'on the economy', mostly in the clubs, with and without women. They shook their heads at the soldiers who did their three-year tour of duty in the barracks, waiting to get back to America.

He loved German women, and the everyday German people he came across, even as he wondered how representative they were of the populace as a whole. He loved the German weather. He loved the German language. He loved German food. He loved German clothes. Oh, and yes, he loved German cars. They drank foul-smelling concoctions and sat in the saunas when Anthony found out about drug tests, although they were rarely tested. They were treated well in restaurants, the Americans who spoke pretty good German and their fluent Dutch friend. Anthony and Terry taught Paul the nuances of German culture not covered in the forty-hour Army Introduction to Germany class.

Terry and Anthony met Paul in the Frankfurt train station, while they were waiting for Anthony's current girlfriend to come in from Kaiserslautern. They had seen him twice before, towering over other passengers, his stride a more refined version of the ballplayer's swagger, several pairs of eyes following his every movement. They watched as women responded to him, waitresses and students and hostelers and wives with practiced peripheral vision. He behaved as if he were unaware of his appeal and only looked up occasionally from his book, for he always had a book, smiling or thinking deeply at something he had just read.

Anthony was slow to warm to people, especially since working in Intelligence. But Terry could walk up to a complete stranger and know their life story in fifteen minutes. He struck up a conversation with Paul. Two hours and several beers later, the three of them were inseparable, when they were together, anyway. Paul had been in the Army for several years already. He never planned to make it a career; he was taking advantage of being in Europe. He mentioned that he was unhappy in his unit, that he had lost his excitement for being in the Army, that he was surrounded by a bunch of horn-rimmed-glasses-wearing punks.

Paul hadn't had to fight since he was a young teen-ager, although he grew up in a really rough place. All it took was that look,

THE REAL LIVES OF DREAMERS

Terry thought, a look that let the look-ee know that he was capable of inflicting extreme pain and regret, whether psychological or physical, a look he never wanted to be on the wrong end of.

Terry saw Paul explode once, as he and Anthony entered his barracks on the Saturday after their first meeting in the Frankfurt train station. The harassment that some Army NCOs prided themselves on had assumed ridiculous and indefensible proportions. People of all ranks scattered when Paul's usually soft voice boomed out profanities as he leapt over the CQ desk like a cheetah, beautiful to watch, but momentarily terrifying. Even Terry discovered that he had involuntarily pinned himself against the wall behind him, fearful that Paul could become unreasonable. The scene reminded him of the twister he had seen expose the roots of two hundred-year-old trees from their moorings beneath twenty-year old pavements and simply stop, all in the space of fifteen seconds, and just like that it was over. So it was with Paul that day. Just like that. Paul looked around, saw soldiers literally shaking in the eerie quiet and, satisfied that he had made his point, quietly walked away. That was the last time anyone bothered him, Uniform Code of Military Justice or not. Anthony arranged to have him transferred to their unit. They played basketball two or three times a week. Paul was the big man who played under the basket.

Oh, yeah, the ball they played! Years later, after a meeting in Manhattan, Terry ran into an ex-GI who had seen the three of them play ball together. He invited him to sit, grabbing a chair from an empty table in one of those delis near Carnegie Hall with the seventeen dollar sandwiches that could feed a family of four for a week.

The ex-GI, whom Terry did not remember at all, said that he had never seen such beauty on a basketball court in all his life, college, pro, whatever.

BARRY NIX

"It was your spirits, man. That's what made the difference. Y'all were on your own clouds out there. We were just glad to be along for the ride."

Those games were highlights among highlights in Terry's life. After they had reminisced a while longer and Terry was alone, he leaned back in his chair and closed his eyes and remembered as if he were there.

Paul would grab a rebound as other leapers reached in vain, surprised at his strength and graceful ferocity as he pulled, insistently and with a guttural 'raaagh!'. Terry would sprint down the right sideline towards their basket while Anthony did the same on the left side. Paul would easily heave the ball almost the length of the court, exactly to the free throw line as Terry and Anthony each moved from one sideline to the other. Anthony would take the ball while moving to his right and flip it behind his back. Terry caught it on one bounce, faked left and glided right for an easy layup while the lone defender went flying. The crowd, for a crowd always materialized when they played, would explode. The looks on their three faces said it all, the same look. This is it, fellas, their looks said. There is no better time than this. Not in wealth or literature or music or between a woman's legs. Not ever will there be a time like this.

When they hung out on weekends, about twice a month before Terry met Lena, and when Paul wasn't catching trains to museums all over Europe, Anthony paid for everything and Terry drove them everywhere on the autobahns in his fast German cars, a different BMW or Mercedes or Audi each year. Anthony worked in Intelligence and was gone for weeks at a time. The Army was using his fluency in English, German, Dutch, and French to their advantage. He kept the Italian to himself.

THE REAL LIVES OF DREAMERS

The deal was that they could not ask questions about his work and he would get them out of minor scrapes, if needed. Anthony truly loved them for not abusing his friendship. He never had to call in a favor to get them out of jail or some other ridiculousness.

Terry opened his eyes. He sat back on the sofa and listened to Leonard Cohen's existential, monotone ramblings of younger times. For the time being, Lena was his Dutch secret. He met her one night in a sandwich shop, after driving to the Netherlands across the German border at Aachen.

It was in Maastricht, the beautiful city of magic, forty kilometers past the border at Aachen. He had driven for several hours after working all day and doing PT, Physical Training; calisthenics, push-ups, sit-ups, and a three-mile run. This was one of those exploratory trips. He was tired and hungry. He had taken a nap, showered, and jumped into his BMW, cruising at ninety miles an hour on the nearly empty autobahn to Bruce Springsteen, Tina Turner, and Kate Bush. He could do this in Europe, jump in the car and find himself in a completely different culture and encounter a different set of historical circumstances, in the time it took to drive from Philly to D.C. He remembered asking himself why he was there, how he had heard of this marvelous-looking city. He found himself in the old section, tired and hungry. He set about looking for a decent meal and a beer.

He walked along the cobblestone paths and gazed into the windows of the clothing stores, then found himself drawn to an innocuous-looking café, though it was a steak he needed, not fluffy pastry. Later, Lena told him that the pained look on his face was a stark contrast to the gaiety of his surroundings. As he opened the door, The Police were singing *Walking on The Moon*.

A long counter, filled with people, was to his right, tables and chairs on his left. He looked around for a seat. She must have had her head down when he made his first pass. Then she was directly in front of him, sitting about fifteen feet away, beckoning, offering an empty chair at her table. He was too tired to decline. He approached the table and sat down, still unaware. He began in English.

"Thank you very much. It's good to sit down. I am sorry. I don't speak Dutch very well, but we can speak German if you like."

This slang-less and contraction-less speech sounds awkward to American ears, but he found that it greatly facilitated communication with non-native English speakers. Besides, it gave him a purer feeling to speak without an assortment of extraneous crudities, colloquialisms, gestures, and intonations. Since that time, he'd always spoken plainer, to the chagrin of the tragically hip.

Then it hit him. She was incredible. She sipped her coffee and took a bite from her croissant.

"You are welcome, American man. Deutsch est okay."

Her voice, sounding like a feminine version of Anthony's Dutch-accented sing-song, but higher-pitched and even more lyrical, grabbed him and laid him down on a bed of roses. Her phrasing rolled him over. He looked up at a goddess.

She was in her mid- to late-thirties. Her smooth skin shone with a particular biracial almond tint. Her clothes flowed and were full of color, set off by an Hermés scarf around her neck. Her hair was long and well-styled. She is almost six feet tall, he guessed, and voluptuous, with full, ripe breasts and the hint of ample hips beneath her long skirt. He gestured to the waitress. He ordered in German,

THE REAL LIVES OF DREAMERS

confident that she was accustomed to German tourists. Strangely, he no longer wanted a beer.

"Kaffee unt zwie croissants, bitte."

Coffee and two croissants, please.

"Du sprecht gut Deutsch für ein Amerikaner. Bist du ein soldat?

"You speak good German for an American. Are you a soldier?"

"Jah. Mein kaserne est in Frankfurt."

"Yes. My kaserne is in Frankfurt."

A long silence as she studied him. He was slightly uncomfortable, but too tired to be really nervous. He suddenly felt astonishingly incomplete and completely taken aback. Relief as his croissants and coffee arrived.

"You are not happy," she announced in English.

He looked into her eyes and continued in English, not finding it necessary to remark on the transition. "I did not realize it until I sat down and looked into your eyes." Oh, please! He meant it, undecided whether he was too entranced to be corny or felt too profound to be trite. He looked in her eyes and did not waver. She looked away, but only for a second, before meeting his eyes again, and decided that his statement, as insincere as it sounded, was, in fact, sincere. She believed in the truth of the moment and the moment told her what she needed to hear and, partly because she wanted to and partly because it was true, decided that he was a poor lost soul who had only in the last minute or so wanted to be found. She had stumbled upon her man.

He looked down and stirred his coffee. A wave of feeling, of sensuality and endorphins, came over him. His whole body tingled and in an instant he was as refreshed as if he had awakened from a deep, late-afternoon nap. He knew the coffee wasn't that strong. Glued to his chair, all manner of superlatives crept into his brain, resisting his best efforts to sit nonchalantly and spread cherry konfiture on his croissant. He smiled a smile he had never smiled before; of expectation, of charm, of commitment, of pure, soulful happiness because he knew this once, this once, that this woman would be with him, that she was his and he was hers, that she would not be afraid the way other women had, that she would meet him on that special soil, that together they would feel the loam in their hands, rich and dark, and revel in their power and their powerlessness. There was only one thing to do now, now that they had internally established their love for each other. They needed to find out exactly who it was that they, each of them, loved. Then, now, and forever.

There is the sound of furniture bumping from outside apartment #6 on a small, mostly residential street in Amsterdam, gradually becoming louder as a man's and a woman's voices are heard sounding desperate and in trouble. There is moaning as an empty bottle is heard to fall from a table on to a wooden floor. Bedsprings are creaking. Floorboards are buckling. There are throaty growls and upper-octave screeches, insistent pleading, even quite emotional begging. There is movement. From a bed to a chair to a hallway floor, the writhing back to the bed, the climbing on…at this Frau Buchalter, bending over in her robe in the hallway, removed her very red ear from the door to the offending apartment.

Indeed, the sound inside seemed to be in full stereo so that hallway doors began to open and energetic women in hastily-gathered housecoats emerged — ample women, not one of them wearing a bra, Klaus Frobert noted gleefully — followed by bleary-eyed men

THE REAL LIVES OF DREAMERS

in a strange assemblage of striped boxers, paisley pajamas, and, for Fritz, the ex-banker who had fallen on hard times, a slightly tattered red smoking jacket.

"Well, Frau Buchalter," Klaus asked as he approached, "what is the report?" Frau Buchalter, aware of her red ear and Klaus's curious stare, made a fuss of bunching her clothes, then waved her hand in annoyance.

"Be quiet!" she shot back in her best stage whisper. "It is almost over." There was a bang inside, and then a scream so chilling it could only have come from the depths of passion.

"Oooh, Terry!"

By this time, everyone else had reached the door. The middle-aged men stood in the hallway and looked to the heavens, their eyes glazed over, silly smiles on their faces. Katrina, Klaus's wife, was the first to speak.

"Open the door, Klaus. She is being killed!"

Klaus, stocky and fiftyish, suddenly wished he were hauling cement up a long, steep stairway. "But a man is screaming, too!"

"He is also being killed! Open the door!"

Then, from inside, Lena's voice is heard. "Ich liebe dich! Schatze! Liebling!"

Klaus looks at Katrina triumphantly.

'You see?! I knew it! That is a real man!" He inserted his right forearm stiffly into the air and slapped it with his left hand. The men laughed, shook hands, and slapped each other on the back. One pulled a bottle of Ansbach Uralt from his robe pocket and passed it around. Everyone drank heartily from the bottle. Katrina, flushed and tingling, looked at Klaus in the light, in the hallway, with almost all of their neighbors clustered around.

BARRY NIX

"Hmmph! Kiss me, Klaus!" He looked at her questioningly for a second or two, reviewing their lives together in an instant. She grabbed his face and kissed him passionately as one last animal-like howl, like the sound of ten hyenas after a bad meal, emanated from inside the apartment. Then, stillness. Utter silence. The women looked down and away. The men smiled and cheered quietly, except Fritz, who was earnestly hoping to discover an untended hole in the side of Katrina's flimsy nightgown.

Meanwhile, inside the apartment, Lena's head was hanging languorously off the foot of her bed, in a diagonal sort of way, half draped in her comforter, unable for the moment to move, floating in a place so serene, so sweet, that she wanted to bring everybody there, maybe on some sort of cosmic bus. Yes, she thought, they could all go, and the wine would flow freely. She felt Terry's strong leg over her thigh. There was wetness everywhere. The sweat on her body began to chill her as her heart rate slowly returned to normal and her breathing became less shallow, but she was thinking only of her cosmic bus and the plans she would make, and who would come, and sleeping arrangements, when she heard a tentative knock on the door. She didn't move. Then, she heard a louder knock followed by several more insistent knocks. She gave up, promising herself to get back to her bus plans later. Somehow, she found the strength to hoist herself up, put on a robe, close the bedroom door, and traverse the now-great distance to the front door. She opened it slowly. It was Katrina and Klaus. Katrina had something in her hand. Good, Lena thought, the bus tickets. Katrina spoke.

"You poor thing. Are you alright? What kind of man is that? What did he do to you?"

She craned her neck and cast a suspicious glance toward the bedroom. She walked through the door carrying a tray of sausages,

THE REAL LIVES OF DREAMERS

cheeses, croissants, and wine, cluttering, distracting. Klaus followed sheepishly, observing that he had never seen such a look of wantonness on any woman as he saw on Lena just then. He wanted to meet this man, this Lena conqueror. Lena reached for some cheese and asked about the bus.

The three of them, The Mars Brothers—so named because their complexions resembled the caramel on the inside of Mars candy bars (after a summer tan, anyway), and because they all seemed to be from another planet, to the constant consternation of the more grounded working-class enlisted soldiers — differed drastically in their approaches to women. Anthony didn't like to get serious with women. Terry had always sensed lingering pain from an earlier experience, but Anthony denied it. None of them had trouble attracting women. They were soldiers, whose pride and confidence, to say nothing of their superb physical conditioning, served as a magnet for the lost, the lovelorn, the sensual, the adventurous, and the unstable. Anthony, though, literally had to fend them off. He possessed an animalism combined with a personal sensitivity that he rarely shared with men. Women could have a good time with him, or not, as he quoted Shakespeare and sang the blues while he took them on his own magic carpet ride. He was dangerous. He didn't care much, or seemed not to, while endearing himself to them, probing their secrets, asking the questions they wished other men had asked, touching their bodies and their souls where other men hadn't, before he left. He just didn't want to do what he didn't have to do, and felt no moral or social imperative to marry someone with whom he had had a good time, but for whom he cared little. Terry considered

Anthony's logic somewhat cold, but understood that Anthony was the freest, if not the happiest, of the three of them.

Paul was Anthony's polar opposite, falling in love at the drop of a clever phrase, a sucker for German-, Dutch-, or French-accented English and a promising smile. His theme song was *"Back in Love Again"*. Remember that? LTD with Jeffrey Osborne singing lead in '78? My God, who wouldn't fall in love with the women he found in a million out-of-the-way places. Terry had seen them glow in his presence, privy to the world of Paul but, usually within weeks, they burned out or gave up, feeling like little more than the exhaust fumes of his never-quite-spent white hot energy. Paul just loved women, and there were too many wonderful women to spend all of his time with just one. He was about having fun and fun with women was the most fun he could have, along with traveling and basketball and music. He loved waking up in strange beds, blinking his eyes and wondering where he was before blurry images filled his foggy brain and faraway sounds echoed with the rhythms, melodies, and harmonies that had been one with the physicality, the scents, the touches, and the tastes that led to the screams and exquisite releases to which they owed their blissful sleep.

And there was Terry. The relationship was the thing for him, the nuances of emotion and desire, the struggle to understand personalities and motivations. He, too, had been disappointed and never expected to love like…this.

He was afraid. He hadn't even told Anthony. The situation was too important to risk a friendship over a careless response or a flippant remark. He was so far gone that he didn't trust himself, stumbling through the day like a drunk, feeling his way carefully when out of Lena's presence, gliding and glowing in a light-headed euphoria when they were together. He was so in love he was walking into walls, constantly nursing annoying little bumps on either side of his head. He was not his carefree self. This was serious; adult serious, a contender for romance-of-the-century serious. He laughed to himself, continuing his impromptu game. Heart attack serious, cancer serious, easy metaphors to toss about when one was still young and felt only slightly mortal. He had never known happiness like this could exist. He liked to think that, although he was still relatively young, he learned from his experiences and was on his way to becoming a wise man one day. He wanted to disprove, at least partially, George Bernard Shaw's axiom that youth was wasted on the young. He was pleased to find that love could get better and, smiling at the bulge in his pants, even better as you got older. He was high in the sky and he didn't need oxygen.

    Lena was ten years older than he and, at any given time, beautiful or plain. Tall when she walked straight, she could also slump hideously when depressed. This always mystified him. No woman could equal her when she was on and she knew it, but didn't hold it against them. Most women seemed to silently thank her for this indulgence and basked in her radiance, becoming more beautiful themselves from the inside out in the process.

    Strong men whimpered when around her, occasionally wishing for the more steady-footed challenge of a battlefield, a production line, or a pair of goalposts when confronted by this particularly vexing and sensual woman. The shy and insecure avoided her as if she were something unseemly sent to upset their fragile Zeitgeist.

    She attracted attention everywhere she went. Her laugh was classic, a lilting "ha-ha-ha!" with her head thrown back, her delicious mouth curled, her upturned face glowing effusively whether in light or shadow, her green eyes pools of ecstasy generously revealing a passion for living.

BARRY NIX

When she was not on, however, when she was low, she was very low and behaved as an anchor attached to a foot of everyone who crossed her path, acquaintances or not. These dreary times occurred more frequently than Terry would have thought possible and he muddled through, unsure of how he had been dragged to such a low place by Sunday evening when they had celebrated his arrival in grand style late Friday night. He was glad to leave during these times, knowing that the source of the problem was not his leaving, but something inexplicably Lena-ish.

When in these funks, Terry often came to the not-so-outlandish conclusion that her whole neighborhood suffered, intuitively knowing of the doom which confronted her; the baker's smile would hold more gravity than usual; the postman seemed particularly concerned. He dismissed these unpleasant interludes as nothing, until much later, given what he received from her; so much love, friendship, culture, and real knowledge that he struggled to give to her equally and, at times, felt that he had almost accomplished this seemingly simple goal, but usually not. Consequently, he was always basking in her love, and always considered himself in her debt.

Soon after the night of the ruckus in her apartment building, after breaking bread with Karl and Katrina for the first time, Lena went into one of her funks and, without comment, emerged refreshed and alive.

Terry was on leave. They had the week together. Frustrated that this one would spoil his much-needed vacation, he had planned to pack his bags after a pleasant afternoon shower and nap when she swept into the room, freshly showered and smelling like hibiscus and coconut. She had applied makeup and was wearing some beautiful light blue lingerie thing. He instantly forgave her, but noticed this time a lingering doubt within himself, which he knew would linger longer the next time, and the next.

She stood in the doorway looking regal, something that almost any woman could do, but only a few realized or had the confidence to pull off well. She raised her arms in her diaphanous lingerie, the flimsy material spreading outward like an angel's wings. He was still in a pleasant post-nap daze, lying across the bed, enhancing the dream-like quality of the moment. Silently, she floated over to him. He was already hard, his erection fully visible through his gym shorts. He didn't sit up. As she moved closer, she pulled on her shoulder straps and her luscious beige breasts broke free. Before he could react, she pounced on him, filling the cavity his mouth created by his surprised expression with her left breast, while rubbing the right one against the side of his face. Terry tasted mint. She had mint nipples! She was already soaking wet, humping his thigh, angling so that her love button was in an optimal spot as she rotated her abdomen against his while pushing her breast further into his mouth. By this time Terry was out of his mind, full of smells and tastes and touching and rubbing. She removed her breast from his mouth, slid down his body, and kissed him so deep and hard that he almost lost his breath. Her tongue gyrated wildly inside of his mouth, and then tried to find his esophagus. She had him pinned so that he could barely move, much less respond. He let her have her way with him for awhile, then grabbed her arm and attempted to roll her over, but she resisted, slipping out of his arms and grabbing his hand to force it back on the bed. Now they were groin to groin, muscle to muscle. With a grunt and a mighty push, he forced her arms up and around as he rolled on top of her, pulled her thighs up and slammed into her. He stroked her for thirty seconds, kissed her like a wild dog, then pulled out and slid his tongue quickly down the center of her body and licked her opening pleasure box from the bottom to her love button, which he mercilessly fluttered, licked, pulled, rolled, and gently mashed with his lips. Now she was breathless, at once pushing him away and pulling him closer, trying to fit his whole head inside her. Terry held on for dear life, determined to ride this bronc until her bell rang. It rang, in deep guttural pulls and moans, wild thrashing and pillow pounding, a great stiffening and a great loosening. He loved to pleasure this woman.

He was still merciless. He gave her only about ten seconds to catch her breath, then put his Johnson against her lips. In a daze, she took him in her mouth slowly. After a few seconds, she warmed to the task and began executing her various tricks with her tongue and lips and teeth, the palms of her hands and her fingertips. He was soon exploding in her mouth. He rested a minute, turned her over, for she was passive now, and entered her from behind, then the front, then the side, then upside down, then round and round. Finally, she rolled him over, turned him around, faced him and faced the wall, rode him and squished him.

They made love that day until they were sore inside and out, until neither had anything with which to lubricate themselves or each other, until time blended into space and they blended into each other, until they read each other's thoughts and knew the colors in each other's minds. Terry had never experienced anything like it before, and never would again. They were intoxicated with the aftermath throughout the day and evening, moving in slow motion, barely able to order and eat, drinking wine and listening to wonderful, lyrical, rhythmic music, and dreaming wonderful, exotic dreams in each other's arms.

Spring 1989

This is the good life in Europe. I am happy. A good job with colleagues I respect. Friends. A little money. And love. My ultimate love.

Terry sat back on a black leather sofa with his demitasse of espresso in a small but very pleasant house outside of Hamburg. He had ten minutes before he had to go to work, in the fifth year of his blissful existence with Lena. He looked around at the art on the walls. There was one of Lena's amateurish oils next to, of all things, one of many Chagall prints. It did not fare well in comparison. The house was full of Chagall and Matisse. Terry finally said 'enough already' before they were consumed by flying matrimonial couples and colorful curved women.

They had gone to Paris in April and spent seven hours at a Picasso exhibit at the Pompidou Center. Walking around wide-eyed and vibrating with the great one's genius, they turned a corner and were greeted by his pornographic line drawings, which neither of them had come across in their reading. They barely made it to the hotel before tearing each other's clothes off. They went back the next day and discovered a Chagall exhibit that wasn't even mentioned in the literature they had read about the show. Terry was enchanted. Lena was taken away. As he looked around the house he began to wonder if she had ever come back.

Art Blakey's *Along Came Betty* was playing on the too-expensive, pure-sounding stereo, a gift from Anthony. He felt perfect. Absolutely perfect. He got up to go when the phone rang. It was Katrina, checking to see if they would be at the party Saturday. Of

BARRY NIX

course they would. The phone rang again. He had to get to work. He answered in the German fashion.

"Hello, Blaisdell."

He was surprised to hear a woman, speaking English. Her voice was strained. "Uh, yes. Terry? Is this Terry Blaisdell?"

"Yes. What can I do for you?"

"Oh, thank God. I wasn't sure about this international calling. Terry, hi. This is Claire. Claire Hargrave."

A voice from the past, after high school and before Anthony, in those hazy, confused, panicky days a million miles away. He had almost forgotten. She had broken his heart. It can't really be her. And if it is, it can't be good news.

"Claire. How did you find me?"

" Oh. It's not important. Terry, do you have a minute?"

She was more sure-footed now, finding the railing of a stairway she hadn't climbed before.

"Yes, Claire. Of course. How are you? Is something wrong." His tone was deep, his voice almost officious, ready to take charge of a crisis. It was coming back to him now. You scared, whining bitch. This had better be damn good. He hadn't cursed in months.

"Uh, well, yes." It had been twelve years, but she never expected him to grow up. That's why she left. Maybe she should have given him more of a chance. Maybe she should have looked a little deeper than equating adulthood with assuming a plethora of responsibilities before one was ready. Maybe adulthood meant a different kind of maturity. Now she wondered what kind of father he would make, or is, or something. The railing was loose, missing a screw somewhere. Grab hold now and climb.

THE REAL LIVES OF DREAMERS

"Um, Terry please don't be too hard on me. I just called to tell you that David died Tuesday. I'm handling the funeral and I know that he would want you to come. He was, uh, sick for a while."

Nothing about this sounded right. He was tempted to hang up the phone, but felt that somehow it would be in his best interest to listen. No, wait. A funeral. Travel to the States. No. Hell no..

"Will you come, Terry? It's in Philly. We, uh, moved there several years ago."

"You and David? Are you, were you, married?"

"Yes. We wanted to tell you, but…."

"Yeah. Sure."

"This is a bit much to take in right now, Claire. Can I call you back and let you know?"

"Yes. Sure. I, uh, maybe we can talk if you decide to come. I'd like to see you. We can catch up. There'll be a first class ticket at the Lufthansa counter. The funeral is Monday. We scheduled it later so you could make it."

"I see. Well, maybe. What's your number?" She gave it to him and said goodbye. So much for perfection.

As he slipped into his new Porsche, a present from Lena, he put in a tape and put Claire out of his mind. He drove down quiet streets with long names populated by quaint shops and old women white-washing steps. He stopped at a bakery, said 'Guten morgen' and was greeted with the same by the proprietors, chubby Herr Gutfreund and his wife, and their customers. They handed him two bags full of tender, flaky croissants and exchanged smiles and pleasantries with him.

He drove and listened to Depeche Mode, then Coltrane's *Equinox* to calm his increasingly excitable heart. He knew he was going to the States. No use arguing a losing cause with himself. But Philly? Lena would have a fit.

He entered the gate of the U.S. Army kaserne, as the installations were known, and passed a bag of croissants to the chubby guard with a smile. Franz smiled and waved a million times as he waved Terry through. Terry parked and walked to his building, a non-descript one-story affair with no markings. It was dark. He was still early. Good. He used his key and let himself in. He walked down a corridor, used another key and opened a door marked TELCOM, turned on the light, and went to his small office. As he waited for his terminal to power up so he could check his e-mail, he began to read. An hour later, after he had gone through the Stars and Stripes and The Frankfurter Allegemeine, and made notes in a telecommunications publication, other workers began to arrive.

Tom, a twenty-year, balding service veteran who was Terry's mentor, as was Charlie, his boss, walked in. He was wearing a funny-looking Sherlock Holmes-type plaid hat and tan trench coat, carrying his bag lunch. His gait seemed un-natural. Terry didn't know why. Tom had a number of ailments.

"Early bird catching the worm, I see. Do you ever rest, Terry?

"No, Tom. I don't need sleep. How are you?"

"I'm feeling older every day. Take care of yourself. Don't get old too early, young man." He leaned into Terry's doorway and lowered his voice.

"I think Charlie's got an opportunity for you today." He smiled and winked and was gone. It was heads-down work until eleven o'clock. Charlie stuck his head in.

"Ter. My office. Five minutes."

Charlie was short, barrel-chested, and short on hair. He generally wore reading glasses, which hung around his neck, and cheap shirts and ties, like most of his GS-15 peers. He was from an Irish family in Milwaukee, another Midwesterner. Terry liked him immensely, had had him and his wife over for dinner several times and had the favor returned. The two of them had closed some breuhauses with Tom. Their friendship was based on mutual admiration and respect, and the feeling that what they did was important. Work was work and fun was fun.

Terry sat at the conference table in a corner of Charlie's office. Charlie, compensating for the difference in their heights somewhat, sat on the opposite end of the table. The office was hardly luxurious, and Charlie was hardly tasteful, in opposition, in Terry's mind, to the ferocious efficiency and skill which he brought to his job. The desk and chairs were usually cluttered with papers and bric-a-brac and today was no different. There were several awards scattered about on different walls, a terminal in a corner, some family pictures on a side table, and a worn corduroy sport jacket hanging on a clothes tree in a corner.

"Ter, you know it's a cluster fuck out there. Policies changing every other day, asses being kissed this way and that. Congress is eager for us to scale down our operations over here. It looks like our department will be cut back to a skeleton crew for troubleshooting mostly. We're going to be busy dismantling operations, determining what we need and where, transferring systems to the kasernes that will remain in operation. So we'll be real busy for a while. Then we'll start shipping people all over, offering early retirement options to some, promoting others, and putting others out to pasture where they can't screw things up too badly. Monmouth or Ritchie, probably.

The brass has been watching you and they like what they see. The scuttlebutt is that they're going to offer you something that will really challenge that steel-trap mind of yours. Being black right now isn't hurting you, in that respect anyway…..I know you don't have a lot of love for Affirmative Action, but the truth is we need to get you qualified black folks through the pipeline as fast as we can…There's just one catch. Anything they offer you will probably be back in the States."

Terry had been wondering when Charlie was going to take a breath. He began to shake his head from side to side.

"No, no, no, what?" Surprise, surprise, Charlie thought to himself. I told those fuckers they should send him to HQ in Heidelberg. I know he wouldn't mind that, but no, they have their plans. Maybe they don't really want him to stay. Maybe he's too smart to be useful to them.

Terry suddenly thought of Paul, whom he hadn't seen since his discharge four years ago, and a blues song Anthony had played for him one day, *'Goin' to Chicago Blues'*, which seemed appropriate to quote just then.

"I'd rather drink muddy water and sleep in a hollow log."

Charlie gave him a predictably baffled look.

"Will there be anything here for me if I stay?"

"I can't be sure, but I doubt it. We're occupying a lot of valuable German real estate and they want some of it back."

Terry got up and walked over to the lone window in the office. He watched some soldiers walking in a straight line across an expanse of grass, stooping to pick up cigarette butts.

"Ter, I'm sorry, but it's at least a year away. There's time to plan and I'll help you any way I can. I just wanted to give you a heads up…..Is there something else going on?"

THE REAL LIVES OF DREAMERS

Terry turned around. Softly, almost in a whisper. "Yeah. I'm wondering if I should go to the States for a funeral. Big decision."

"No…. Well, that solves that…….. Forget it, Ter. You don't want to do that. You'll start to question everything. Leave it alone. Is it back in Minneapolis?"

"No. Philly."

"Philly?! Oh God, no. Not that cesspool."

"I haven't decided yet. Do you think I can get away for a couple of weeks?"

"Hell no. I've got to do my best to keep you here. But if you gotta go, you gotta go. You know you're going. You're already intrigued by the possibilities. But, Ter. Seriously. Look at me now. Things have changed a lot. Reading about it isn't being there. There's gonna be things you won't be prepared for. I wish you wouldn't go. Take two weeks and take Lena to Stockholm, or Barcelona." Terry looked unconvinced. Charlie had to keep trying for his friend's sake. They would eat his generous soul alive back there.

"Look around you, Terry. This is real. You've worked hard and you've got a good life that you're enjoying, and rightfully so. Your life won't become any less real because of what you see in the States. Lena's love for you won't become trivial because you look around and suddenly feel guilty for your emotional and material prosperity. You're a sensitive guy. Don't go." Terry was listening, but Charlie could see that he still wasn't getting anywhere.

"How does Lena feel about it?"

"I haven't told her yet. This would be solo. She's due back from Munich today. She has no desire to go to the States. None at all."

"She'll have a fit."

"I know."

BARRY NIX

After work, Terry played three hard games of racquetball with two players he'd never beaten, victory always just out of reach. He lost the first two. At the end of the third game, he banged his knee on the fiberglass wall chasing a ball, but still managed to scoop under it and fire a game winner that pinched the corner only two inches from the floor and dropped, unplayable. He cherished that victory, saw it as a turning point in his life somehow, re-played it in his mind again and again. He rested for ten minutes and lifted weights for half an hour.

As he left the gym, refreshed after a sauna and a shower but limping slightly, a company of soldiers was running its last leg on the track, only twenty yards away. The runners were soaked with sweat and singing cadences. Some fell out of the group as hard-bodied NCO's urged them to dig deeper and find what they needed to finish the run. He realized he was getting older, losing a little steam each year. He stood there and drifted away. He saw himself running with Anthony and Paul the way they used to, Paul always a step or two behind, running faster when with his faster friends. They sang the standard airborne cadence.

> *'Get up, step up, shuffle to the door*
> *Step right out and count to four*
> *Sound off! Sound off! One and two and*
> *Three Four!'*

He wanted to know. Where are my friends?

Lena had a fit. It was after dinner, by candlelight and Segovia. They could hear the Spanish guitar master scraping the strings

THE REAL LIVES OF DREAMERS

as he played. This music was beyond romantic, Terry thought, although the setting was a lover's dream. It was art, pure beauty, too beautiful for simple romance. It demanded unrehearsed passion and an unflinching free-fall into the depths of lovers' souls, into dreams made real.

Terry refilled their wine glasses. They moved to their favorite big, overstuffed chair and she sat on his lap, his body still tingling from his workout. She leaned back in his arms. He stroked her hair and nibbled on her ear. He waited for her to speak. It didn't take long.

"Shall I cancel our plans for this weekend?"

"No. We'll have fun… I hadn't seen David since 1979." He had already decided not to mention Claire. There was no need. It was history. "We had great times together, jumping in and out of different businesses, trying to figure how we were going to get rich."

"So why did he turn his back on you, his friend?"

Her love and seeming innocence, her basic questions posed like a child, kept him honest and had furthered his growth as a man. Love, he surmised, either makes you grow up and behave as an adult, or exposes your immaturity and selfishness for all the world to see.

"I don't know. He had his reasons, I suppose. I was a good friend. But I've also not been there for friends. There's enough guilt to go around. We shouldn't take our friends for granted. Friendship is important. I had really forgotten about him."

"He did not deserve your friendship. Even now you suffer just to think about it. You should not go to the funeral."

"Don't worry, schatze."

Segovia was finished. A bass began a slow song, then guitars asked a question. Teddy Pendergrass came in and pleaded, *'Can we be lovers?'* He was playing dirty. She melted in his arms. He nudged her up and they began to dance slowly.

"Terry, you know this song makes me weak."

His eyes welled up with tears. "Yes, schatze. Me, too. I love you, Lena. Don't ever forget it. I still love you too much. You still give me butterflies in my stomach."

She started to cry, too, looking up at him. "You silly man." They kissed each other, a soft, gentle, loving kiss for the ages, and fell to the floor as Teddy's pleading became so intense, so heartfelt, as Lena told Terry how happy he made her, and they rocked each other, wiped each other's tears away, until they fell asleep in each other's arms, a heap of love on the floor.

Another day. Which day? One day closer to his departure. A whooshing sound. The Silver Surfer surfing in space, past planets and stars. He stopped and looked down from his perch in space, then took off again. Whooosh.

Terry opened his eyes. He looked over at Lena. She opened her eyes.

"I don't have a good feeling about your trip."

"I'm not crazy about it myself. Come with me."

"No. I know you need to go alone, and I have no desire to visit America. My friends have told me about the crime and the dirt and the uneducated people."

"You know there's more to it than that. I came from America."

"You are a freak of nature. We all know that. I never hear anything positive about America anymore. Your soldiers are terrified of living as civilians in their own country. So many rich people and so many people living in, in, das Elend…"

THE REAL LIVES OF DREAMERS

"Misery."

"Yes, in such misery."

And later, after work and dinner, he tried again.

"You sound as if I've already left you for some romantic American dream. My dream is right here, right now. I will only be a visitor in America."

"I have read articles which disturb me very much. There is so much trouble in the world. America is losing its power, its economic and its moral power."

"Writers exaggerate."

"Not these writers. You are not taking me seriously."

"Yes, I am, Lena. I don't know what to say. I will be gone for two weeks, maybe less. I haven't been back in eight years. I'll just look around a little bit, see what's happening. Our lives will not change. I will be the same man when I return."

"Perhaps. Perhaps not."

Katrina and Klaus's party took place in a Greek restaurant in Hamburg that Sunday afternoon. Terry looked around at Germans, Africans, Indians, Dutch, and Americans, children and dogs, his group, his friends, talking and laughing and drinking and dancing.

Lena sat on a table, surrounded by six or seven men, young and old, hanging on to her every word. Klaus led a winding, snake-like line of children around the restaurant like a merry Pied Piper, swaying back and forth to a song Terry never heard, the chorus repeated until it was etched in everyone's brain for the rest of their lives, recalling this party, *'Let's Have a Good Time'*. Lena looked over and threw him a kiss. He smiled, shaking his head back and forth.

As the song ended, Klaus fell into him and the children squealed and clapped in delight, falling themselves, like dominoes, on to each other one by one. Klaus wiped his moist brow as Terry pretended not to notice Katrina's loving glance thrown in his direction. Klaus pointed to Lena's table.

"You must be a confident man."

"Or a fool, eh?" They had a good laugh as children tugged on Terry's jacket, urging him to take Klaus's place.

"When are you going to have a child?," Klaus asked.

"Good question. Soon, maybe. Come on." They both danced with the children and swung them around. The adults clapped. The children, flushed, out of breath, and proud of themselves, bowed.

Terry listened to John Lee Hooker on the flight to Philly. He felt oddly sad and tired. He had told Lena he would only stay a week. And he meant it. John Lee sang, in that haunting, rich, whiskey-soaked voice, 'I reached over, and you was not there.' He rested.

Paul met him at the airport. He didn't look well. He had picked up some weight. From sitting around studying all the damn time, he said. And he hated Philly. It was no longer the town he grew up in. He didn't know anybody anymore and the people were much meaner than he remembered, into some 'attitude' thing for some reason. And cheating was rampant in his classes. He had just been too involved in various projects to leave. He was close to finishing a degree in computer science and talked excitedly about the future and the money-making possibilities for those situated to take advantage of the enormous changes about to take place. Terry hated computers, figuring they were years from doing what he needed them to do. He thought the programming was purposefully designed to be opaque, and the jargon carefully created to exclude those not in the know.

"Oh, no. You've got to get to the higher level, the business level. That's where the action is. There's some tremendous work going on at Stanford and MIT. And they're working on the user side, too. These developments will change the world," Paul said. To Terry's surprise, his excitement was contagious.

At dinner, Paul apologized for not having more time to spend with Terry. He had research projects to finish and exams to take. He seemed poor, but happy in his world of theory. Terry slipped two hundred dollars into his jacket pocket when he went to the men's room. Before they parted, Paul gave him the name of the best places to get a cheese steak, along with an explanation of important new technologies and some companies to watch. Terry didn't pay much attention to the stock market, but promised he would look into it.

As Terry drove around, he pondered how his life had changed. He was glad Paul was so thrilled about the future, considering he had put ten years in the Army and had little to show for it. Not much money put away, no established career, but a life fully-lived, with no regrets and few apologies, a head full of memories to relish, a mouth full of stories to tell. He relied on himself to an almost absurd degree, never wavering, sure that no unforeseen disaster would come his way. Terry was very pleasantly surprised that he was finishing his degree. He was working hard, and more outspoken than ever. Was there anything he didn't have an opinion about?

Aside from a couple of postcards, neither of them had heard anything from Anthony. He had talked about finishing his doctoral studies in anthropology, but they didn't know. After discharge, five years to the day after they reported to basic training, Anthony had spent some time in Eindhoven with his father, worked on his house and brooded, then gone back to the States to pursue his blues and his doctorate. He needed some time, he told them. He would find them in a few years. Well, five was more than a few. Five was several, and Terry didn't like it one bit. He felt abandoned; first by David, who disappeared after their partnership dissolved, just before he met Anthony. Later, Anthony disappeared into thin air. Was something wrong with him? Were his friends not really his friends? Life is too short not to value each other. He didn't understand. He never excluded anyone from his circle because he was madly in love, not like a lot of men did, proclaiming marriage to be the death of all fun, or trivializing their prior lives as if none of it really mattered except as preparation for defeat, their inevitable capitulation to the feminine war of attrition, growing up and squarely facing the drudgery and responsibility that was to be their lot in life until they died.

The next morning he got lost as he drove to the funeral. According to the map he was only a few blocks from his hotel, but the neighborhood was particularly seedy. He watched a raggedy black man talk to himself as he walked streets with torn-up pavements in front of boarded-up stores. He kept driving and watched the transformation to the downtown commercial sector. Unimpressive. He longed for Hamburg already.

The Baptist church was old and big, remodeled and annexed to accommodate the demands of time and a growing congregation. There was a smattering of white mourners in a sea of several hundred. Terry marveled at the black women in their funereal finery, wearing colorful, intricately-detailed hats that defied description. And prosperous-looking black men in suits always gave him a sense of pride, except when accompanied by bow ties, bean pies, and rhetoric. He was amazed at the turnout. Apparently, there was a lot he didn't know about David and the new world taking shape. He felt as if he had a sign around his neck, so out of place did he feel everywhere he went. Had he changed that much? Had everything and everyone else? He used to be able to travel anywhere and feel at ease. So far, he was not enjoying life in Philly. People eyed him suspiciously, this light-skinned stranger in his European-cut suit. He had never heard so much cursing in his life as when walking down the streets of that dirty town. People seemed to revel in their ignorance. Inside the church was different, though. Praise the Lord. The choir finished a rousing number. Shhh. Here comes Reverend Wilson.

Reverend Wilson was very dark, dark enough to forget about acceptance outside of certain areas, dark enough to have withstood taunts from light brown-skinned schoolmates, yet somehow strong enough to have weathered them and much more. Terry, no stranger to teasing and questioning on account of his own differences, wondered what his life had been like, how he had seemed to prosper. His wise eyes were full of pain now as he scanned the pews facing him. Probably in his early sixties and standing about six feet five, his face wasn't very lined, but etched with character. There was plenty of curly mixed grey hair on his head, and sideburns a little longer than the current fashion, more akin to those worn in the late sixties. Terry guessed that maybe it was athleticism that saved him, maybe a keen intellect, maybe a hard-bitten approach to life. Maybe he was one of those legendary church hustlers. Then again, maybe his life had been a pleasant one. Enough guessing. People didn't know anything about anybody else, and it was usually too much trouble to take the time to find out. This Reverend Wilson appeared to be a man Terry wanted to meet. What will he say now? Shhh. There was excitement in the air. Reverend Wilson got up from his seat on the stage and carried his notes and a bible to the podium. Terry realized that there were several feet of pew space between himself and the next mourner. The rustling of skirts and the hushing of children stopped. The voice from the podium was a rich baritone, amazing in its inflections and modulations.

"Please allow me to extend my sympathies to the family for the loss of our friend, David Taylor…

David Taylor was a good man. A good man who attempted to follow the road down which his heart and soul led him, and who made some mistakes along the way. He was a smart man, a brilliant man, determined not to let the circumstances of his modest upbringing dictate the circumstances of the rest of his life. He made a lot of money! And he took wonderful care of his family, both spiritually and materially, and shared his gifts with his church and his community. He shared, not because he was concerned with politics, or about what people thought, but out of a genuine concern for people and for humanity. And there are several young people in the best universities, who earned their places there, and who are excelling, who are glad he did…His is a dying breed…

He had good manners! He did, of course, speak perfect English and could, when called upon, speak the dialect of our people from the delta of Mississippi to the fields of South Carolina to the urban landscapes of Chicago and Philadelphia, and make your sides hurt from laughter."

Chuckles from the audience.

"Yes he could…This man enjoyed livin', y'all! He knew he could because he had no guilt in his heart about not doing what he could to help others, while avoiding the sin of greed. He enjoyed money and a certain amount of finery, but valued people over material things. He was not a perfect man. He was, in his last days, a troubled man, a man in tremendous pain, suffering mental anguish for which no one had the answer…and from which he found no escape. Many of us sincerely tried to help, but to no avail. And I must admit, our actions were not entirely selfless.

For when a man like that! A man full of hope and optimism, joy and a love of life, when a man like that! Like David Taylor! When *his* star begins to fade, the rest of our lives become di-mi-ni-shed!.... and we realize how much we depended on him to lift us out of our self-absorption, to make us feel that we can be what we thought we could be, what we have to be to get through this time on earth, and what we must become to enter the Kingdom of God! ………We need men!" He pounded the podium and everyone in the church jumped. Then, he paused for a long time as he looked around at the faces in the pews.

"No man is perfect, but men are what we need, and it hurts me so much when a man like that, a man like David Taylor, a man who could have taught us all so much more, an imperfect man who tried hard….when a man like that loses his way, we feel a little weaker, we question ourselves a little more, don't we? A man who makes the rest of us ask ourselves, 'How hard am I trying?'

"And most of us know the answer to that question, don't we? Socrates said that an unexamined life is not worth living. And Cornel West replied that an examined life is full of pain, but must be faced, nonetheless…The departure of a man like David Taylor, a man gone in his prime while so many of infinitely lesser stature prevail, his departure forces an examination, an introspection, of who we are…and what we value in this life…while preparing for the next world."

BARRY NIX

Reverend Wilson was respectfully mobbed after the funeral, his status apparent, the love of his flock overwhelming to a stranger unused to a mass outpouring. Terry couldn't get close enough to thank him. He didn't know anything, he decided.

Terry realized how long he had been away from black women in numbers when she opened the door. She was about forty-five, in a charcoal grey dress that hugged her generous curves. The light grey and gold silk scarf that hung from her shoulders drew attention to what couldn't be perfect breasts, 42-D, he guessed, but just as easily could. Oh my, the hips. He had to look up. A mixed grey perm, black earrings. My, my. Her smooth face, the color of a walnut cabinet, featured almond eyes and a full mouth in a shade of peach. She was trouble. His knees buckled and a barely-audible, high-pitched 'Hmm!' escaped from the back of his throat. He felt instant guilt, but reasoned that his actions were reflexive and involuntary, thus absolving him from responsibility. Oh no, not that smile.

"Oh, hi! You must be Terry. Claire described you perfectly." Terry found that strange, since he had seen the ravages that time dispatched on so many.

"Yes. Hi. Yes, I'm Terry. Terry Blaisdell. I was David's friend, er, a friend of David's, in Minneapolis." He followed her into a large, elegant foyer. Several people were milling about in each of several rooms off the main hall. She turned to face him. Her voice was like sunshine on a pussywillow, her tone molasses on cornbread.

"Hi, Terry. I'm David's aunt, Cordelia. So you're Terry, the world traveler. I've heard a lot about you."

"Jewel of the sea."

THE REAL LIVES OF DREAMERS

"Excuse me, honey."

"The name Cordelia. It's Welsh. It means 'jewel of the sea'. I knew another woman named Cordelia once."

"I'll bet you did, darlin'. Imagine that. All these years and I'm just finding that out. I never really thought about it. I'm not much for water, though. Let me fix you a plate, Terry." Given her sophisticated appearance, he wondered if the hominess was a put-on.

"Did you make any of the dishes?" He knew some things wouldn't change. Black women cooked and brought food to funeral wakes. Oh, the food.

"Yes, I did. I made the peach cobbler."

"I'll come back for that, thank you. But I'd like to see Claire first. Is she up to seeing anyone?" He had to get away from this woman.

"I think so. She's in the kitchen."

"Thank you."

"Here's my card. In case I don't see you again. Call me if you need help with anything, or would just like to talk to somebody while you're here."

"Thank you. Thank you very much."

"You have such good manners, Terry. It's refreshing. We don't see that enough these days."

"Well, thank you again. Bye" He walked in the direction she pointed. He looked at the card. She was a CPA with her own firm. Interesting. He scooped a napkin from a table full of food, wiped the sweat off his brow and took a deep breath, then put the card in his jacket pocket, never thinking, given his happy situation, that he would have occasion to call her.

Claire was in the bright, airy kitchen. She looked like a woman in charge, efficiently bustling about handling sundry requests, not what he expected for the grieving widow. Several people sat at a table with full plates of turkey, candied sweet potatoes, collard greens, biscuits, and cranberry sauce; attempting, then giving up, conversation between mouthfuls of food that made them shake their heads and murmur *hmmm* every once in a while. More people were in a corner with drinks, talking quietly. She looked over and saw him.

"Terry! Oh, Terry!" She ran the few feet to him and hugged him hard. "You came."

"Yes, I came. Of course I did. Are you alright?"

"Yes. I'm fine. We knew it was coming. He had been very sick. I'll explain." She took his arm and steered him in the direction of the group in the corner.

"Let me introduce you to everyone. This is Dr. and Mrs. Williams, Dr. and Mrs. Johnson, and Dr. and Dr. Healey. Everyone, this is Terry Blaisdell, David's friend from back in the day. Terry was in the military and stayed in Germany."

"What are you doing now, Mr. Blaisdell?" Dr. Williams, he guessed, asked.

"Enjoying life mostly, but I'm also a telecommunications manager." Williams' face turned smug, his tone turned to condescension.

"Tell me, is military intelligence still a contradiction in terms?" The others smirked behind their drinks.

Terry looked in his eyes for a moment as he re-grouped, caught off guard by this pompous ass. Without moving his head he looked around at the group. These were the people Paul had warned him about. His soldier's instincts took over. His face became harder. He attacked the soft underbelly.

THE REAL LIVES OF DREAMERS

"No more than compassionate doctoring." He turned to Claire. "Can we talk?"

"Of course. I'm sure everyone will be fine here." Williams looked sheepish, almost in shock, his shallowness revealed, dismissed as a peasant. The others sported small smiles, guilty by association.

Claire led the way to an upstairs study. A large crystal vase sat on a table, overflowing with white, yellow, and red roses. Terry spotted a collage painting on the far wall. It didn't look like a print. He walked over and admired it for a minute, not able to place why it looked familiar.

"Are all of your friends that personable? Ah, it's a Bearden! Original?"

"Yes. David was an early collector. Beautiful, isn't it? He's really a good person when you get to know him. Dr. Williams, I mean."

"I'm sure. Aren't all effete snobs?" He studied the painting. She was uneasy. She exhaled slowly.

"Well."

"Well. I hadn't heard from David in years, or from you."

"Ten years. We enjoyed your postcards, until they stopped coming. And the Belgian lace. And the crystal." She pointed to the vase on the coffee table.

"Let's sit."

They sat down. "How did David die, Claire? He was only forty-six."

"Well, as I said, he had been very sick. He had been HIV positive since '83, from a blood transfusion. He was one of the first, but he kept himself healthy. He made a lot of money in real estate and made some shrewd investments, but it was his work with kids that he really loved. Then this crack epidemic hit in '86 and quite a few of his success stories became failures. People just wanted to try a new way to get high and, instantly, they were addicted. There were some scary times. His immune system couldn't handle the stress and he developed symptoms, so he got hold of some heroin and gave himself an overdose, just like so many of the friends you shared in the old days. He stopped getting high after you left, so I know it was intentional."

Terry was having trouble enough digesting it all.

"Well, he didn't always make sense, did he? Neither did you. Anyway, our marriage was...... I loved him. He felt so much guilt for not staying in touch with you, and for not doing more to make your partnership work. He left you some money, a hundred thousand dollars."

"Hmm. That's nice. I've got money. It's friends from the old days that I need!"

"I know, Terry…But just so I know, will you take the money?"

"Of course I'll take the money."

There was a knock at the door.

"Yes?"

A girl of about eleven, graceful beyond her years, opened her eyes.

"Come in, Sandy. I'd like you to meet Mr. Blaisdell, Daddy's friend from the old days."

"It's Cassandra. Hello."

Claire rolled her eyes.

"Hello, Cassandra. It's nice to meet you." He was confused, again.

"And it's nice to meet you. I've heard a lot about you."

"I wish I could say the same. You're a fine young lady."

THE REAL LIVES OF DREAMERS

She spoke German. "Perhaps we could talk sometime."

He responded in kind. "Of course. I'd like that."

"Mom, I just came to check on you. You seem to be in good hands."

"Thanks, Honey. I'm fine. We're just catching up."

"Okay." "*Jus*, Mr. Blaisdell."

"*Jus*, Cassandra."

Cassandra left.

"She speaks good German."

"She's attending boarding school in Switzerland."

"There's something else about her, too."

"Really? What else, do you think?"

"I don't know. I can't quite put my finger on it…… Why did you leave me?"

"Don't ask, Terry. You had a good heart, but you were the wildest, flakiest, gettin'-highest man I ever met."

"I loved you. I'm askin'!"

"You loved any intelligent woman with good poontang! You were living your own life!"

"Did I ever mistreat you?!"

"No, Terry."

He was pacing manically now. "

He stopped pacing and sat down, then got up, paced again for a moment, and sat down again before taking a deep breath and speaking softly.

"But why, Claire? Why then, without a word? I could have changed."

"It happened one drunken night. David and I met and held each other's hands, wondering how you would turn out. You weren't a very responsible business partner, you know."

"Was I really that bad? We were just feeling our way around, making it up as went."

"No. David had a plan. You didn't have enough faith in him to follow his lead. You were too wild and head-strong and he didn't have the strength, he didn't have the personality, to fight you, to argue his point. You really hurt him! And I….you were driving me crazy. I just couldn't take that trip with you. Do you have any idea….?!"

Terry leaned on a wall trying to remember. It came back to him in snippets. There was the distance, and the partying. Maybe he was too impatient.

"I guess I don't," he conceded.

Terry got up, went to a window, and looked out. A man and a woman were talking in the back yard, drinks in hand.

"I wrote to you. I sent you presents. Nothing. I don't even know why I'm here."

"I know, Terry. I know."

Later, in his European-style hotel room in the Olde City section of the city the next morning, he was sipping coffee and reading the Philadelphia Inquirer for the first time in several years.

On the radio, a commentator and his guest, a psychiatrist, began discussing father-child relationships. Then:

"It's always been my opinion that a man is not a man until he's a father, or a mentor, to someone."

Terry looked up from his paper and stared at the radio.

The next day, he called Claire. She was resting. Cassandra spoke to him and asked him what he had planned. He mentioned a trip to the museum. She surprised him by asking to tag along. He agreed. That afternoon, at the Philadelphia Museum of Art, they walked slowly through a fairly dark room full of Turkish tiles and fifteenth-century handmade Persian carpets. They talked and discussed certain pieces.

"Mom said you were wild. You don't seem wild to me now."

"She told you that, huh? These are different times. I'm happy. I'm in love. I'm at peace with myself…and my demons."

"Mom said you did drugs."

"Yes, I did drugs. The drugs we did then were like candy compared to what's out here now, though. They were different times. Before crack and AIDS…and a lot of things. Life was a blast. Talking about it now makes me feel old. I was never addicted to anything. But I knew a lot of people who were, some good people who lost their way."

"And life wasn't a blast anymore, huh? My father used to say that. 'Life was a blast.'"

"He was a good one from what I've heard."

"He was a saint."

"That's sounds like something a Catholic would say."

"I attended Catholic school here before boarding school in Lucerne. He used to say he was mixing Catholic discipline with the Baptist spirit."

"Hah. That sounds about right."

They talked for a while, appreciating the art.

"How's your mother handling things?"

"She has some bad days."

They continued to walk and ponder.

"Would you like to come visit me, and my wife, in Hamburg?"

"Sure. It might be a blast."

"Listen, if you need anything, if I can do anything, any time, you just...."

She smiled, sensing his unease. She stepped over to him and gave him a big hug. Returning her hug, he smiled and wiped his brow.

Later, after lunch at the museum restaurant, they kept on, silently agreeing to embark on a day-long art appreciation marathon, feeling that it would lend an additional luster to their new-found friendship and communication. Exhausted, they sat on a bench, looking tired, breathing deeply, absorbing where they were, surrounded by paintings of Degas, Pissarro, Monet, and Renoir.

She spoke first. "This is intense."

"Yes. It is."

That evening, sometime after six, he sat in a chair reading The New York Times and listening to new jazz CDs - more of Paul's right-on-the-money recommendations - and sipping from a glass of Bailey's Irish cream.

At the same time, although it was sometime after midnight in Hamburg, Lena, Klaus, and Katrina sat in Lena and Terry's house, sipping wine after a late dinner. Klaus said something funny and they all laughed. Although she looked tired, Lena got up and coaxed Klaus from his chair for a dance to *The Boulevard of Broken Dreams*. Katrina got up and joined them. They spun languorously to the melancholy saxophone. Lena wondered what Terry was doing as she savored their conversation from earlier in the day. As the song ended and they caught their breaths, waving napkins in front of their faces and lovingly wiping each other's brows, Lena thought about how happy she was. It's a shame, she thought, and fell into Klaus's arms, dead before he caught her.

Terry, firmly ensconced in a comfortable place, enjoying his second day in Philly immensely, drifted off to sleep to Bryan Ferry's ultra-sensual *Boys and Girls*, a soundtrack to innumerable lovemaking sessions with Lena. As the phone rang, he wondered who would call him after midnight. He had talked to Lena only a few hours before. She seemed distant already. He wondered about her behavior as he picked up the phone on the third ring and, again, changed forever. He was not the same man when he returned to Hamburg.

It was raining lightly, the drizzle of the in-between. A procession of black-clad men and women, mostly German, many from the party in the restaurant only a week before, walked along a straight dirt road, lightly as if in a ballet, between two rows of carefully planted, perfectly symmetrical, fifty-year old trees in full bloom.

Terry and Klaus were among the pallbearers. Katrina, sobbing, led a group of mourners behind the casket. She watched as Terry stumbled, not from the weight on his shoulder, but from his new burden. He looked to his left and saw Lena as an apparition, barefoot and dressed in a translucent white gown, dancing a dance of joy, looking at the somber throng of several hundred as if to ask why. He was stunned, but Katrina seemed to have seen Lena, too. A look, between time and space and tears, passed between them. He wondered what new world he had begun to inhabit.

A mourner, a big, strong block of a man, his undabbed tears filling the corners of his red eyes, touched Terry's elbow and silently took his place among the pallbearers. He had been one of Lena's rapt admirers at the party, one of the hopelessly lovelorn, Terry had joked. There was nothing funny about it now. He would have to break bread with this man, he thought. He expressed his gratitude with a solemn nod.

He stepped aside and fell in beside Katrina, who immediately clutched his arm. Her eyes were open wide. She started to speak, but decided not to. Terry turned back to look at Lena, but she was gone. They were a few steps behind the other mourners and looked down at the moist imprints left behind by their shoes on the wet ground as they followed them.

The rain stopped. The sun appeared, bright and unknowing. In the limousine with Klaus and Katrina, as he gazed through the window at the artfully-arranged lines of trees on either side of them, a little boy and girl, each about five years old and resembling a young Terry and Lena, appeared beside the limousine, holding hands, laughing and skipping down the road. As the limousine sped up, the boy and girl looked on as if to ask, 'Where are you going? Why are you leaving?' Sadly, they waved goodbye and sat down in the middle of the road and threw dirt at each other. The dreams had begun.

T he reading of Lena's will. He needed nothing. He had had everything he wanted. Nothing else mattered. There was no going on. Katrina had made him come to this place, the very tasteful office of Lena's attorney, drunk, after throwing him in the shower and selecting his underwear. Klaus was helpless. He never possessed any skill in these matters. He worked with his hands and his soul. He lived for Katrina. She was the only one Terry listened to these days, these miserable days they all wanted to go away, but which had to be lived, like untreated asthmatics experiencing an attack, heaving for their emotional breaths and praying for a re-opening of their scarred lungs.

Herr Schmidt, an older, distinguished, wise-appearing lawyer who looked amazingly like Max von Sydow, welcomed Terry, Klaus, Katrina, and an unknown middle-aged woman warmly as they filed somberly into his office. Terry's eyes were glazed and far away. He wanted to tell Mr. Von Sydow how much he enjoyed his work. Katrina, the obvious center of strength in the group, bade Herr Schmidt to commence.

"I will speak English so that there is no misunderstanding. Is that acceptable to everyone?"

Everyone but Terry nodded. Understandably, he was distant and still.

"Very good. Mrs. Blaisdell possessed a few secrets which she asked me to reveal if this time should come. She was one of the finest women I have ever met…I will miss her very much…

So! Please allow me to introduce Frau Herlich. She is the Executive Director of The Seaman's Charity Association. Shall we proceed?"

Everyone nodded.

"Very good. This will is dated March first, nineteen eighty-nine, eight months ago. 'I, Lena Blaisdell, being of sound mind and body, have led a secret life. I apologize to my friends and to my husband, but I did not want you to see me differently, for you have made my life a perfect one. At this time I am unbelievably happy, so I do not want to change one thing in my life, but I have a feeling that things will change very soon. I have no explanation for these feelings, except to say that I have recently heard a distant calling of unimaginable purity, and it has gotten closer in the last month, so I feel that preparations are in order. Do not mourn me too much, for I know that I am happy here.

My father was a modern pirate and smuggler during the war. I do not know the exact details, but he was an evil man until he found me, his secret daughter, after my mother died. He sought redemption..."

"Redemption. Wie heise das auf Deutsch?" Klaus asked.

"Redemption. Uh, uh, die Erlosung."

"Ah. Danke schon."

"Bitte schon."

"He sought redemption by establishing The Seamen's Charity Association and by performing other good deeds. He left me money, which I invested with Herr Schmidt. But now, it is time that money did good things. I am giving it to you, my family and friends, to enjoy and to make other people smile.

...To the Seamen's Charity Association I leave, in addition to the endowment established by my father, fifteen percent of my wealth. To Klaus and Katrina, I leave ten percent. To Herr Schmidt, I leave five percent. To my husband Terry I leave seventy percent of my wealth to enjoy and to do the good things which he has dreamed of doing since he was a boy."

Herr Schmidt put the paper down and looked up solemnly, then smiled.

"That is all. So. Congratulations. The recipients will share approximately eighty million marks in assets."

Klaus and Katrina gasped and looked at each other, amazed. They heard a loud thud. They looked over and saw Terry on the floor, Frau Herlich leaning over him. He opened his eyes and tried to get up. He hit his head on the bottom of the conference table and passed out again. Herr Schmidt rushed to get water. Klaus sat in

THE REAL LIVES OF DREAMERS

his chair, dazed. A moment passed as Herr Schmidt returned. Terry woke up, flailed his arms and sent the glass of water out of Frau Herlich's hands and onto Herr Schmidt, who fell backwards onto Katrina, partially exposing her ample thighs and bosom in a silky brassiere as they crashed to the floor. Klaus tried to say something, but nothing came out. Gently helping the embarrassed Herr Schmidt off of her, all the newly comfortable Katrina could think of was how much she wanted to be in Terry's arms.

Paul and Anthony, Klaus and Katrina. They were his foundation after Lena died. As military men, the Mars Brothers had grown comfortable with the possibility of going to war and dying themselves. Several times, Anthony had come closer to facing death than he'd anticipated when signing up on that bored day in August; but this was different.

Terry would not be consoled. Publicly, he seemed to be adjusting, but he was a proud man, and Lena would not want the world to know what they had, he told himself, but anyone with eyes who saw them for more than five seconds knew what they had, and the sheer beauty of it brought some women to tears as they hoped with every fiber of their being that they could have it, for just a short while, for they knew that nothing that good ever lasted very long. It was beyond contentment, beyond great. It was cosmic, a soaring rocket carrying two people, weightless with the wonders of their love, looking out at impossibly beautiful skies as the earth faded beneath them. He had no preparation for anything like this, for he had never dreamed he would love so completely, and he had only a little while before gotten used to it.

The grieving was incredibly hard and he knew it would never really stop until the day he died. It bent him over in pain. His head rang every day. His eyes ached.

Klaus and Katrina bought a big German Shepherd and rented a house and forested land in the country. They invited Terry to stay with them for awhile, if sweeping into his house, packing his bags, and dragging him out into the crisp, pre-dawn November air could be considered an invitation. He graciously accepted.

One day about a week later, Klaus came into his room as he sat listlessly, watching students tearing down the Berlin wall on a silent television and listening to Pucini.

"Terry, my friend."

"Klaus. Sit down."

Klaus stroked his head gently. He had learned much about the human heart since their friendship began that bumpy night over cheese and sausages and Lena's going on about a bus.

"Katrina is shopping. I am going away for several days, maybe weeks. I must travel. I leave you with Katrina. She will comfort you. Please accept her comforts as they are intended, with love."

Terry thought his behavior a little odd. Klaus was usually very simple, very predictable. He was tired. He didn't question his meaning.

"I will, Klaus. Thank you for everything." They embraced and Klaus was gone. Terry went to sleep and dreamed of Lena.

He awoke to find Katrina in his bed, in his arms. She kissed his forehead and put a finger to her lips in response to Terry's questioning eyes.

"Shh. Dinner is ready."

He showered and they ate a delicious dinner in silence. There was a different feeling in the house with Klaus absent. Despite his initial misgivings, he felt warmer and more comfortable than he had since Lena's death. He fell into Katrina's arms again and fell asleep there before she nudged him and he made his way to his bed. Katrina was living part of her own dream, unsure how to proceed. Later that night, she came into his room and made love to him. At first, he wasn't sure what was happening, for he was involved with his dreams. By the time he came to his senses Katrina was gathering up her nightgown and tiptoeing to her room. The next morning, he started to speak of it but she put a finger to her lips and he ceased trying to say what he couldn't say anyway. He managed to read for most of the day, about Pissarro and his friends Cezanne, Monet, and Renoir; about Pissarro's poverty as he struggled to support his family and discover Impressionism and, later, his experiments in Pointillism with Georges Seurat. Thinking about the suffering of others helped; to suffer for art, one of Paul's favorite themes.

After dinner that evening, Katrina came in as he was drying himself after a bath. He had taken a long walk in the woods, throwing a stick to Zippy, their dog. Wordlessly, she dropped to her knees and took him in her mouth. He didn't know how to respond. He needed help to deal with the pain he felt. Paul, again Paul, always said that sex and exercise could get a man through just about anything. He did nothing. He let himself be taken to a new world as he granted Katrina her desire. She let her robe fall off and he saw her body for the first time in the fading light of dusk. It seemed to be twenty years younger than the pleasantly-lined face and neck that sat on it, so smooth and supple.

They lived together and made love for four weeks, their nightly screams punctuated by long stretches of silence at first; until the color was restored to Terry's cheeks; until all of his appetites were restored; until he was rested and partially healed; until he went running for miles in the woods with Zippy the big dog; until their days together became sunny with conversation and laughter and long car rides along winding country roads; until Lena came to him one night as she did every night, with Katrina in his arms, and announced that he was ready to go and perform good, good deeds; until the first week of January, 1990.

Klaus returned on the morning of Terry's departure. Katrina was happy. She had healed Terry and, at the same time, worked him through her system like a drunken binge, exhilarated by the experience but content with the aftermath. She was several pounds thinner and genuinely happy to see her husband. At fifty-four, slightly older than Klaus, she had emerged from menopause to a sexual thunderstorm of desire and discarded inhibitions. She had quite a few surprises for Klaus. She threw herself into his arms. Klaus smiled warmly, exhaling a long sigh of relief that his gift to the two of them had also been a gift to himself. The three of them enjoyed a hearty breakfast together and Terry departed, away to his new life. He had decided to start over in Philly, where Paul was working in software development and systems architecture, an Internet plumber, he called himself. Lena said hello in first class.

It was a party attended by well-mannered but unassuming people of different ages. There was drinking and loud discussions over loud music from a concert video of Terrence Trent-Darby shown over several monitors placed around the room. They spoke in German, French, Dutch, and English. Lena introduced Terry to Wolfgang Frank, a thin, handsome, effeminate middle-aged man.

"Pleased to meet you."

"Oh, Lena, a good-looking American with good manners and who also speaks good German. It is a pleasure to meet you, young man."

"Thank you. But not so young, I'm afraid."

Wolfgang shifted to English. "Well, I compliment you again. You are not in the military, are you, Herr Blaisdell?"

" No. Not anymore. I was, though, for a few years. Lena has kidnapped me and forced me to lead an unhappy existence in your country."

"Yes, your suffering is obvious. She is a horrible woman. She has a big house full of captive GI's somewhere in Munich. Even your CIA has been unable to find it. I'm sure you'll be joining them soon."

He fended off a light hit from Lena.

"Wolfgang, you liar. Terry does not know your terrible sense of humor. He will believe you."

"I will think twice before believing anything Wolfgang has to say."

Wolfgang is drunk enough to think Terry is as funny as Alan King. "Lena, I still can't get over it. So clever."

"Have you been implying, Herr Frank, that Americans with a certain degree of cultivation are rare?"

"As rare as Steak Tartare, Herr Blaisdell."

"You are terrible, Wolfgang."

Wolfgang switched gears, into high melodrama. "Ha! You must be in love, Lena, defending Americans. You should have heard her before she met you, Herr Blaisdell. 'Oh, those stupid Americans. They know only one language. All they talk about is money. They don't know how to dress. No taste, no style, no culture.' Then you arrive and she is defending Americans. What of the truth, Lena? I ask you, what of the truth?"

He knelt on one knee before her. They had apparently performed variations of this comedic farce before. Lena was the center of attention, again, bemused partygoers looking to her to explain herself. She didn't disappoint. She was all flourishes and grand gestures as she projected outward to her growing audience.

"Get up, you silly man. The truth is like the wind, blowing cold or warm, but it must be faced and when all is still, it forces you to prepare for it or be swept away. Terry is the warm wind and he has swept me away. I am hopeless."

Well, it's one thing to call each other little lovey-dovey and pumpkin cake and all of that malarkey in private, but to be honored by this woman who was held in such high esteem was more than a brother could take, even if delivered with frightfully bad prose. Wolfgang wished someone would look at him the way Terry looked at Lena. He got up and bowed to her, a tear in one eye.

"Once again, Lena, you leave me speechless. No small feat, you know."

After Wolfgang backed away with another melodramatic flourish, Terry teased Lena.

"I have learned so much from you. It's hard to understand that you felt that way about all Americans."

"Wolfgang exaggerated. Of course I knew that there were wonderful Americans, but I had not met any. At least I was able to recognize and appreciate a wonderful one when I met him. That is the big problem for your races in America, no? Recogni….recogni…"

"Recognition, yes." Yes, proper recognition was a big problem.

THE REAL LIVES OF DREAMERS

Pennsylvania
1994

Terry had always dreamed of acquiring huge amounts of money, living the grand life, and making contributions to society. The irony of it having been made possible by the only person with whom he could ever have been happy never escaped him.

He constructed a three-phase plan which consisted of education, wealth accumulation, and a philanthropic retirement. Making money in the early nineties really wasn't that hard. Low interest rates, undervalued stocks, exploding technology, and Paul in his ear the whole time as a well-paid, part-time consultant. He couldn't believe his good fortune. He paid a lot of money to keep his name out of the papers, a rich black man. He kept up appearances as a slightly wealthy financial executive.

The crazy thing was that he was far from the only one, or the best performer. It was happening every day, new millionaires created at the same time as hundreds of thousands of people were thrown out of work, many of them forced into marginal existences as old ways of life and long-held traditions died unmerciful deaths. He had a lot to learn about this new world taking shape. He finished his undergraduate degree in accounting, then earned his MBA in Finance from the University of Pennsylvania's Wharton School, motivated and connected.

8

Anthony
2002

Anthony, feeling great after having lost thirty pounds that had dogged him for more than two years, stretched his six feet four inches on his chenille sofa, one of those solid, heavy pieces he liked. It fit well in his living room, in a used-to-be-rural suburb fifty miles outside of Philadelphia. Framed prints of memorable art shows sat on a mantle shelf and leaned on the chocolate brown accent wall. Everything had its place. A teak bookshelf, full of books, occupied another wall in the living room. He had avoided elaboration here, in this rental, which served as a base for his planned surprise reunion. He saw several rooms of furniture he liked in an acceptable catalogue, somewhere between House Beautiful and Architectural Digest, and ordered everything. It would do nicely for a year.

Sunlight flowed into the room. Trombonist Steve Turre played *Morning* on the high-end stereo. The music was so rhythmic, so joyous, so pure and uncluttered, that he instinctively raised his hands in the air in a celebratory gesture, ritualizing an imaginary victory over some dour, non-musical philistines who had begun to tap their feet and smile in spite of themselves.

He stared at an original oil painting, arranged for in a bar in Skippack by an old artist who favored the German Expressionists. When the song was over, he picked up his goblet of wine and leaned back to continue his conversation with yet another Internet acquaintance, Jennifer. He was in his Big Woman Period, preceded, in undefined intervals, by his thankfully brief Runway Model Period, his Athletic Woman Period, his Extreme Intellectual Woman Period, and, of course, his Gay Period, which had been so socially problematic that it was hardly worth it. He was glad that he could choose to walk away from it; so much tragedy in those days. He was, as Terry put it that day long ago, one of many Picassos of sex.

He discovered one day, by accident really, that he liked big women and they liked him. It was upstairs, in a less reputable section of a reputable bookstore in downtown Philly. He hadn't even known of its existence. There were several cutouts, something about books and magazines with no covers sold at a discount that he never quite understood. Among them was a magazine called *Gent*. His reaction was as surprising as it was immediate, more purely sexual than anything he'd known before. He was neither a stranger nor a devotee of pornography, though he anticipated that in coming years the latter would prevail over the former. Here was page after page of beautiful, natural, big-breasted, round-hipped women. He left the store, embarrassed, with an armful of magazines, the entire stock of old Gents, really, and very, very grateful that he was wearing a long coat.

Jennifer was big enough to keep him interested, but not big enough to attract undue attention. She was shapely, creative, and smart, really smart. She hadn't needed to delude herself into that recent post-feminist American 'I'm smart because I think I'm smart' syndrome, its sufferers resentful when the conversation strayed, quite logically, into territory of which they were surprisingly ignorant. And she worked out, she told him. Of that, either, there was no doubt.

My, my, my, Paul would say. Mm mm mm. That was how Anthony liked his women these days and the Philadelphia area was a damn good place for someone with that particular predilection to live. Occasionally, he ventured into really big woman territory with those he wouldn't be seen with, but who showed him a really good time, treating his playstick like a very lucky lollipop at an extended lollipop fest. These were often women with psychological problems, usually poor or working class, so an extended stay or dates in public were out of the question. He made no promises and offered no apologies, but left them enough money to dismiss any dreams of a future and smile when they thought of him again. He preferred these lonely women to whores. They were so grateful, and so sad.

He looked over at Jennifer as she straightened up a little. She bent over and he got hard. She finished and sat down next to him and they talked for a few minutes before they devoured each other like starved animals that had come upon an unexpected buffet after a long trek in the desert.

She had been active in the Fat Acceptance movement until politics and agendas differed. She looked to the Internet for friendship and found plenty of fat acceptance, chubby chasers, apologists, parties, and forums. It was useless to try to change American culture's macabre fascination with the too-skinny. She found friendship and an undreamed of underground of sexual possibilities. Her sex life had never been better; neither had her sense of herself. Men were really something, she mused. So many of them loved big, fleshy women. In secret, of course. Others feigned sickness at the thought of sex with any woman bigger than a size six. Where did this come from? Did it have any basis in reality? Was sex with a big woman an acquired taste? Was it something to do with ideal motherhood, fragile, ante-bellum southern womanhood, fear of the Amazon, performance anxiety, the oppression of maleness, the fear of economic parity? I dunno, she thought. She was just happy to be with a man who liked big women, who genuinely enjoyed *her*, and who treated her with respect.

Oils and prints of Peter Paul Reuben's' work were almost *de rigueur* in her circles. Flesh and warmth and size and curves were valued in their subterranean society, a society that seemed at times more concealed than those of drug addicts and trans-sexuals. But their day was coming. The thin women think we all lead miserable lives, she thought as Anthony put two fingers inside her, but our time is coming. She screamed in pleasure.

He encountered smaller women who cowered, wondering about their chances in a physical confrontation if a love affair with this big man went south. Hit a woman? He found this thought process, based in reality or not, incredibly sad. Such was the state of affairs. He despised woman-hitters, but to say so to a relatively small woman sounded trite, in the way that simple, truthful declarations often do. He supposed that, at times, like speaking French, the context mattered more than the actual statement. So be it. It was all academic anyway. Smaller women didn't really hold any interest for him in a purely physical way; only to direct him to where the big sluts were. Falling for someone, of course, was always something different. The physical took a back seat to that certain sparkle, that gleam. It had been a long time since he had seen that sparkle, though it seemed closer now.

The Internet was a God-send to off-channel activities. His email inbox was full of pictures and possibilities. What a life. Happiness without love. The pleasure he was feeling was absolutely exquisite. He was fifty-two and the pleasure was exquisite. 'What have I done right today?' he asked himself.

Two days later, while listening to Buddy Guy and Johnny Shines, he recalled the pleasures of that day and how he had climbed on top of her. They rolled around and laughed, her large, heavy, perfectly-shaped breasts slapping his face, her thighs a geometry lesson for his two big hands, traveling, negotiating the half-moons that made up her ass until he found the wetness between her legs, open and inviting. The agenda of the day was fun. He could learn to like this one, he thought. She had good taste, too. Unlike many big women, she was confident. How many had he met who thought their lives were over, so why bother to dress well and pay attention to their hair and make-up? As far as he was concerned, Jennifer's achieving her stated goal of losing thirty pounds, or not, would be perfectly acceptable to him and keep him crazy in bed. He was sure she could lose some weight if she wanted to. He knew from past experience that it was all in the motivating. Besides, his body wasn't what it once was, either.

Money always bought a certain amount of freedom, but money and age were truly liberating. He cared not a damn about things that used to keep him up nights. He would laugh at the first black woman who scowled at him, eager to let him know of her displeasure at seeing him with a white woman, as if she had a stake in his happiness, as if he owed her an explanation, as if she would be willing or able to offer a suitable alternative. They had had their chances. So many damn chances.

As one comedian who hadn't lasted too long had asked, 'Why should *you* be happy?' He was through suffering at the hands of black American women, and knew several good men who shared that opinion. He never voiced this opinion around Terry, for Terry loved black women. He kept finding the good ones. Anthony didn't buy the idealism about there being good and bad ones of all races. We were all products of our culture, the culture we had foisted on us or the one we consciously chose to adopt. He despised the hands-on-the-hip, neck-twisting black woman, so at home with herself and her ignorance. More than once, he had been almost physically attacked for issuing his cynical proclamations, issued from a cave of pain and disappointment, of course.

His love of the blues and jazz always seemed to get in the way of personal relationships with black women, so many of whom escaped into the love of Jesus, rejecting secular living generally, and his beloved music particularly, as something evil simply because they had known so many who made the wrong choices. He couldn't stomach anyone who wasn't engaged with life, with the society they lived in….well, let's not dwell on that. Outside of romance, he wondered again — though he felt, sadly, that he knew the answers — why he had never been accepted for who he was in different black communities, why his potential contributions were dismissed out of hand; and again it bothered him, like an athlete with a slightly sprained ankle, in otherwise excellent shape but unable to play his best game. He went to another room, picked up one of several guitars on stands against the wall, and absent-mindedly began to strum something by Sonny Terry and Brownie McGhee.

BARRY NIX

He had felt enough of that pain to enable him to sing his particular blues. He was an outsider and, though his accent was not nearly as noticeable as it had been even five years before, he was always made aware of it. What a narrow world too many of them live in, he thought, its limits defined by their victimization, real and imagined, finely honed to ridiculousness, totally out of scale with the realities of daily existence, holding themselves back with their claims to folksiness, to keeping it real, only wanting jobs for money, taking the money and running back to their insular little society, refusing engagement with the larger world as they sneered at those who tried to get along, devoid of intellectual questioning and responsibility to the higher self, to self-actualization.

Just when more white Americans, but far from all, were willing to judge them by the content of their character, or so they said, as they lost their own collective character. How boring, he thought, as boring as junkies and teenage mothers and cursing comedians. How low. How low they had brought him, his people, half of his bloodline. He was glad his father wasn't there to see this state of affairs, but felt, anyway, that he should apologize to him and those in the honorable past who had endured so much and hoped and bled and sweated and been humiliated and killed for so much more in the future.

Aside from Terry and Paul and Kimble, he seemed unable to communicate or get along with many native-born American black folks. It was only the musicians and academics with whom he was able to find common ground, yet he found acceptance from members of every other culture he encountered. He had friends from all over Europe, from Mali, from India and Lebanon, Senegal and Israel, Barbados and The Dominican Republic. He and Paul and Terry, three adventurers of the spirit, had not been welcome in the group,

THE REAL LIVES OF DREAMERS

having violated several unwritten group laws, chiefly that of being open-minded enough to consider the possibility that other groups possessed humanity, that other groups were suffering daily and that some had also suffered throughout history; rejected because of their willingness to accept the responsibility that came with freedom, the understanding that life is just damned hard. It was a tragedy of the highest magnitude, Paul had told them, the dumbing-down of a whole bunch of people.

In their Army days, Kimball, the dark, deep man from the Chicago streets — even if he did wear countrified-looking clothes, as Paul said — had been one of their few friends back in the unit. They invited him along on excursions — to a good German clothing store first, Paul said under his breath — but he declined. He had their respect, especially Terry's. He understood that there were bigger things going on.

Paul. You mothah fuckah, he thought, only thinking what he would not utter because he lacked the flow, the naturalism that would enable him to deliver the phrase earnestly without being laughed at, a European-American imitating ghetto naturalism. It wasn't something he lost sleep over, though the rhythms of Paul's language were often things of beauty.

And Terry. Poor Terry, the idealist. He remembered Terry's attempt to hire his first employees after graduating from Wharton and deciding to stay in Philly for some reason, a strangely parochial place for a traveler. He observed his friend's frustration and disappointment, the realization that he had to painfully alter his dream, the one he had worked so hard to position himself for, like an amputee who had to re-learn walking after training for a marathon. Terry learned, but cursed the need to do so frequently. Eight years ago? It couldn't have been eight years already. He felt old. He felt sorry for

Terry that day. He felt sorry for all of them. It wasn't only Philly, he learned. Things were the same everywhere in the States. More of the same.

Anthony had been in town to celebrate Terry's graduation from Wharton and to lend assistance to his entrepreneurial endeavor in center city. Entering Terry's new suite of offices humming with activity and construction at one end, he passed some young black people in their early to mid-twenties, most appearing awkward in ill-fitting suits and starch-less shirts,. He didn't know Terry was interviewing for positions other than broker. Further down the hallway were a pleasant-looking, young Indian man and a Korean woman with a brick house for a body and lasers for eyes. She watched him as he walked past, burning holes in his back. He hung around in the offices, answering the phone, moving boxes, and offering his opinion for the décor.

Cordelia stuck her head in and announced she had the test results, some basic questions designed to assess critical thinking skills. Terry looked at the tests for several minutes and frowned, then smiled, then frowned again. He handed them to Anthony without a word. Anthony couldn't believe what he saw. The Korean woman hit it out of the park, providing a particularly thoughtful analysis of global demand for microchips. Rajneesh Ashwarmin also did well, though he was a bit reluctant to draw definitive conclusions without more data. Most of the others were, shall we say, appalling. Terry went wild.

Terry walked into the conference room looking to kick some ass and take some names. Cordelia walked in behind him carrying the tests. She handed them to him and took a seat in the back next to Anthony. Terry raised the tests above his head and waived them back and forth. Ashwarmin and the Korean woman had been given twenty dollars each for lunch and asked to come back to interview with Terry. He introduced himself and launched his tirade.

"I am very disappointed with what I see here! These, for the most part, are not the tests of critical thinkers. The math was decent, but the reasoning was flawed, horrible actually. Don't you read the business press? Don't you know what's happening in the world?! Or were you too busy trying to impress your friends by making sure you bought the right sneakers?!" Cordelia shifted uncomfortably in her seat and shot Terry a look that was meant to give him laryngitis. Terry took a deep breath and continued.

"Welcome to the real world, people! The geeks are making all the money! The geeks are designing the software and financial instruments that you think you're too cool to learn! Do you think I'm going to hire someone who can't write a decent essay, who can't give me a reasonably accurate assessment of the American economy?"

He threw the tests onto the table.

"No!"

They jumped.

"Do you think I'm running some pussy-assed social program for losers? I am looking for qualified, I said *qualified*, people to train, to train in excellence, to sweep the floor with the competition! By qualified, I mean people who can write well, who can think on their feet, who are hungry, who possess integrity, who have the common sense not to walk into an interview looking like clowns!"

A young black man started to say something.

"Shut up! There is nothing to say!"

He spoke directly to the young man.

"Do you know what it took to get black people into these schools, to earn some respect, to be accepted as capable of doing intellectually demanding jobs? It took blood and hard work! I don't see much evidence of that here…"

He lowered his voice and calmed down a bit.

"So you say, 'Who does that so and so think he is?' I'm just a guy, a brother who worked hard, caught a break here and there, and wanted to help bring some other people along. So much for idealism in America in nineteen ninety-four."

He looked around, wondering what to do, then picked up a wooden chair and threw it, viciously, to the floor. It broke into several pieces, sending shards of wood skittering on the floor between the test-takers. There was absolute silence. He turned and left. The test-takers looked around at each other and slowly started to get up to leave. Cordelia rose and spoke.

"Wait here."

She ran into the hallway and cupped her hands over her mouth. Anthony stuck his head out of the doorway and watched her catch up to him.

"Calling Terry the Tyrant! Calling Terry the Tyrant!"

He whirled. "Don't start."

She caught up with him and took his arm "Don't you think you were a little hard on them?"

"No. You saw the tests. Where's the commitment? Where is the pride?"

"Terry, you're a survivor. Where are the people you went to high school with? Dead, or in dead end jobs, mostly, right?"

He is agitated. He doesn't want to hear another lecture about how different he is. He had been prepared to tough it out if he had

THE REAL LIVES OF DREAMERS

to. He just got lucky. His preparation put him in the position to take advantage of the opportunities presented to him.

"You know the answer to that. Don't patronize me."

"Terry, I'm sorry. I'm not trying to patronize you, but you were the exception, not the rule, honey. I think you realize it on a theoretical level, but you don't want to face up to it on a practical level."

"Well, thank you, Dr....whomever." She was exasperating. He liked it.

"Come on, dahlin'. Let me work with this group. Let's train them, mold them."

"Screw 'em. Let 'em suffer in the street. Maybe they'll go back to the library."

"You don't mean that."

He mocked her, then smiled just a little. "You don't mean that...No. I don't...One month. Five hundred a week each. Get whomever you want, including somebody from a charm school. I want excellence and good manners, some savoir faire. Maybe one will make the cut. And the rain in Spain falls mainly on the plain."

Cordelia stood on her toes and gave him a long kiss on the mouth, rubbing her body hard into his. He was caught off guard and more than a little excited.

"Where did that come from?"

"From way down deep inside, honey. Should I apologize?"

"No, don't......you're full of surprises."

Paul returned from a meeting with a young, entrepreneurial computer scientist later in the afternoon, still bouncing to Monk's *Off Minor* and a spirited, music-filled ride on the Schuylkill Expressway, upset that he had missed the action. Terry, still agitated hours later, took them to one of downtown Philly's many new restaurants for dinner and plenty of micro-brewed beer. The restaurant was big and boisterous, perfect for Terry's mood. He invited Cordelia but she muttered something about too much testosterone for her to be comfortable. Terry considered the reference primarily directed at Paul, who didn't let women get away with much. He said that American women weren't accustomed to being held accountable for their anti-male thinking and resented it when they were. Paul didn't hold Cordelia true to type, but she nonetheless felt uncomfortable in his presence.

Anthony pondered what he characterized as the American-ness of her attitude, despite his regard for Cordelia. He wouldn't stay in America too long, he decided. They spoke in low tones, only for themselves.

Terry could hardly sit still. "Fucking idiots we're graduating from universities these days. Damn! Tell Ant about all the cheating at Temple, Paul."

"He knows."

"Damn right, he knows. Fucking idiots!"

"Welcome to the New World, Ter", Anthony chimed in, somewhat fruitlessly.

Paul found his soapbox of disappointment and despair.

"Don't native-born Americans want to be smart anymore? All I ever wanted was to become a smart motherfuckah, like the cats who wrote those books I read when I was a teenager. Smart motherfuckahs with soul. Now it's only the money and the image. Get the credentials at any cost. A country full of lazy fucks looking for someone to tell them how wonderful they are and that everything's all right. Maybe we'd be like that if it weren't for the Army, huh?"

"Hell no, we wouldn't", Terry retorted.

THE REAL LIVES OF DREAMERS

"I know one thing," Paul continued, "black folks had better get hip to the deal before it's too late. This technology thing is going to jump off huge. Nobody's gonna want to hear that 'victim' shit. Let me tell you, the Indians and Chinese are smart as hell! I'll work with 'em any day of the week. And the women are fine!"

"No one in the international community respects black Americans anymore, you know, except the jazz musicians," Anthony said. "Even most of the athletes are like children, selfish and materialistic."

"You're damn right," Paul said. "Think about Bill Russell, Kareem Abdul Jabaar, Jim Brown. These were men! Men of the world who at least tried to understand their political roles as black men. They wouldn't be caught dead dancing and prancing on the court or the field after making a good play, after doing their damn job! What bullshit!"

"Damn, damn right," Terry put in. But my question is, 'What's on the horizon?' More bullshit? Are we gonna be talkin' about the old days and all the lost potential for the rest of our lives?"

They became quiet, realizing that they just might be subjected to this fate worse than anything they could have imagined, when, only years before, they had looked onward and upward. It was Paul who broke the silence, in a somber voice, as if he were the wizened, ancient wizard Gandalf in Tolkien's *Lord of The Rings*.

"I think so. Children without fathers are doomed to repeat the mistakes of the fools who came before them."

He took a long swig of beer and became more energetic, returned to himself, the cussin' philosopher.

"There will be individual success stories. In terms of the group, though, you'd better hope this rap music shit dies down fast,

BARRY NIX

because it's becoming more and more negative and more and more influential on these fatherless kids."

They ate their salads and drank their beers in relative silence. The reality of the future descended upon them heavily. Terry was almost in tears. The future, the dreams. How could he be so rich and so depressed? He remembered how critical he was of the spoiled rock star in the movie *The Wall*. He brought his depression on himself, Terry thought at the time. He was beginning to understand, God forbid, beginning to relate to that self-obsessed fuck; self-obsessed because of the savagery of the world outside. He wished he were as tough as Paul, who could tell anyone to kiss his ass, from the streets to the ivory tower to the boardroom. He was the most self-contained, spiritual man he would ever know.

Paul, though, hated the person he felt himself becoming; hard and cold, looking for a surrogate son to teach all that he had discovered in his life. None appeared; too late to father one now. He didn't have the necessary patience; not yet. He became immersed in the goings-on in his own head, retreating more and more to his interior cultural oases. He thought of the perfect mixes he was compiling from his CD collection, his interior historical record.

Anthony sipped some pils and wondered how a country with so much energy and so much musical creativity could be so clueless. But he couldn't stay away. He was endlessly fascinated, no matter how far ashore he traveled. He always came back, not only to be with his friends, but to try to fathom the contradictions.

They managed to snap out of it after gorging themselves on thick steaks and cheesecake, but only for the night.

A̶nthony smiled and woke up. His mind continued to drift. He smiled as he thought of Jennifer again. Well, well, surprise, surprise, surprise. He thought of women, the good and the bad. Speaking of bad women. Ha! He contrasted his state of mind with his desperation as his three-year marriage to Angie was about to end, during his initial exploration into black America.

She was caramel-colored and thin, and dazzled him with her ambition and her energy. She soon became repressed and showy, with a core of pure nothing. She had spoken of the importance of family to co-workers and friends, yet was the most selfish woman he'd ever met in a life full of selfish women. She looked great in clothes, but eventually failed to excite him in bed. She considered herself above the tequila and bourbon of the blues, preferring smooth jazz, the audio equivalent of watered-down Sangria.

It helped that they looked good together and she had an MBA. She was his entrée to the African-American upper middle class. Big deal. Hadn't he loved her? Of course he had, way back when. He wasn't that shallow, but he was damned if he could remember any defining moments in their time together before marriage. Things went downhill faster than an Alpine avalanche. Two years together and six years apart. He could barely conjure her face when he closed his eyes.

She came from an elite black family in Virginia. He loved and respected her father as a man like his own, from the old school, well-dressed, educated, and articulate, every word carefully enunciated, a lover of learning. He had learned so much from old Charles, about the indignities he suffered as a boy, how he discovered books at an early age and never really felt poor because he traveled to so many places in his reading, how he was actually surprised to learn, years later, how poor his family really had been. It was Charles who lectured Anthony on the finer points of forming a meaningful life in a society that was more racist than he could imagine just a few decades ago, yet offered more opportunity than many had the courage to admit today.

Of course, his own father, Jimmy Turner, had washed his hands of America years before. The best advice he could give Anthony, he told him, was to stay away. Anthony chose otherwise, so Jimmy called some friends who offered clues for survival in a hostile land. Anthony thought the perceptions of some of these friends to be unrealistic and said as much. They politely told him he didn't understand how the white man was.

After dinner once or twice a month they would sit in Charles' study, an ornate affair decorated with mahogany walls and plush burgundy carpeting. Books occupied every shelf and overflowed onto most table tops. The heavy, overstuffed sofas they sat on contained intricate patterns and rested on solid wooden legs turned by black craftsmen in 1930's North Carolina who, though distinguished, were refused entry to the furniture unions of the time.

It was Charles who made sure that Anthony could draw the distinction between racism and personality clashes, and made sure that Anthony understood how intimidating he could be because of his looks and his intelligence. Regretfully, not long into their marriage, Charles was unable to convince his hopeless daughter that Anthony was deserving of respect as a husband and a man. That was his fault in a way, Charles told him, for he had treated his wife as well as any man, but stepped out when he wanted, in a time before liberation and feminism, when men in his town took care of their families and took time to go to the juke joints once or twice a week, homes of the blues, to play poker, drink whiskey, and take the favors of nice women who were willing to grant nice men almost any favor in exchange for a few drinks and a few dollars.

When Angie found out years later through some cruel accident, of course, when Charles was an old man and had settled in to enjoy some semblance of peace before dying, she went stark raving mad. Despite all that he had accomplished in his life, in the civil rights movement, in the streets, and in courtrooms; despite the deep, warm, sparkling and infectious smile that he bore witness to on his wife's face every day after forty years of marriage, Angie would not relinquish her self-righteous, holier-than-thou, I-don't-care-about-the-times, all-men-are-the-same, late-twentieth-century indignation. She stomped her Prada shoes on imported Italian tile. She waved beautifully-manicured hands in the climate-controlled air and displayed her politically correct, hopelessly muddled, absolutist, too-pampered-to-be-able-to-relate-to-any-other-existence, mediocre thinking for all the world to see. Her mother, Nancy, was shocked, but had long ago known that her daughter was spoiled beyond redemption, although she was sure they hadn't over-indulged her, relative to her peers, anyway.

Trouble began when Anthony forsook his corporate aspirations (some experiment that turned out to be) and retrieved his albums from the closet in the back room upstairs. He set up a little studio and dabbled in composing, determined to study music at his relatively advanced age. He gave himself a short refresher on music theory and practiced piano to a book. His playing improved quickly. Several scalar runs presented themselves to him with relatively minor effort this time, having eluded him in the past like the prom queen who had eluded the class geek and then offered herself freely as if she had been available all along.

His first pieces reminded him of some of the old blues players before producers found them, rough but ready, full of soul awaiting just a little refinement and some good sidemen to modify the timing and contribute some good solos. Not that he was that good yet, not by a long shot, but there was something there. By this time he had listened to so much music that he could scat a nice solo almost effortlessly, and had lived so much life that his voice dripped with honey and vinegar in every wail and soulful moan. Of course, he still didn't *look* like a blues singer, obviously coming from money, but that didn't matter. Every syllable vibrated inside of him and resonated with the soul of a man on a long search, never giving up, never settling for contentment when he was sure that pure ecstasy was just around the corner, refusing to sit back in his easy chair and pass out forbidden candy to happy grandchildren who climbed all over him while their tight-assed parents scowled in the kitchen, doting and restricting their movements, always afraid of the minor injury, always afraid of risk, afraid to end up like him, wizened and sad, never having known the mountains he had scaled in his mind, the places he had been, or the many types of happiness he had known.

He was so excited by this development, his musical progress, that he ignored Angie, which, of course, because she had been accustomed to an inordinate amount of attention all of her life, drove her to near insanity. She scoffed at his music, not realizing that an at least accommodationist comment was her last chance at anything resembling a peaceful co-existence. Upon the realization that she was unwilling to change her attitude and deepen her understanding he left, suddenly and with a smile on his face, as she stood in the doorway in amazement, hands folded, weight resting on one Prada-clad foot, unable to understand because she had been such a legend in her own mind, with the best taste, the best clothes, and the best pussy, she told herself, oral sex being for sluts, one of which she definitely was not, the late-night soirees with her boss while her husband found his muse notwithstanding.

What Angie hadn't understood, and would never understand, was that he didn't care who she slept with as long as he was getting his, emotionally and sexually. He never really believed in monogamy anyway, considering it a capitalist and puritanical crime against nature.

Besides, Charles had died. He and Nancy mourned deeply, while Angie, spinning balding tires in the rut of her self, could not. There was no longer any reason to stay with her. At the age of thirty-five she had already committed so many grievous sins against the really good people in her life he believed she would be doomed to grey years of miserable reflection once her life began to spiral inevitably downward, eventually becoming the lonely, white-haired woman with the ever-present smile and kind words who, those who got to know her would think, couldn't possibly have engaged in that sort of not-so-youthful idiocy. He was so glad that they hadn't had children he was beside himself. He had seen to that after he realized she was not the mothering kind.

She enjoyed a successful career, but she was a disappointment to all who knew her outside of work. Every day her parents asked each other what they had done wrong, until they had not even the faintest idea. Nothing showed up on their internal screens.

They had doted on her, but had also instilled, or thought they had, a sense of responsibility and discipline, satisfied that they had achieved a delicate balance of countervailing qualities which could have made, which should have made, for a splendid young woman with a healthy sense of herself and the world. They thought they had sent her off to college, to Cornell, with brains and, just as important, good sense. They never knew what happened there. She became cold and conniving. They should have tried harder to convince her to attend Spelman in Atlanta.

Anthony had come along and gotten her to loosen up, to enjoy life again and, from the dizzy smile on her face when Charles and Nancy popped in one Sunday morning, lovemaking, too. But that only lasted a short while. Since then, she had walked around with a misguided sense of entitlement, as if happiness were hers by birthright, and to be had without much effort on her part. She began to reject all men out of hand, especially black men. He hoped she was suffering. Like John Lee Hooker sang, it served her right to suffer.

Nancy refused to let herself be miserable about her evil child. She had some living to do. Charles had never told her, or even tried to tell her, what she could and could not do or where she could and could not go. She had been by his side, his buttress, because that was where she felt happiest and most valuable. She had grieved his death, but, with Anthony's help, had emerged whole and renewed. I'll be damned if we didn't have a good run of it the last twenty years! She knew people who were so eaten up by the hurt and anger of their early years that they didn't know how good things had gotten until it was too late, when one of them was sipping all of their meals through a straw, usually the man, while the woman's obesity made the routines of daily living an ordeal.

She looked at herself in the mirror and patted her hips. Not bad for an old gal, she thought. After the initial panic following Charles' death she dragged herself to the gym. She hated it there, but it was better than working out at home alone. It was drudgery any

THE REAL LIVES OF DREAMERS

way she looked at it. She hadn't lost much weight, but she was firmer and more proportioned. Lately, she had taken to walking along the trail that ran behind their, now her, house. She was going to sell it soon and move to an adult community. Did they really let them in at fifty-five now? She remembered reading an article in the New York Times Magazine about the love life of a man who lived in one of those places. He was having the time of his life, falling in and out of love and screwing up a storm at seventy-five, living the Viagra life.

She smiled to herself as she thought about Anthony's courtesy call last week. Her travels, including the mandatory widow's cruise, had rejuvenated her, but not to the extent that some would think, for Charles hadn't been there, except in her dreams. A few times her depression had gotten so bad that she was tempted to jump into the ocean, but thought of the commotion it would cause and changed her mind. The dreams had stopped. Martinis had helped. Yes, she was depressed and admitted that it was a natural enough thing. She resolved not to give in to it for too long, but it was difficult. Anthony had called and detected the panic in her voice, which she hadn't expected to be there. He was worried and insisted that he meet her for a cup of coffee. To her surprise, she said they might as well have lunch. Had she really taken extra time to get ready? She was a recently-widowed sixty-five. Why was she almost giddy at the prospect of her ex-son-in-law taking her to a courtesy lunch?

He was there when she arrived, a small place off of South Street where they could read the menu without muttering to themselves about exotic but unappetizing items to sift through. He had some old-fashioned qualities about him, she thought, having voiced to her the opinion that traditions had their place and should not be gotten rid of merely to serve someone's misguided notion of change for change's sake. That was refreshing.

When he saw her approach, he was something out of a Marx Brothers movie. He almost fell out of his chair. When he brought his tall frame to its full height he banged his head on a beautiful pendant light that must have been made of some very heavy material. It looked like it almost knocked him unconscious as his head sent the light careening wildly, casting eerie shadows over other tables, attracting attention to himself, which he didn't like to do. He had already broken into a sweat by the time he took her hand, apologizing while surreptitiously, he *thought*, taking in her entire body. She hadn't been looked at like that in twenty-five years, and the man whose gaze and remark Charles happened to catch was sorry for weeks afterward.

Seeing that he had been found out, surprised and confused at seeing Nancy so obviously out of her self-described doldrums, and so healthy, my God, Anthony looked down at the table and mumbled something about her looking healthy and vibrant. Vibrant, now that was a word. She instantly forgave him his male indiscretion and thanked him. She felt vibrant. Yes, she *was* vibrant and she ate and drank and talked with abandon. Anthony was a strange one and she understood why women liked him. At one point, she was so drunk and vibrant that she had to restrain herself from...what?

There was another reason he was smiling. He had finally earned his doctorate. She was flattered that he had chosen her to celebrate with him. They enjoyed themselves thoroughly that afternoon and vowed to look out for each other, and they did.

The years since the Army had been strange ones. Anthony hadn't been able to quite get his footing. All three of the Mars Brothers craved organization, so they gravitated to corporate structures, where the money was. After his marriage disaster he went back to Eindhoven and spent a year decompressing and remodeling the house Belinda left him. He found it rewarding and spent more energy and money than he originally planned. It turned out very well.

Friends from his and his father's jazz network told him that he was an artist, a genius of mood. They always wrote good music when they visited him, they said. Naturally enough, the word spread throughout Europe and the States, delivered by his network of virtuosos. After several requests, he hastily assembled a portfolio and found himself much in demand and discussing his reading of architecture on three continents. Despite his protests, he was contracted to work on several homes during his second whirlwind year back. It was his spirit they wanted. He could hire whomever he needed. He did fine. His fee was now quite high and he had as much work as he wanted. He worked, if you could call it that — designing, creating, and collaborating — eight months of each year.

His work was informed, naturally enough, by his prior readings, his travels, and his studies. He was an ABD, all-but-dissertation Ph.D, for two years, then took a year off and completed his dissertation in Ann Arbor. The world now had a new, documented, methodologically-accepted, University of Michigan-certified, linguistic anthropologist. It was perfect for him, 'the study of language in the context of human social and cultural diversity, past and present'. He told everyone who asked that he studied people and why they spoke the way they did. That usually satisfied them. They usually enunciated more clearly after he explained. Now he had to decide where he would devote his time, each discipline refusing to play mistress to the other's favored role as spouse.

This was a strange time, post-September 11th, Anthony thought. He asked himself again how much it had changed Americans. People seemed to be reading more, trying to make sense of things. He certainly was. He was in the tail-end of his weekly day of indulgence, a private ritual of spiritual exploration, emotional catharsis, and intellectual digging. Today, it had been two martinis thrown back while he searched his music collection for seventies reggae. The day's program had been dictated by the airing on PBS of a documentary on the life of Bob Marley. He wanted, needed, to continue his revived feeling of the Jamaican revolutionary fervor of the early 70's. After listening to several Marley songs — Natural Mystic, Jammin', No Woman, No Cry — he began to feel moods he hadn't felt in nearly twenty-five years. He played Toots and The Maytals, Burning Spear, and Peter Tosh, too. He nodded the reggae nod, that spliff-induced mantra to rhythm, or riddim as they called it, Jamaica, and fanciful tales of biblical salvation and the rising up of poor people to take their just deserts from the manipulating capitalists of the world. Then he searched for worthwhile words written about Bob Marley on the Internet. He was inundated with music files, reflections, and photographs. It had been a good morning.

    He had paid to have all of the worthwhile music on his hundreds of albums that weren't available on CD digitally converted and stored. They sat on a small external hard drive with a rather large storage capacity and were playable on his stereo or one of several computers he kept with him. They were duplicated on another hard drive and stored online, along with his architectural files. Music had resumed its rightful place in his life, at the top. There were some one-of-a-kind files, though, stored in a safety deposit box in Zurich, along with some other, rather damning articles.

THE REAL LIVES OF DREAMERS

He missed Paul and Terry. Their time was almost upon them, the enactment of their pact. When Anthony had mysteriously been given orders to return to the States that day, they had made a pact, the three of them, the Mars Brothers. That last day, even tough-as-nails Paul, occupying the entire backseat, didn't bother to hide the tears in his eyes as Terry, in his element in his BMW and on the Autobahn, drove him to the airport in Ramstein.

Anthony had been their leader and their rudder. He said that they would meet again when they all knew it to be the right time, when they had lived enough to come back to each other. He changed, becoming more reserved as life and people revealed their hands more each year. He let himself show just a little emotion that day — especially after Paul bear-hugged him, apologizing profusely as Anthony dropped his bag and grabbed his chest to catch his breath — because they really needed to see it from him; Terry, the money-hungry romantic, and Paul, the questioner, irrepressible, angry, and always chasing his elusive, shape-shifting spirit.

Anthony suddenly realized what he had done. He had abandoned them, these fatherless travelers, orders or not. Although he was not much older than they, he had had more help in defining for himself what it meant to be a man, and they looked to him for direction and structure. He hadn't felt ready to lead anyone in these matters, but that didn't matter. The important thing was that they had been ready to be led. It had been his job to lead and he hadn't led, at least not to the extent they needed. As the tears flowed down his face, he sincerely hoped that he was overstating the gravity of his sins. Either way, it was time.

9

Dr. Wisniewski

The good Dr. Wisniewski was nervous. He was always nervous these days, except for the few moments after he had been teased to orgasm by Miss Nicole, his new-found dominatrix, the only person who could make him relax. He had never had so many orgasms. He submitted. He had never been so submissive. He dared not question its origins for he doubted he would like the answers. Was he better for it, or just another type-A experiencing his comeuppance?

He feared he was exhibiting addictive behavior. They took unnecessary chances. All other activities, associations, and responsibilities were left as recklessly as classes on the first warm day of spring. Yes, she was the first warm day of spring, free Yankees tickets for game seven of the World Series, a Guggenheim fellowship in Florence, backstage with Leonard Bernstein in '65, a red Ferrari. Yes, she was all that! It was all good! He looked at a plastic rendering of a three-dimensional face cut away to reveal a red brain, held it in his hands, and began to address it. He saw it light up.

"Oh, good grief, man," the red brain said. "Get a hold of yourself. Are you really in love with someone whose kindest words to you have been a positive critique of your window cleaning efforts? What about your addictive behavior?"

"Oh, yes," Wisniewski answered. "Let me see. Unnecessary chances, obsession, irrational behavior, probably delusional. Yes, that's it. No doubt about it. Should I go cop some heroin?" he asked gleefully. "Should I go rob an ATM in front of a police station? Ha ha ha."

He danced around his office like a lunatic and swore he saw the brain alternate colors between the left and right sides. The phone rang and rang and rang again. It stopped. Sharon Taylor, pretty, with warm brown skin, late fifties, well dressed, glasses, an efficient air about her, knocked on his door. He had managed to seat himself at his desk, but not to restore his usual pasty color to his red cheeks.

"Yes?" Sharon came in.

"Dr. Wisniewski. It's time to get serious, honey." Sharon had never been anything but staid and professional with him. She certainly had never called him 'honey' before. He sat a little straighter. He had never noticed her large breasts before, either. They seemed happy under a beautiful green and yellow print dress. She had so much more style than those too-cute twenty-somethings that she supervised, he thought. She put her hands on his desk and looked in his eyes.

"You've got some serious goings-on today. It's not the weekend yet. I know what you've got. I've seen it many times before. Now listen to me, Doctor. You're a brilliant man playing with fire. You've been wound up way too tight for way too long and you're ready to let go. Just remember it was that tight wind that got you where you are today. And it's not automatically going to last forever. It can be gone like that, in a flash." She snapped her fingers.

He came out of his reverie, sober and more grateful than he could say. She saw the change in him immediately. He stiffened. His eyes became sharp and clear again.

She smiled.

"Okay. You can keep some of it. You don't have to go all the way back to the old Dr. Wisniewski." He smiled and relaxed just a bit. He looked up at her.

"Thank you, Sharon. That was exactly what I needed."

"You're welcome. Now, that woman is coming, that psychic woman, at 2:30 and it's 2:15 now. Will you be ready? Let's get ready."

"Yes, Sharon. I'll be ready. You're right, of course. Thank you. Thank you very much."

"You'll be okay? I won't have to come back and check on you, will I?"

"No, thank you, I'll be fine." She turned to leave. And then, only slightly wickedly as he studied her ample behind as she walked away, "You're the boss, Sharon."

THE REAL LIVES OF DREAMERS

10

Reunion

Solitary brother, is there still a part of you that wants to live?
Solitary sister, is there still a part of you that wants to give?
Seal

Terry walked into the hospital looking like all the other terrified souls who come to visit a sick or dying loved one for the first time. At least he had an idea of what to expect. Paul, whatever he looked like now, was most likely lying prone with his eyes closed, smiling, cussin' at the world and dreaming to a Coltrane soundtrack. He wished he hadn't given his driver and personal assistant the day off. He was lost when fending for himself, having purposefully cocooned himself in luxury and privilege years ago; fewer disappointments, less….no time to think about that now. He signed in at the security desk in the lobby and took the elevator to the fifteenth floor.

He emerged from the elevator to the sight of two young, very overweight black orderlies lazily pushing their empty gurneys. Without acknowledging his nod and smile they studied him intently and with some hostility; he in his Hawaiian tan, expensive summer clothes, designer sunglasses and combination cell phone-calling, organizing, computing, web-surfing, stock-updating, news-tracking, restaurant-reviewing, crime-spotting, global-positioning, slim line silver-looking piece of electronic gadgetry in his right hand, Porsche keys in his left.

"May I help you, sir?" the nurse at the desk asked in a singsong Jamaican lilt.

"Yes. Paul Warner's room?"

"That's 1522, third door on your right."

"Thank you."

"You're welcome."

This would be his first meeting with Nicole, his reluctant co-conspirator, having only spoken with her on the phone and agreeing to regular payments from Paul's account, well, loans technically, since Paul wouldn't even acknowledge that he was a partner in Blaisdell Investments. Paul was in some kind of guilty denial about his wealth. Sure, he had taken losses lately. Who hadn't? Although Terry had not been screaming from the ramparts about how much the firm had made, his books had been open for Paul's perusal at any time. While doing well with his consulting he had jokingly asked Terry to plow his dividends back into the firm. A wise move. He was far from starving now. He never had to work again if he didn't want to. If he were awake he could see the hospital care that private insurance bought.

He knocked lightly on the door. There was no answer. To his left, Nicole was standing by the window looking out at parking lots, taller buildings, and, off in the distance, the waterfront, engrossed in her thoughts.

He was glad he saw her first. He was shaking as he finally gathered his courage and looked at Paul, directly in front of him, looking too young for his age, in funereal peace, lying at about a twenty degree angle in what looked like a very comfortable Swedish bed, and hooked up. His hair was longer than Terry remembered. He was bigger, but still handsome and powerful under the sheet, his arms nicely toned. He had a two-day stubble and his jaw seemed set. His eyes seemed to be moving under closed lids. Was that a slight smile? At least he was human. A slight gut showed itself as he turned on his side. Didn't people in comas usually need to be turned? What, Paul, do you have your own coma style?

He hadn't been in a hospital room in years. He had invested in a number of healthcare firms, start-ups and second-round financing mostly, but they were doing exotic research in labs along the Route 202 tech corridor. He suddenly felt older and vulnerable as he involuntarily moved his right hand up to his heart to check its rhythm.

He realized that most of his knowledge in this area consisted of technology and costs, the theoretical and the quantitative, and the sympathetic listening to the odd second-hand report of an employee's relative's battle with cancer; nothing as real as watching your friend lie in a coma and wondering if he would ever wake up. He felt ridiculously unprepared to handle the emotional reality of the situation. If it had been anyone else……Damn!

Softly, very softly. "Nicole?"

She turned. 'My God, she is fantastic!' was his first reaction. Her eyes were dark, big and distant, but not sad. Her red hair, more of a henna with brown streaks, was longer and more unapologeti-

THE REAL LIVES OF DREAMERS

cally feminine than most women her age wore it these days. Her tan suit looked new and expensive. Her shoulders were set back. She had been standing mostly on one leg in that sexy way that confident women do, and that generally drove him crazy. She looked her age, about forty-six, and she looked fabulous. She peered at him and did a double take, squinting after having been lost in thought gazing into the sunlit streets below..

"Terry?"

They rushed into each other's arms and hugged warmly, then kissed on the cheeks. He couldn't help but notice how Stairmaster-solid she was. She didn't seem to need much consoling. She hadn't been crying. Not a hair was out of place. There wasn't a wrinkle in her beautiful tan suit. Now he really didn't know what to say or how to behave. When they came out of their clutch, she held him by the arms and looked at him.

"Terry", she said and smiled a very peaceful smile. Terry wondered if she had either cried herself out or come to terms with some very unpleasant realities. He hadn't been feeling very peaceful himself, but the hospital room, Paul's prostrate form, and Nicole's calm presence quickly took him out of himself, like a couple of shots of Jack Daniels. That feeling left quickly, except for an imagined hangover when he attempted to talk.

"Nicole, I...I..."

"Shh. It's okay. Let me look at you. My, don't you look like the tycoon Paul told me you always wanted to be. He talks about you and Anthony, but especially you, all the time. Do you know how much he loves you?"

Terry looked puzzled, the way he often appeared in Paul's presence. They never talked about loving each other. They didn't even think in those terms. That was for women. They didn't need to verbalize what they knew to be with each other. That was mushy shit. Verbalizing the truth didn't make it so. He tried to talk, but all that came out was a short, high-pitched squeal.

"Shh. You're gonna wake him…." A natural, but unrealistic, concern. After all, waking him was the goal. They smiled at each other as the logic struck them. Nevertheless, they spoke in muted tones.

Nicole seemed to have already made peace with herself in that room, but Terry still had too much to process. He released her hands and slumped down in a chair and put his face in his hands. He started to shake. She rushed over to him and held his shoulders as she stood next to him and cooed, like a mother soothing a child after a fall.

"I'm sorry, Terry," she sing-songed, "I must seem cold. I'm not cold. I just have a feeling that Paul is where he needs to be right now. He's taking a break from the world. He'll come back to us when he's ready, and when we're ready, maybe. I'm not sure, but I can't be too sad. You see, he shouldn't be in a coma. There's no real reason for it. The dreamer is in an extended dream."

"What do you mean?"

Nicole then told him the medical facts of the case as she knew them. Terry shook his head and sat back in the chair.

"I need a drink."

She walked to the closet and reached under some sheets stacked on a shelf. Terry heard the rattling of a paper bag. He closed his eyes again. He felt a strangeness. There was something about this room. Already, the outside world had seemed to melt away. When he opened his eyes, he felt her gentle hand on his shoulder. She handed him a paper cup.

"Jack Daniels", she said.

Perfect. He took a couple of swigs.

Time (how much time?) passed.

They talked about Paul and his visions and his outrageous conversational comments and his seeming conservatism, too, and how it all fit together for him, but was so hard for others to see.

Except for her eyes, which assumed a deep red tint as time passed, the Jack Daniels hardly seemed to affect Nicole.

"He always told me that the biggest crime, even more than living an unexamined life, was to live without imagination. It drove him crazy to walk into a house with no books, no music, and no art. 'How do these people live?!' he would ask me."

They talked and laughed, but they didn't cry. Nicole would quickly change the subject when Terry's eyes started to cloud, and accuse him of being a sentimental drunk, which was true just then. He enjoyed this time with Nicole, drunker than he'd been since his time in Germany, maybe drunker than at her birthday party. Her. He could not speak her name. No, don't, he told himself. He couldn't stand for those memories to flood his consciousness just yet, not now.

He searched for the proper metaphor for what she had done to him. In a drunken haze, he noticed that his chair was surreally comfortable.

"Yeah, she eroded the soil of my emotional stability," he slurred to himself, "a little bit each year. She gave me the blues!" That was the best he could come up with. Pitiful.

"Lena or Cordelia?" Nicole asked, but he didn't hear.

He managed to pull himself up. He looked around and saw Paul's contented smile. It warmed him. No, he wasn't finished here yet. He stretched and realized that he felt like having a cheese steak with everything on it, some mango juice, and a Tastykake coconut creme pie. He waited while Nicole excused herself and disappeared into the bathroom. They floated out of the room and into the elevator and descended into the darkness of a drunken night, in search of the perfect deli.

Later, stuffed and momentarily happy, he looked out of the hospital room window at the headlights of cars crossing the Ben Franklin Bridge into Philly from South Jersey. Nicole slept in a chair by the bed as he let his thoughts roam. He let out the long sigh of the recently-aware, awaiting only rest and the time to implement a new plan. He was tired of his life, tired of the demands of success, tired of immature young employees with no morals, tired of pretentious rich investors, tired of complaining poor people with no education and no discipline, tired of egos and talk, always of money, money, and money, houses and cars, always trying to outdo each other with this or that luxury vacation and this or that fast boat. He was fine with the doing. It was the talking he objected to. So many of the wealthy were so boring. He remembered how he had been disinclined, at the impressionable age of twenty, to make a lot of money because so many of the rich people he'd met till that time had disgusted him. Twenty-five years later, here he was, disgusted again. Like so many others bypassed in the frenetic nineties, he had missed several opportunities to associate with people of character who would have been glad to eat some cold chicken and potato salad with him. Regrets………regret.

"Don't be too hard on yourself", he whispered to himself.

"You spent time with Phillip and look what happened. That fucking crook. There were others, too. Your judgment was faulty, that's all. Time to get out, then."

But mostly it was the work; the tethering of oneself to the office, despite the best that money could buy outside of it; the stress, despite the workouts and adequate sleep; the boredom with ordinary life, despite the sensual overload; the relentless flow of information, the marketing, the onslaught to sell him everything as he cursed the necessity of going through everything, checking everything out, never tuning out for fear of missing the newest product or service or computing language or platform or business model or communications standard that would be the next big thing. Good God, was this any way to live?

No, but it had changed so fast. It seemed like only a few months ago when he felt a seemingly endless exhilaration, cursing the need to sleep, meeting young geniuses and old hands who still wrote in COBOL and FORTRAN on mainframes. He had interacted with some of the finest minds of his time and was imbued with an unwavering belief in science and its ability to help illogical humans. The loss of those times was as real to him as Paul's coma, worthy of their own funeral service. Not that Paul….

The successful effort to raise thirty million dollars to fund a project to enable scents to be transmitted over the Internet was the last signal to Terry that this new thing was going awry. The con artists and defrauders had slipped in under the radar in the excitement, storming the beaches of capitalism itself, ripping off the greedy as well as those who only worked hard and believed in a system that was supposed to take care of them after they worked themselves to premature aging. They would get a separate burial, the crooks, after the trials.

'Did you really expect, Mr. Venture Capitalist, that investing in the ability to produce scents over the Internet would be a meaningful service, and that it would produce profits for your investors? And what about you, you off-the-books, off-shore, above-the-line, expense-hiding, amoral accounting fuck?'

It was time to enjoy life again. The bubble had burst and the disbelief had settled into economic decline, depression and the telling of stories. The stories they would tell their grandchildren! You should have seen it! they would say. Everybody was making so much money! (Of course, everybody was not really *everybody*, but it sure was a lot of people, wasn't it?) Then they would go into their spiel about the IPO's and three hundred percent annual returns on stocks that were no longer traded, businesses liquidated on auction web sites, enough computing power to run countries sold for a song. And their eyes would glaze over as their grandchildren, probably too young to understand, possibly disinclined to listen carefully if they weren't, gave them that 'you old coot' look. Forget this, he thought, it's nowhere thinking.

All of this, he thought, slamming a fist into a palm, after I spent so much time in the last several years pleading with poor people to learn the economic system, to believe in the creating and sharing of wealth, only to look like a fool, unable to adequately answer the questions of those who were, finally, almost-believers.

So, smart guy, what now? Maybe he should help the feds go after the crooks. Hmm. One thing was sure, everybody would be kept busy.

He remembered one of their last conversations. It must have been two years ago, at least. When did time become his enemy? He had heard yet another report on poor housing and schools and the need for safer communities in the inner city. The person being interviewed, the head of some community group that had gotten lucky and received federal community grant money nonetheless managed to, in thirty seconds, blame the government and racism for all of the problems of the inner city, effectively leaving the impression that the residents there were powerless sheep with no sense of determining their own fate. Drug addiction and poor parenting and a popular culture that glorified crime weren't mentioned. He found himself screaming at the radio as he drove past long lines for lottery tickets. He went to see Paul.

"Too many poor people loved being poor before the government reformed welfare. Fewer expectations. Fewer demands. Now they see that competing is hard. Especially if you're honest."

Terry was just a little more forgiving.

"C'mon, Paul, you make it all sound so cut and dried."

"That's what I used to say to the old people. I was so full of hope and wonder and possibilities! Then I got mugged, smacked upside the head, beaten within an inch of my life, and left for dead."

Terry was sympathetic, but couldn't quite see the relevance.

"I'm sorry. When was this? Are we changing subjects here?"

"Reality, Terry! Reality kicked my ass and left me for dead! I was left with nothing once I began to understand how people are. Do you think that stopped me from trying anyway, arguing that, 'no, you can't give up. There are hard-working people that need the help you can offer?' No, it didn't and I'm scarred because of it, scarred because people can't just accept help without imposing their fucked-up value system on the helper, more concerned about the shoes he's wearing than what comes out of his mouth. People ask for help, but they just want money. They don't want a roadmap that points the way to success. They don't want the fishing rod, just the fish, and it damn sure better be snapper 'cause they don't like trout."

"Man, you are so dramatic! Reality kicked your ass and left you for dead. But you're right, to a certain extent. But I wish that people, all people, were more..desiring of what our generation of educated black men has to offer."

BARRY NIX

"That's right, and we're the generation with probably the best perspective because we remember the fight for civil rights and nickel candy bars, and we've functioned in a new world, too. We're the transitional generation, the ones who were offered the carrot. Sometimes it was poisoned, sometimes it was too sweet, sometimes it had to be washed off real good. But it was there for more than a few of us."

"What about your carrot, Paul?"

"It was there, but this rabbit's legs weren't strong enough to jump up and get it. I had to exercise them for a few years first. I don't blame society for that, except maybe some along the way could have pushed a little harder, gotten me out of my own head. But mostly it was me, my personality. It wasn't easy. I needed to find myself at the same time I was arguing against self-indulgence and narcissism. I was living instead of planning for a career. Then I found myself wise and underemployed. And yours?"

" It kept moving every time I got close. Until...."

"Yeah. Until is right. The Forbes 400."

"Oh, please."

"Like it or not, you're an important symbol".

"Yeah. You're worth a lot and you haven't had to make it by rappin' and usin' the word nigger."

"What an accomplishment."

And later. ".......least of all our kids and relatives. The fathers who take fatherhood seriously are rejected by feminized males with a distorted view of the world. Like the women have all the answers. Pussies in Desert Storm crying for their mamas on camera. Women who think they're superwomen and only need a man to carry a box, no understanding of the pleasures of real manhood. We're all fucked up! Everybody's fragmented! There's no unity in anything.

THE REAL LIVES OF DREAMERS

So, somebody divided and conquered, I guess, but who? Because I don't see anybody winning in this mess. 'We must be oh, so tender,' the liberals say. 'We must repress the primal instincts of men.' Fine, muh fuckahs. Can't chop down trees, slap your woman around. Can't make money, give a baby to a teenager with no self-esteem. Make a lot of money, ignore your kids; one's anorexic, one's in a cult, and one's just plain crazy. Raising kids is woman's work anyway. Well, I'm a music-listening, culture-pushin', chest-poundin', hard-fuckin' man and I don't apologize to anybody. Fuck 'em. I'll go off in a cave somewhere. That whole concept becomes more appealing every day anyway."

Terry realized there was no stopping Paul once he got that stagecoach moving, whip in hand, horses' feet barely touching the ground. Terry was merely the old, grizzled one riding shotgun, watching out for bandits and holding on to his hat and hoping they would get where they were going soon. "You could become a monk."

Paul slowed the stage down to turn a corner. "I've considered it. The spiritual life, the life of the mind, is very appealing. I'm not with the religious thing, though. It's all mythology and power anyway. Talk about fragmented! It's all the same, only the artifacts are different. Besides, those cats live hard! Up early in the morning, tending gardens, no talking, working in the fields, probably no cappuccino, no Thelonious Monk. A monk with no Monk. A man's got to have something."

He was finished. They had arrived at their final, improvised destination of the moment, none the worse for wear, Terry supposed, but he was scratching his head, stiff from the ride and wishing there had been other passengers along to help him make some sense of the journey.

Relaxed again after working himself into a lather, he looked over at Paul. He sat back and went limp as he became one with that ultra-comfortable chair. He began to dream, of long-ago times in Minneapolis, of people he'd known, of Germany in those days, their time.

"Damn you, Paul!" He opened his eyes, not knowing he had slept, not remembering the fading of daylight, the surrendering of dusk to darkness, the lighting of the candle on the nightstand, the sad departure of Nicole, his brief comrade-in-revelry, the concerned face and kind eyes of the nurse who covered him with a cashmere throw from Paul's house, none of it could he remember; but he remembered her, despite all of his ranting, his begging her to leave him alone, despite fighting the good fight as she crept out of the recesses, despite closing his eyes and holding his ears to protect himself from the siren-call of her beautiful, ultra-feminine soprano voice. But it was useless. He gave up and slumped down in his chair, the chair that owned him now, that refused to release him, as she sat down on the bed by Paul's knee and spread her beautiful pastel blue nightgown outward, as an angel would gather its wings, as she smiled a maddeningly pleasant smile and called him darling in Dutch.

"Shautige."

Lena was back.

He and Lena were in Paris, strolling the Champs' Elysees in April. Springtime in central Europe was to die for anyway though, wasn't it? Perfect day followed by perfect day. Then three months of a perfect summer. Sunny and seventy-five degrees, with a little sprinkling most afternoons at four-thirty to keep everyone honest. GI's from the States' hot south, the humid northeast, and the rainy northwest, even from California, couldn't believe it. The weather was, to their sensibilities, as perfect as weather could get, and they luxuriated in it as a valued resource. They were mostly young and very healthy, far from family and all that was familiar, as they began to stretch their legs alone in the real world. Our three wunderkinder had already felt the strength in their legs of life and run some good races, had fallen as they approached the stretch in others, scraped and scarred in one or two instances, for life.

"I am here, shautige."

But Terry was feeling crowded. Lena got lost as too many lost memories demanded to be found. Like the field exercise in the fall of '87. The Incident.

Terry was tired, but it had been a good sixteen-hour day, all of it spent outdoors in the German countryside. Trees and tents, dirt and grass. Meals in aluminum plates. Hard-leg GIs all around. He absolutely loved it. For the first two weeks. This exercise, though, would last three and a half weeks. The best shower he had ever taken had been upon their return from the last exercise. He was looking forward to his next, best shower.

He had two jobs this time out. That was fine with him. He had trained over and over how to deliver first aid, respond to a nuclear, biological, or chemical attack, distinguish a saddle from a valley on a map, and drive a Jeep over rough terrain. But there hadn't been enough shooting and real combat training. That was for the infantry, he supposed. We just communicate with outmoded equipment; safe but boring. He was the lone finance representative sent to the field for the company, joining others from several battalions to oversee paychecks, problems with direct deposits, overdrawn accounts and the like. His other job was as unofficial director of morale, a task usually assigned to a senior non-commissioned officer, but given to him on merit after he pulled off a hugely successful company party for four hundred soldiers and their families at minimal expense.

He walked to the Operations tent and plopped in a green, metal folding chair after taking off his helmet and web gear. He waited while barrel-chested Sergeant First Class Kelly talked on the phone. Terry tried to spend as much time as he could around Kelly. He always learned something. Other NCO's were suspicious of Terry and his endless questions from everything about the inner workings of the Army to their career tracks to their opinions about the officers in the battalion, but Kelly shared his knowledge freely, not threatened by Terry's over-eagerness. Kelly's reddish-blond hair was a little longer than the other NCO's, but short enough to adhere to regulations. There were rumors about his tour of duty in Vietnam, ranging from how much heroin he'd used to how many women he'd married to how many enemy he'd killed. He was overweight, but solid and not obese, and too valuable to let twenty pounds get in the way of his efficient de facto running of the battalion. Besides, he had pull at Army Europe HQ in Heidelberg. A lieutenant of his in 'Nam was on the short list for Major General.

Kelly hung up the phone.

"Blaisdell!" he shouted, despite the fact that Terry was less than ten feet away.

"Sergeant First Class Kelly! Terry shouted back and smiled.

"You ain't tired, are you, Blaisdell?"

"Hell, no, Sergeant Kelly. I'm ready to fight a war!"

"Good, good. Godamnit, Blaisdell, you're my kind of soldier!

THE REAL LIVES OF DREAMERS

"Thank you, Sergeant Kelly! And, Godamnit, you're my kind of NCO!"

They both laughed.

"Blaisdell, you're so full of shit your eyes are brown. Listen, Ter, I've got somethin' for ya, if you're up to it. And keep this to yourself. I know it's been a long day, but I thought I'd run this by you. Your buddy, Turner, is being dropped in by helicopter. I'm not gettin' any information on this one, but my guess is that he just came off a mission and we don't need to ask any questions, ya unnerstand?"

Terry, as suddenly serious as Kelly, shook his head up and down.

"You wanna go get him? If you're too tired, let me know. I don't need you crashin' into a tree and makin' me fill out more damn paperwork."

Terry was energized now. "How soon?"

"The chopper's due in at twenty-four hundred hours. It's about a twenty-minute drive."

"I'll go."

"Alright. Report back here at twenty-three fifteen and top off thirty-six. No papers on this one, Terry."

"No papers? Damn."

"No papers."

Terry didn't trust 'no papers'. He was going to cover his ass. He went to his tent, an Army Large, and found his aluminum and Army green nylon cot among the two rows of twelve each. The German rock group Scorpions was playing softly in a corner as a quartet of soldiers played cards to a single bare light bulb in a naked socket overhead. Others were sleeping. Two were in their cots, reading themselves to sleep by flashlight. There was the sound of two or three loud snores. Paul looked particularly uncomfortable as his long legs hung off his cot, but he was out for the count, smiling, as he usually did, in his sleep. Dog-eared paperbacks, espionage novels by John LeCarre, rested on the dirt floor under his cot. What did he know? Terry dropped his gear and walked over to the table.

"Hey, muh fuckah," Kimble said.

"Hey, muh fuckah," Terry replied. "Ah'm tired as shit."

"Fuck that. Get in this game and let me take some of your money, muh fuckah."

"Nah. I'll just watch for a while. Gotta head out soon."

All four card players looked up.

"The fuck they got you doin' now?" asked Patterson.

"Can't say. Besides, I volunteered."

"Oh."

That was all that was said about that. Terry would long for those days when a simple explanation was enough. Leave it at that. Shut the fuck up and move on. And no, I don't want to hear about your day. No such thing as full disclosure then. Not for him, anyway. Muh fuckahs communicated with their actions more than with their words. They didn't talk unless they had something to say.

Terry shot the breeze with them for ten minutes, then went to his cot and slept for exactly thirty, when he felt a tap on his shoulder, then a whisper.

"Time to get up, muh fuckah."

Terry blinked, groggy, then shot up, ready to go.

"Thanks."

"Yeah." Kimble moved away silently in the dark.

Terry got himself together. He began to write on a piece of paper.

THE REAL LIVES OF DREAMERS

Paul,

I'm going to the airfield to pick up Anthony. Keep it to yourself. No papers on this one. I'm covering my ass.

Terry

He put the paper in an envelope that he picked up from the soldier on CQ, twenty-four-hour duty in the tent, the one that had to stay awake and provide assistance as needed, no matter what else he did.

Terry walked to Kimble's cot. He was reading the Stars and Stripes. He looked up. "Muh fuckahs in the states are goin' crazy."

"Yeah, they are. Later."

Kimble sat up. "Yo, man. Stay alert."

"Always."

They gave each other as much of a heartfelt smile as their code of two macho muh fuckahs who respected each other would allow. It was a smile that, if shared in a slightly different variation between a man and a woman, would cause a woman to open her legs in willing acceptance, or a man to drop to his knees in submission, but in its present form declared, in very specific terms, that each would "go up that hill", the ubiquitous hill over which a known enemy presented unknown hazards, with the other; the ultimate trust. There was, to them, no greater compliment.

Terry opened the flap of the tent and walked into the brisk night air to be greeted by the never-ending hum of generators and the brightness of strings of light bulbs hung in strategic pathways. As he walked away, he looked for a clearing, found one, and went over to it. His concern for Anthony fused with the gratitude and humility he felt for the show of respect that had just been directed at him. He leaned, inconspicuously he hoped, against a tree and breathed the clear air of the German night and smelled the trees, the dust, the gasoline, and the warm metal from just-parked Jeeps. He let himself cry, almost silently. He had much of what he wanted in life already; the love and respect of people whom he loved and respected. He took two huge sobs and got himself together. He looked around, straightened up, and walked with his chest out, emotionally sated, rivaling the afterglow of lovemaking. He was rested and free and strong.

He walked to a communications trailer and knocked.

"Hey, Simpson, do me a favor and time stamp this without lookin' at it."

"Sure, Blaisdell."

Simpson returned it stamped with the date and time. Terry eased back into the tent and put the folded envelope with the time stamp in the top right pocket of Paul's fatigues. Paul didn't move. Kimble, lying down again, looked on silently.

After checking in with Kelly, Terry found Jeep number 36 and filled it with gas from the cans in a roped-off area.

As he drove into the brisk night air, bouncing on the uneven, winding dirt road, very careful on the turns, he wondered what Anthony had been up to this time, as if he'd ever been given a clue. He smiled as he thought about the game Paul played with Anthony as he, Paul, armed with the few facts he knew of Anthony's comings and goings, tried to glean some tidbit of information about exactly what Anthony was doing, or had done. Paul parried and Anthony thrusted. Paul retreated and tried to outflank, but Anthony would have none of it. Paul referred to scenes in spy novels, but Anthony remained noncommittal. It really was a game, of course, because Paul would never encourage Anthony to compromise himself. Had Paul really intended to win he would have been more circumspect in letting Anthony know how much he knew. Anthony knew that Paul was highly informed and thinking seriously about the intricacies of world affairs. He occasionally tossed Paul a harmless bit of almost-information, perhaps verifying the accuracy of a novelistic portrayal of an event in the not-too distant past, expressing wonder at how one or two authors came by their knowledge of their subjects. Paul was genuinely appreciative of these puzzle pieces.

"So! I guess you went to Hamburg looking for that Red Brigade punk that escaped from prison, huh?" Paul hated terrorists and followed their movements in the papers.

"I didn't say that. How did you know about him?"

"It was in the papers."

"It was?! They need to keep that stuff bottled up for a while."

"So you *were* there."

"I didn't say I was there."

"Well, where *were* you then?"

"I didn't say I wasn't there, either. Maybe I was there."

"Or in Paris at the economic summit. Or that little get-together of foreign ministers in Antwerp, taking care of an attaché or two in just the right way, heh heh."

Paul would never fail to raise Anthony's eyebrows with his careful readings.

"I'm just a low-level guy. You're operating under this James Bond fantasy that I refuse to encourage."

"You have all of the talents to be James Bond, except maybe a cold-enough heart that would be unaffected by dirty but necessary deeds done dirt cheap. But you're probably right. Maybe you're just chasin' horny officers sleeping with their enlisted aides, or drug-dealin' soldiers makin' runs on the autobahn."

BARRY NIX

"Or saving the world from nuclear destruction every week. Give up," Anthony laughed.

"Just thought I'd see if I could get a reading. Good job, soldier. You're keeping the world safe for Democracy!"

All of that would stop, though, after Anthony returned from this trip.

Anthony emerged from the noisy chopper in a green nylon flight suit carrying a green nylon Army valise. He saw Terry standing by the Jeep and shielded his eyes as the helicopter took off. He walked, iron rod-straight and with a purpose, toward the Jeep. Terry walked to him, hollered a greeting and reached for the valise. Instead, Anthony surprised him by grabbing his arms and giving him a bear hug, squeezing him hard.

"Terry," he said calmly. "Thanks for coming. Where's Paul?"

"This one's a solo. Orders. No papers."

"Oh. Right." They jumped into the Jeep. Terry started the engine and began to drive back into the dark forest from which he came.

"You know he would have come if I'd told him."

"Yeah. Just as well. You got any hash?"

Terry reached into his fatigue jacket and handed Anthony a black plastic film canister. It contained a small folded pipe and a tiny zippered bag with a chunk of black hash.

"Afghan, huh?"

"Yeah. Be careful."

"Okay. I can't talk. Do you mind?"

"No, Ant. Do what you need to do. You hungry? Need anything else?"

"No, Ter, thanks."

Terry drove in silence, taking just one hit off the hash pipe, watching as Anthony took four and carefully replaced the fixings, driving into blackness, navigating expertly with only the headlights as guides, feeling for the twists in the road, searching his friend's face for hints of psychic damage (for he never seemed to be in physical danger), wondering what dangers he had faced as he and Paul worried and fretted more than Anthony would ever know, more each time as he re-entered the mouth of the lion that he seemed to know so well, and wondered what would come back to haunt their friend in the future and, because they loved him for life, what would haunt them.

Anthony sat low in his seat and drifted as the motor hummed and the hash lifted him above, but not out of, his surroundings. He vowed never to smoke weed again. It scattered your brain. Hash left you clear, functional, until you smoked too much; just right for his time in life now.

He had to brief headquarters in the morning. Fuck 'em. He'd be ready. Ready for the subterfuge, the grandstanding, the hollering, the accusations. How about the truth, fellas? Any room for that? Hell, no. He would lie, and in his lying state truths that were understood, but not to be uttered. There would be a nod, a meeting of another pair of eyes across the room, and a question, 'Are you sure?', as long as they thought he was on the team, playing ball the way they had determined it needed to be played. They behaved as if they thought he was a cowboy, but he wasn't really. Maybe they knew exactly what he was.

The all-volunteer Army was many things to him, a vast humanity of the ignorant and barely civilized, the upwardly mobile of average intelligence, high IQ renegades (unrecognized, with an ax to grind), and brilliant planners, strategists, and tacticians. It trained the country's warriors better than any in history. It made men out of non-beings, molded the un-formed, strengthened the weak, and rejected the recalcitrant and returned them to their sullen environs. At the same time, it ruined the curious, the free-thinkers, the creative, who also wanted only to contribute, but found themselves in the druck of the rote, cast off as freaks for voicing original thoughts where only orders mattered. The conferences had taken place at higher levels. There was no need for discussion. Only execution along the chain of command. Necessary and foolish. Right and wrong. It simply was. It was never 'it depends'. Execute. Accomplish the goals of the mission whatever the cost, almost. Do what has to be done.

This was not the evil that weak-spined complainers thought it was; people who would never be able to face the necessities of freedom. It was the lack of imagination in the lower supervisory ranks, both enlisted and officer, which he despised; that and the almost non-existent political awareness which left them unable to place any action, or reaction, in context. There was actually some discretion available in choosing how to accomplish goals, but what is discretion without imagination, without awareness of current thinking? It is slavery to what worked ten, fifteen, twenty years ago, in a different time, in a different situation, with different technology, that's what. It was these people who stifled the liberal-arts educated enlisted soldiers, effectively blocking their entry into the creative ranks within the Army. The only thing wrong with the Army way of doing things, as he saw it, was the people who inhabited that system, much as the pure ideas of intellectuals floated down to the untrained masses, who interpreted the noble as the prurient, the search for true freedom as the operating license of the decadent, skipping over the boring reading to get to the good parts.

They knew they had to accept certain personality traits to get certain others. You want sensitivity with that killing? Intelligence with that blind patriotism? Efficiency with that chaos? No, he wasn't a cowboy. But he was able to gather in the totality of the picture better than most. He saw the necessity of certain actions before they did. He was resented, barely trusted (earning them his enmity, for he was nothing if not loyal), but grudgingly respected. He got the job done.

This time, though, he would admit nothing. There would be no implications. It was too serious. It would be by the book. He would see to that, guiding them each step of the way, if need be, for they would want to cooperate. Besides, it had all been so unexpected. Or had it? What did they know? Had they anticipated his response? He did not like being used, but realized it was part of the game. Maybe they had read him perfectly and got just what they wanted, a dead traitor.

He had trouble believing the finality of what happened. He so wanted to turn back, to reverse actions, to un-hear what he had heard, but precipitous events had taken place long ago. The die had been cast before he joined the game. He didn't try to talk himself into feeling shame or guilt. Was there something wrong with him? Hell, no. You don't betray your country. Period. Especially when in a position of trust. And especially not for money.

It was seven PM the night before. Anthony sat eating dinner at a small table in a fashionable Indonesian-Chinese restaurant in downtown Cologne while diners around him spoke in the 'Kolnish' dialect, to his mind an abomination of the German language that should have been outlawed by the courts. He put his fork down from his sweet and sour pork and reached for his glass of Spätlese. A middle-aged German couple walked in.

"*Guten abend*," they said, in the tradition that floored Paul when they went out. He thought it extremely civilized and could not imagine a roomful of strangers in America speaking to each other except over a sporting event.

"*Guten abend*," the sitting diners said, almost in unison.

As he sat there, Anthony thought this was one of those moments he would never forget, that at any time in the distant future, he could place himself in this restaurant, taste the wine in his mouth, pat his stomach in comfort as he recalled the fine meal, see the particular faces around him, revel in his hard, taut body, feel his soft silk and wool patterned sport jacket as he rubbed it between his fingers; the lighted candle on the table, the apprehension of the much-anticipated meeting to come, how much he loved his job, how useful, how alive he felt.

Then there was the blurriness of a life-changing event, the physical pain of a betrayal of the collective self, and the floating, the floating, as his abdominal muscles loosened and his head swam as he listened to the tape, the decisiveness of the moment without hesitation, the fear in the eyes of those around him, the acquaintance who became the target — his silly, arrogant smirk twisted into a grotesque mask of fear, smelling his own death at twenty-seven, questioning his own decisions and motives, realizing at the last possible moment that he had gotten it all wrong, like a mathematician who had covered a classroom full of blackboards to arrive at a conclusion originating in a faulty premise, as he knew to them he was the symbol of all that was wrong, then the darkness — the hatred of the righteous numbed by action, the papers recovered, the mopping up, no tracks, only sadness, sadness, and depression, wondering if his father would be proud, calling up images of an arrogant Lieutenant in a field in Holland forty-four years before, pounding the green grass with his fists, screaming and shaking, looking to the black sky, then exultation, categorization, filing away, pushing back, archiving, and home, for now, to the forest, to a Jeep with Terry, his rock, beside him, guiding him through the thicket of his strewn synapses, reassuring him of good and friendship and trust as tears refused to flow out of aching eyes, down a tired face, as he realized his head would not explode under his hard helmet, as he returned to the present. To life. To sanity. To freedom.

The morning after his Jeep ride. Breakfast in a huge mess tent, Credence Clearwater Revival at a decent volume over the speakers, surrounded by men in green, laughing and joking, doing a double-take at the stereotype-defying tasty food, bathing in the glow of ultimate camaraderie. Anthony gave his briefing. There were few questions. The mood was somber. After they checked his weapons, the ones they knew of, for recent firings, he was given three weeks' leave. He ate, smoked, and screwed his way from Hamburg to Munich. That night entered his consciousness in the oblique way that acknowledged its existence without dwelling on the particulars. They could wait. For fifteen years.

Paul awakened with a grunt. What was Terry doing here? For some reason, the sunlight seemed unbearably bright. He looked up and saw the startled look of the dark-eyed Amazon of his recent dreams. She was fiddling with his covers. What a knowing smile she had. She wiped her mouth. He was very confused. He cleared his throat and reached to blow his nose. Nicole had left a box of tissues nearby. He blew his nose, took a sip of water, and leaned back. Too much confusion. Sleep is better. Now, where was I? he wondered. Oh, yeah. I used to keep 'em laughin', didn't I?

It was the Saturday after the field exercise that changed Anthony, after they had worked like dogs to get their vehicles back to 'go' status, cleaned them up and passed inspection, along with all of their gear and their weapons. It wasn't over until that seventy-two-hour turnaround was over. Then the fat lady sang a funky song, put a red dress on her rump-shaker, and prepared to party, waiting for exhausted soldiers pushed on by the need to let off a lot of green Army steam.

Anthony, Paul, and Terry were in Paul's barracks room drinking beer and jumping up and down to Parliament/Funkadelic, loud, before heading out. The officers and senior NCO's were gone, most off to spend time with families deprived of their presence for three and a half weeks. There was a knock on the door and Kimball, Jones, and Walker walked in. Terry handed them sixteen-ounce bottles of St. Pauli Girl and everybody was thumpin', laughin', and talking trash. Four more GIs, white guys pausing tentatively at the door, showed up. Kimball rushed them in with a furtive look up and down the empty hallway. Johnny Mac, the nickname given to the leader of this particular group of tentative white guys, wondered about the black guys. These guys seemed to know how to have fun without acting like pure idiots. The Mars Brothers, and the darker-skinned Kimball, from Chicago, always talked to them and made them feel welcome. They were older than most of the other guys, seemed to come from a different time, looked to different references for their behavior. Kimball brought out some hash and Terry rushed to put a towel under the door. There was a party goin' on.

"Oh, shit," Paul said, "you must not want me to go anywhere, muh fuckah."

Kimball. "You need to leave them German girls alone anyway, muh fuckah."

Paul slid into his heavy dialect, laughing. "Ah know you must be crazy, muh fuckah." He quoted a song he'd heard Lou Rawls sing in '67. "I'd rather drink muddy water and sleep in a hollow log."

"Sheeit. You one crazy sombitch!"

Terry started instigating. "Wait, Kimball. Look at Paul's eyes. He's got that twitch. Look at his mouth. I think he's goin' there."

"Don't start no stuff and there won't be no stuff, Ter," Paul laughed, almost drunk from one beer. His cheap drunkenness was legendary.

"Yeah, Blaisdell, I see it. He's a funny-lookin' muh fuckah anyway."

"Kimball, you just fucked up. You gonna get it now."

The room erupted in laughter. Paul took a long swig on his second beer, grabbed the hash pipe out of Kimball's hands, and toked long and hard.

"Y'all bettah hold me off him. Ahma hurt him!" Kimball shouted in his mock serious way. He lunged as the others grabbed him, laughing hysterically.

Paul encouraged him. "Sheeit. You don't want none a' this. You know I'm tha ass-kicker around heah! I'm a kick your ass so bad you'll need to order a new one, and then I'll kick that one, too."

By this time, Kimball was laughing so hard he couldn't keep up the charade. He fell back, laughing, on a bed covered by an Army-green, scratchy wool blanket, made to specifications and tested occasionally by the bounce of a quarter on its surface.

"I give up! You're a funny muh fuckah. You'll *laugh* a muh fuckah to death!"

This puffed Paul up. He gave the pipe back to Kimball and fished a chunk of hash wrapped in plastic out of a pocket and tossed it to him. Then he turned around and Mulebone was in the room. Mulebone was a character that Paul had been working on ever since he had seen Richard Pryor's Las Vegas concert on video the year before. Mulebone, according to Paul, was the brother to Pryor's character, Mudbone. When the GI's in the room saw the look in his eyes, they laughed, knowing what was coming, except for Jones, who had just gotten in-country the week before and was trying hard to take in all that he was hearing and seeing, in addition to missing his mother in Gary, Indiana. He looked flummoxed as he watched Paul and. This was not what he expected from his first duty station. The others laughed harder.

"The show is on, Jones," Kimball said. "This muh fuckah's a riot."

Paul, in character, put on his Army cap backwards and cocked to the side, turned a chair around, and sat down with an exaggerated, put-on, scrunched-up, angry look on his face, holding the back of the chair in front of him. He started in on Jones, sounding like an old southern codger, mad at the world.

"Who you, muh fuckah?" Jones looked even more confused. He opened his mouth but nothing came out. Now the men in the room, Terry, Anthony, Kimball, and Walker and the others, arranged around the room on chairs and on the side of Paul's bed, standing

THE REAL LIVES OF DREAMERS

by the door, sitting on the miniature refrigerator, cross-legged on the floor, each with a nice buzz on, were falling over each other laughing. Jones sat there looking like he wanted to go outside and do push-ups.

"Did you hear me, muh fuckah? Who you?" Terry was almost choking with laughter. Jones, higher than he'd ever been in his life, couldn't speak. He didn't know whether to be fearful or exhilarated. Was this another manhood ritual thing? He noticed there were no women in the room. They pretty much kept to themselves.

"You a strange muh fuckah, ain't you?" Kimball played the foil. "Eh, Mulebone, you leave this young soldier alone. He don't know what to say."

Mulebone mocked Kimball. "He don't know what to say. He better find out! This ain't no mama's boy camp!. Ah'll whup you up sump'n terrible if you say anotha word. Who asked you anyway? You bettah go out and get you some poontang 'fore Ah tell you 'bout yo'sef."

The room erupted with laughter. Then, to Jones. "You had any poontang since you been here, young buck? Ah bet you lookin' at that purty thang from Kentucky. Got a ass lahk a tank and can suck the chrome off a tailpipe. Dat gal done had mo' men than Bayer got aspirin. You know Bayer aspirin is right down the road heah, too. I bet you didn't even know Bayer aspirin was from Germany, did you? Ah *bet* you didn't know that. Yeah, you young folks swear you know evah damn thing, don't you. Ain't got no use fo' a old fool like me. Well, Ah got plenty left in me, don't you worry. You know what John Lee Hooker said, don't ya? Look at him, y'all. God-damn boy don't even know who John Lee Hooker is. You bettah git some blues recuds while you heah, CD's or whateveah they makin' these days. God-damn young people today. Got me all upset, agitated. Gimme some a dat beer, muh fuckah. Anyway, yeah, John Lee Hooker said, 'mah fathuh was a jockey and he taught me how ta ride. Once in da middle, den side ta side'. Now, young smart-ass, Indiana momma's boy, what he mean by dat? Come on, tell me. Ah knew it. You don't damn know, do you. Dat's cause ya ignant 'bout womenfolk. Y'all wanna learn sump'n 'bout womenfolk? Well, Ah'm heah to tell ya."

"A woman, see, she diffent dan a man. She don't want what you want. Most o' da time, anyway. 'Ceptin' if she's a good slut. We'll talk more on that later. Now, as I was sayin', all you want is some good, sweet pussy. She wants a feelin'. And if she thinks you cain't give her dat feelin', well, you mo' outta luck than a seven-foot jockey, 'cause you cain't ride. Well, anyway, John Lee, see, is tellin' you you gotta know what a woman wants. Ah talk to young fools, some of 'em look jes' like you, they don't know shit. Dey say, ' Ah'm getting' dat pussy, let her get hers.' Well, dey might git it once, but dass all dey gettin'. You gotta play wid it evah now and then, ya know. Oh, yeah, ya gotta play wid it. Ya gotta git her ready, ya gotta know where dat little man in the boat is and ya gotta give him an ocean to row in. Muh fuckah, Ah'll bet you jes' leave that little man tryin' to row on dry land, don't ya, ya damn young know-it-all? See, once dat little man is swimmin', he gonna let her know eveahthang is alright, see. Den you got her. She know you give a damn 'bout how she feels and she say she can get freaky witcha an' you happier dan a pack a hound dogs in a cave fulla foxes."

Kimble was beside himself, sputtering and spilling beer. That made the others laugh harder, slapping each other fives and doubling over, pleading for Paul to stop. Well, why did they do that?

"Ah ain't finished yet, you muh fuckahs. We gotta have a toast, to that Kentucky gal, and all the sluts like her who give a man

THE REAL LIVES OF DREAMERS

comfort. A man needs comfort, you know. Ah luvs me a slut, 'long as she's clean. Oh yeah, she got to be clean." He raised his glass.

"To sluts, muh fuckahs!" They raised their glasses and shouted. "To sluts, muh fuckahs!"

Mulebone sat down, seemed to get more serious, and went on. "Yeah. Yeah. You see, son, a slut ain't no joke. She performs a valuable community service that people don't wanna reco'nize out in the open, see. All dese hardlegs in heah, most o'em is goood men. A woman'll try ta make 'em feel like they ain't no good if they don' wanna settle down and get married right away. An' she walkin' 'round like she got golden poontang or somethin'. Sluts love to share, see. That's what we was put on this earth to do, share the good things in life. An' what's better than sharin' poontang, know-nuthin' young boy? Dese men here, they jus' want some satisfaction, lahk that English boy, Jagger, he knew what he was talkin' 'bout, see. They git dat pressure built up, they just need some release. It's that damn simple. Now you keep lettin' that pressure build up, that's how you get these freaky goin's on, these evil goin's on. It ain't rocket science. It's just fuckin'. Now, you all, evah one a you in this room. Raise your glasses to fuckin'!

"To fuckin'!"

Paul got up and stood up straight and tall, finished with Mulebone. He turned his cap around to the front, looked military again. In his most booming command voice, he instructed them.

"Now waive your arms in the air like you just don't care! Burn this muh fuckah down! Move on up! We're winners! Say it loud, I'm a bad muh fuckah and I'm proud!"

"Yeah!" they shouted.

The young men in the room went off, clapping and shouting and cheering in an orgy of testosterone heaven for twenty more minutes before settling down for another hour, reluctant to leave, not sure that what they had been looking forward to so eagerly could compare to what they just shared. Then they went out into the world and followed the precepts of the ancient one, and made their girlfriends and wives and slutty partners of the night happy after paying particular attention to the men in the boats, the sensitive love buttons, the happy clitorises, then slept the peaceful sleep, dreaming warriors' dreams to a Fela Kuti soundtrack, and loving life.

"Have you learned anything yet?" the one with the English accent asked. Paul could not answer. "Silence. Hmm. That is good. We will continue."

They were each unique, different rivers emptying into the same sea, each background and set of experiences contributing the sticks and small fish acquired along the way, the joys and detritus of lives fully lived, until they became nearly one, but not really.

Anthony was in search of an essential understanding of the blues and all it entailed. A noble journey lovingly documented.

Paul was living, just living; an improvised life hewn from an imaginary all-night jam session with Bird and Dizzy and Monk at the Five Spot in New York, Jimmy Heath and Benny Golson at Pep's on Broad Street in Philly, or present at the creation of Samuel Barber's Adagio for Strings at The Curtis Institute or up the road at his home in Bryn Mawr. Gone. Men and women and music and the times of his life, real and imagined. A lifetime of learning and improvisation, of Ralph Ellison's underground man's covert preparation bringing forth overt action, the chord changes of the theme laying the groundwork for the solo in the tempo of the moment.

THE REAL LIVES OF DREAMERS

Terry wanted the money. Not without accomplishment, either before or after, the defining periods of the upwardly mobile, the 'before money' period and the 'after money' period, as different as night and day despite any attempts to 'keep it real' or to 'not change'.

"Did you worry about money every day of your life?"

"Well, not every day."

"Are you now, or will you ever again be, worried about money?"

"Well, no."

"That in itself is an irreversible change."

"But I'm still me."

"And a fine person you are, without the stomach cramps, economic anxiety and the bags under your eyes, bags of restive hope. Now your wallet and belly are full. You can afford to be generous and engaging. You are free to explore life, to achieve your greatest potential. You are a different man."

Paul was hard on women. Come to think of it, Paul was hard on everyone, especially himself. He was constantly befuddled by the illogical actions of people who complained about their lives and, at the same time, confused about how to make his way in a world he despised. He despised hypocrisy. He despised pretension, knowing it more fully than Terry before he drowned in it, not his own, but that of those in his rarefied world. He praised achievement and cursed himself for not achieving more, for only dreaming and reading and observing. He worshiped art, but pitied those who were burned by the flames of its creators. He wanted no part of artists — though he knew himself to be one, still hiding — or those who thought they were artists, and who lived according to their take on the pre-defined, alcohol-soaked, woman-abusing, self-indulgent precepts of the gifted. The men, that is. And the women. Brilliant and illogical. He loved them, even after they left his bed for others', and for no particular reason. Just as well. He couldn't imagine any of them mothering his child, should they decide to have him. Flighty and moody because they could be, they were more childish than he could ever imagine being allowed to be. Except Julie.

She was strawberry blond, with a beautiful, strong body that intimidated most men. Feminine, classy, and athletic. Confident and vulnerable. She could throw him across the room and then cry on his shoulder, curling up on his lap, her beautiful mouth kissing his shoulders, perhaps the only woman he ever thought he didn't deserve. She loved him fruitlessly, in the wrong time and place. He spent lonely nights wanting her years later, but couldn't find her. He would have done anything to hear her voice in his ear. He couldn't believe he had been too, what, too much in motion (?), to love that extraordinary woman properly.

That was a year of dangerous living and extraordinary women. He was always going, a constant blur. He didn't enter a room, he blew into it, beginning as a thunderstorm, gradually assuming hurricane strength, leaving nothing unchanged in the wake of the winds of his personal power. His energy was disconcerting, for it was derived from the artists he generally despised — pathological liars, gigantic egoists, the supremely gifted — but he wanted to be more civil about it, whatever his true avocation. Alright, yes, he was an artist, and to try for normalcy was fruitless. But one could have manners, couldn't one? Was it really necessary to destroy hotel rooms, beat women, become addicted to everything, and destroy those who cared about you in the manner of Charlie Parker, Jackson Pollack, Debussy, and Picasso, to create greatness, to be great? {Hey! Hold on, Jack. Bird's friends didn't feel burned. Most of them wouldn't change a thing.}

THE REAL LIVES OF DREAMERS

Okay, but still. Couldn't one's own suffering be enough? Maybe not. He had found himself swallowed up in niceness and around nice but bland people so that to genuinely express oneself was considered a sign of insanity rather than imagination or scholarship. Did he possess value amid their insignificance, despite the fact that, to their way of thinking, they believed him to be the loser, the loner, on a relentless search destined to end in despair and, quite possibly, tragedy? They effectively said, 'Just take the money, fool, and don't concern yourself with culture'. He was left talking to himself and to his enemies, always in absentia, because they refused to engage in arguments they would certainly lose.

"Is Art by its nature defiant? If so, defiant of what? Of tradition? Of discipline? Of meaning? Of cogent observation?"

"I'm a writer."

"You don't know the language."

"I'm a painter."

"You don't know how to draw."

"I'm a dancer."

"You don't know the language of the body."

"Who are you? A bourgeois artist with your fancy traditions, that's all. You are the enemy. We must get rid of you."

"Who are you? The vanguard of the ignorant, the ransacker of libraries, the foreshadower of our precipitous cultural fall, the decline of the species, that's all. We must get rid of you, but you multiply like pod people in *Night of the living Dead*."

"Libraries. Books. Life is action and makin' money, not thinkin' all damn day."

"You must examine your life. You must have a philosophy for living; aspire to a standard of living your life"

"You talk funny. I ain't got no time for no standards."

BARRY NIX

"I know. Leave me."

"I'm every damn where. You can't escape me."

"Oh, yes I can."

Leave this person. Lock your doors.

But wait. Go back. Can't you keep a line of thought? Go back to Julie, to loss, to a smile that makes you weak in the knees twenty years later when you have the good sense to know better, more than then when the opportunity presented itself, unable to give up your quest for the unknown, paying a heavy price, burdened, burdened. Play some jazz, daddy. Play some jazz. Burdened. Remember when you came back to the States? Play it loud. Oh, oh!

Paul believed in omens. He always had. He believed in them when it rained cats and dogs when his first wife (what was her name?) landed in Frankfurt after the weather had been perfect for three weeks. His cosmology wasn't a religious one, but an anthropological alchemy of secular spiritualisms, in touch with ancient worlds and modern flows. Usually, the events which he determined to be omens were so obvious a departure from what transpired before that their conclusions were foregone. They simply presented themselves and signaled a sea change, a warning that the rollicking good times were over.

As the plane descended in Philly, it finally sank in that the military stage of his career was over. He had been among a group at Fort Dix, given a last opportunity to re-enlist, to claim injuries sustained, to breathe American air again on neutral ground before being sent to the civilian slaughter. He knew what to expect before he reached the airport itself.

THE REAL LIVES OF DREAMERS

It was in the apron that he was re-introduced, as he headed toward Philly again, that she saw him, this young woman approaching him, wearing her sense of entitlement, and he felt it, despite his seventy-dollar T-shirt, his luxurious tan and sparkling teeth, despite his welcoming, pleasant smile, exquisitely-toned arms, flat stomach, his easy gait and peaceful demeanor. A reaction he hadn't seen in six years, a hesitation, a drawing in, a shrinking away in fear, an attempt to deny him his enjoyment of the moment, his peace of mind, an immediate reminder that, yes, there was black and there was white. He was stateside again.

He thought many things after passing this woman, after most of a decade away from the sickeningly familiar, after pleasant years of being treated as an American without conditions or qualifiers. Yes, many things. He thought he wanted to go back to Europe, to the smiles and the welcomes to which he had grown so easily accustomed. He thought. He thought he was going to be sick as he looked back at the plane and wondered why he had returned.

But he pushed forward, suddenly more depressed than he had been since the demise of his last love affair. Marliese, his lovely Marliese, whom he begged to marry him, who tried to deny the depth of their feelings because she knew he would leave. Marliese, so steadfastly German, so determined not to come to America, love or no love, not to leave her <u>heimat,</u> her homeland.

"Money doesn't mean that much to me," she responded, "I cannot trade my soul for money. I would still love you, but your country would event.. event.. event-u-a-lly make me lose my soul. Germans go to America to become rich, then come back home to live."

Marliese loved to generalize and exaggerate wildly, a trait of his to which she had helped herself, often leaving a listener who lacked humor or a sense of the absurd flabbergasted. She found it liberating. This declaration, though, she believed to be a truism, a satisfying rant against creeping American cultural hegemony. He had educational plans and, because of a dearth of information about English-language programs in Europe in those pre-Internet days, and because he had to, at least for a while, he returned anyway. So now, only a moment or two after disembarking, awed about the future and beginning a new stage in the drama that was his life, he was holding his stomach after it knotted up on him, his shoulders gradually slumping as he walked past sloppy, obese service people, and mostly black, he noticed, a new sight for him, after living for so long in a rarefied world of very fit soldiers and healthy Europeans. They looked at him as if he were some strange foreign film with subtitles they were too lazy to read, no matter the payoff.

Two weeks later he walked in the sunshine outside of the Veteran Administration's regional office in Germantown. He had just secured his educational benefits. His program of study in computer science would surely be approved. His savings and the VA would pay for his education. He would have enough to live on. He wouldn't have to work unless he wanted to, assuming he didn't mind living like a poor student after the high times he had known. He felt wonderful again as a sexy black woman walked toward him and smiled. He had missed Philly's black women, remembering how they excited him fifteen, twenty years before, gracious and warm, wearing short Afros and short skirts. But things had changed. He was in form. He smiled back and asked for directions, looking somewhat confused. She was oh, so eager to help. It gave her more time to look at him. She raised back on one heel and turned to her best side. He mentioned something about a home-cooked meal and taking her for a ride. They rode and rode and rode, into her sunsets and into his dreams.

BARRY NIX

> I woke up this morning
> Got a jug and laid back down
> I woke up thinkin' about the future
> But the blues were all around
> The Persuasions

Culture shock. Take the electrodes off! Please!

Paul soon found that he could fill volumes describing what he didn't know about his Philly in 1988. The magnitude and enormity of change since 1973 were stupefying. But it wasn't the cell phones and the financial instruments, the new racial climate and the increasingly sophisticated software, but the overall culture in disarray that baffled him. He quickly came to understand that black folks hadn't achieved anywhere near their potential in any calculable way and it depressed him, wrapped him in a fog, shut him out. He was soon as miserable as he had been in his last year in the Army. It really was, after all, a microcosm of the larger society. He had hoped it wasn't, not really, perhaps only the back end of a particularly unforgiving bell curve. The backbiting, ignorance, soul-lessness, anti-sensual attitudes, ham-handed logic, and plebian tastes sent him running to libraries and digging into old soul music, the blues, and bebop.

He spent weeks reading, trying to figure things out. Shelby Steele and Henry Louis Gates helped, as did Stanley Crouch and Cornel West, Paul Johnson, Lewis Lapham, and Gary Willis. He learned, too, on the basketball courts, as good a barometer as there ever was of manhood, graciousness, responsibility, camaraderie, and virile negativity. The brothers were particularly bitter to white players and particularly nasty with each other. They were generally far less talented, far less physically conditioned, and far more ballhoggish than he remembered. Why? Because most of them didn't have fathers and they listened to that drivel they called music?

Too many of them had no skills and weren't trying to get any. They couldn't read and write well enough to fill out a job application and lacked the discipline to show up on time or to put their backs into a task. Those who did show up in service jobs made all who depended on them wish they hadn't. They were loud, thuggish, and horribly profane, daring anyone to say anything in response. Even patient black business people wouldn't hire them. They repeated lyrics from their heroes' rap songs, idolizing any gold-chained idiot who could coherently express a thought or a truism that anyone who had ever read a book knew and took for granted. The sheer ignorance and worldly un-sophistication, and its massive scale and pressure that attempted to co-op the entire ethnic group, amazed him.

As a die-hard integrationist from the old days, the overtly racist attitudes of so many black people, then seeking legitimacy under the rubric of African-Americans, were appalling and more damaging in a self-inflicting way than anything he had ever before heard. Someone had gotten them to believe that there could be elegance without substance, charm without a grasp of language, wealth without intellectual currency, and rights without responsibilities.

He partially blamed the lowered expectations of liberals, the kind ones who wanted to literally pat black males on the head like faithful dogs, who really didn't believe that any black man could be as intelligent as they were, which wasn't all that intelligent after all, especially in a holistic sense. 'Oh, gee, isn't that cute? You made little rhymes about fucking people up. Of course you have a first amendment right to destroy the culture of your peers. We'll make you a star. Be sure to pontificate. Oh, about anything simple. I'll tell you what. Between your songs about fucking people up, (but use the

N- word, okay?) and dirty bitches, why don't you make a nice little rhyme about how you love God? Yes, I know you do. By the way, you don't know anything about investments, do you? Don't worry, we'll take care of it (pat, pat). Here's some money for your new cars and champagne. These girls need to see evidence today, you know. That's okay, don't thank me now. Just wait.'

He found that apologist liberals responded negatively when unexpectedly confronted by a black man in the city who could actually think, even had some training in thinking logically. They were in such disbelief, their cultural filters so opaque, that they were unable to hear what was being said to them, so sure were they that the person they saw not three feet away could not possibly possess the kind of insight necessary to make them question themselves. Consequently, they assumed the paternal/maternal role. 'Oh, son, you really don't understand.' Fuck you. He told Terry and Anthony, exaggerating only slightly, that, except on television, a comfortable distance away, no one likes an educated black man, each for their own reasons. Oh, you could be trained in your job, but don't see things too clearly, don't be too aware. That's much too upsetting. People were too entrenched in their beliefs, unable to venture out of their comfort zones. Change is hard. Rapid change is very hard.

He gradually realized how different military society was in ways he hadn't really expected. He met too many working professionals who still refused to grow up, forty year-olds who still fought adulthood and maturity, refusing to take each year as it came while they idolized a seriously flawed younger generation for no reason beyond their youth. They spoke only of their high school days and how they lived then, hating their mortgaged, married, two- and three-kid lives. They were devoid of interior lives, resigned to their own powerlessness because they weren't rich or famous, and wondered why he wasn't as depressed as they were, especially because he was black. They were intimidated by the fact that he enjoyed something resembling an enlightened freedom in his youth, and baffled by his travels, his reading, and his love of food. There were no conversations, only spoken competitions; there was no sharing of ideas, only one-upmanship; and there was no satisfaction in personal competitions, only hollow victories.

On the other hand, there were many black people in Philadelphia who were entirely too deferential to white folks and entirely too lacking in their own lives. His can-do, entrepreneurial attitude didn't play well. He was accustomed to being looked in the eye and given a task or a mission and expected to acquit himself in an outstanding manner, excuses or legitimate failure not accepted. The attitude was 'learn from everything'. He stood too tall for the 'Philadelphia Plantation Negroes', as he called them. He had to leave, but he never got around to it.

School was tough at first. It had been a while. He took a full year of math courses, from pre-calculus to probability, differential equations, and mathematical computing. Then he was ready.

As an older student with no doubts as to who he was or where he was going he found undergraduate study thrilling and undergraduate interactions unbearable. During an exam, a Venezuelan girl he liked asked him for answers when the instructor, a full professor, left the room for a moment. Shocked (how naïve was he?), he said he didn't cheat and never spoke to her again. In another class, the instructor left and it sounded like a debate forum. He turned around and faced a flurry of papers flying and loud whispering. He put his head back down. Like kids caught struggling to get their hands out of the cookie jar, they nearly flew back to respectability as the door opened and the instructor returned. He was appalled. He felt old.

BARRY NIX

They laughed. It's all about the paper you can document, not how much you know. Get a grip, old fool.

Another time, a young black male looked at him hatefully when Paul asked him to be quiet in the library which was, by his fast count, eighty percent full of East Indians and other Asians on a regular, non-exam-cram week night. Asians made up eight, yes eight, percent of the school's enrollment; a new mathematical formula with astounding repercussions.

He was able to schedule his work and complete assignments with an efficiency he hadn't dreamed of in his earlier university days. He slowed down on the basketball court, too, adding to his disgust. He was excited only by his education and he sometimes wondered, without missing a beat in his studies, what it mattered when all around him his people were self-destructing. Young black women were getting the job done, but an acquaintance, a senior, told him that the number of black males in his classes had diminished by three-quarters since his freshman year. This did not bode well for the future. Paul wanted more company than that.

He went back to North Philly looking for the people he had grown up with in the streets. He found tales of violence, premature death, addiction, and the occasional success story of college and a good job. He went to Berks playground one morning and saw Justin. Paul wanted to talk about the old days, but Justin had never left. He wanted to sell Paul some Amway products.

One summer morning he was driving on Broad Street near Cecil B. Moore Avenue, so named for the ex-Marine who, upon graduation from law school told his sister that he would remain in Philadelphia because there were so many dumb people there and he could prosper. He went on to become a leader in the civil rights

THE REAL LIVES OF DREAMERS

movement in Philadelphia and was responsible for a number of advances.

Anyway, Paul was driving and then he saw Spottis, who had knocked skinny Paul around on the court for a whole summer. He made it his business to toughen him up. He did. Paul became a maniac under the boards, snatching rebounds with authority and a grunt, 'Aaaaaagh!', and becoming much stronger than his appearance would indicate. Paul never forgot that summer. Spottis helped him become a man, pushed him to see what he was made of. Paul could have just folded and sat on the sidelines, but he didn't. It hurt, though. He nursed lumps and bruises every night. He became a top street player, creative and independent. He was always grateful to Spottis and wanted to tell him so, but wait. Spottis was staggering into the middle of Broad Street in a torn t-shirt and loose, raggedy jeans that gave ground to a huge stomach, and he was openly smoking a joint. Paul parked his little Golf in the middle lane and got out.

"Spottis!"

Spottis looked around with glazed eyes, but he recognized Paul immediately after more than twenty years.

"Hey, Paul, man. How you doin'?"

"I'm alright. How are *you* doin', man? It's good to see you." He suddenly felt very prosperous. As he approached him, Paul saw that Spottis looked worse up close, and he smelled bad.

"Yeah, man I'm good, thanks to the grace of God. You want a hit on this? Yeah, man, God is good. I had some trouble with that smack but He helped me shake it. Now I'm just waitin' for this little young girl to come on out with me."

He looked around to see if he missed her.

"Well I'm glad everything's okay. You know, I was just thinking the other day. Remember how you knocked me all over the court that summer. You weighed about two-thirty and I was about a buck thirty-five drippin' wet?"

"Yeah, man those were some fun days. We went at it, didn't we?"

Paul discreetly looked around to see if one of his professors was watching him interact in the middle of Broad Street with a born-again, reefer-smoking man who was down on his luck.

"Yeah, man, we did. Listen, I just wanted to thank you, Spottis. You know, you helped me a lot…I really appreciated it. I took that with me, man."

"Aw, man, that's cool. Look here, man, I got to go find this girl. You sure you don't want some of this shit? Yeah, you look good, Paul, like God's been takin' care of you. Take care, man."

"Okay, Spottis, you take care, you hear?"

"Yeah, man, I just got to find this big-legged girl."

They shook hands and Spottis stumbled across the street.

Paul had paid a debt he'd dreamed of paying for years and it didn't matter at all. It never had.

The Mars Brothers met in Manhattan the June before Paul's January graduation to catch a Taj Mahal concert. Paul was in heaven after working like a dog in school eleven months a year, singing along to almost every song, especially Catfish Blues. He had just finished final exams and was due to start summer classes in another week. After the concert, they went to a luxurious steakhouse in midtown.

THE REAL LIVES OF DREAMERS

"Don't you ever stop?" Anthony asked over appetizers. He was newly in love, he claimed, to a woman named Angie, although it didn't seem to affect his demeanor nearly as much as it would Terry's or Paul's.

"Nah. Gotta keep going. Besides, I'm having fun."

"You just continue to give me that good advice, Paul, and do whatever you need to do." Terry handed Paul a wad of cash. He always tried to return checks.

Predictably, Paul responded with a "What's this for?"

"Just take it. You're making me money. I don't know where you get this information. I know people and I'm not getting anywhere near the quality of information you're giving me."

Paul wrote down the names of a few obscure journals and trade magazines on a napkin. Terry looked over at him. He was changing. He wasn't as carefree anymore, though things seemed to be going well for him. It had been a long road, for sure.

Love or no love, Anthony saw a 'healthy' black woman walk in and started squirming. He got up and walked to the bar. He gave the bartender a CD and a twenty. Soon, Skip James' falsetto blues poured through the speakers. A couple of drunken investment bankers tried to sing along, holding their beer bottles like microphones. As he returned to their table, Anthony caught a glimpse of the 'healthy' woman, who flashed a smile. The smile he returned was only a cursory one. No, he decided. Too much stomach. He turned and found a gorgeous Latin woman looking at him. She was breathtaking and wearing a beautiful white and gold necklace that gratefully sat around a silky neck and looked down on ample cleavage the color of a stained oak banister. A well-dressed man approached her table and signaled he was ready to leave. He was very attentive. She shrugged slightly as she got up, and smiled before heading out with her date. One more beautiful woman gone.

Terry watched this scene unfold with interest. Life was good again. Here were his guys. Paul, though, was worrying him. He had made some strange comments earlier that signaled to Terry that he needed to get out more. Already, he seemed to be getting lost in his books and in his own head, a wonderful place, apparently. And Anthony was looking hard. Interesting.

Paul was drunk when Anthony returned. Oh, he was cool about it, but his bell had obviously been rung. Still sleep-deprived from studying, he was on the verge of sleep now, shaking his head occasionally to wake himself up. Anthony ordered him an Irish coffee and he was soon animated again, insisting on dragging them to a late set at The Village Vanguard to see Roy Haynes. Once there, they squeezed into small chairs at crowded tables and didn't care because they didn't move for two hours. Terry hadn't been to many jazz concerts lately and he was speechless. Anthony twisted his tall frame sideways, closed his eyes, and smiled. Paul nodded his head to every nuance of every rhythm, eyes wide open. When it was over, Paul didn't care about half of the things he cared about before he walked into that club. There was nothing like live music. Two major artists in one night. Damn! They floated in a cab back to their hotel. The next morning, they had a huge buffet breakfast together. Several men looked over as if they were gay. Anthony took it in stride. Paul disliked it, as he sought to engineer some supremely masculine act that would defer that kind of attention. Paul left to hang out in Brooklyn. Anthony had some research waiting for him in Louisiana bayou country. Terry flew to Prague, a new boom town.

$\Large A$nthony rolled over in his bed, smelling jasmine and sex and beer, smells of his life. He opened his eyes to bright sunlight poking through closed curtains. Jennifer wasn't there. He reached over to his night stand for the remote, thought about listening to NPR, but changed his mind and played the CD that was in the player. John Lee Hooker's moaning and baleful guitar softly playing woke him up right, then put him back to sleep, to dream, to visions of that night so many years ago, and Henderson's pleadings.

Anthony imagined that over the years the participants had tried to rationalize the events in that safe house in a German forest. The traitor Henderson's linear thinking would not permit him to even consider the immorality of what he had done, satisfied that because he had suffered through a series of perceived racist events that he was justified in offering somewhat valuable information to the highest bidder. Besides, the Army didn't care about him.

His ignorance was shocking, before Anthony realized how common it was and faced it often enough to know better, before books with titles like *Twilight of American Culture* and *The Death and Life of Great American Cities* were written. Henderson knew nothing of political affairs. His moral compass was stuck and wouldn't budge with a whack, or even two or three.

For money. Anthony wondered what he would do for it if he hadn't grown up with it, wondered what his father hadn't told him, and the hold his money had over him.

But now he had a big problem, so big that he was shaking as he went outside with Russell to clear his head and talk it over. And he never shook. He was in charge. Henderson was caught red-handed, the smoking gun and all that. The Russian agent, middle-aged, extremely intelligent, and obviously contemptuous of Henderson, facing the possibility of extreme pain upon his return to Moscow with some disdain, wanting to live and with little else to lose, had been very cooperative. Henderson was beginning to see that his life would never be the same. None of theirs would, probably, Anthony surmised. It's a terrible thing to be sitting in a restaurant enjoying life when suddenly everything changes forever for so many people because of the idiocy of one man who didn't get enough love as a child, who never developed a coherent sense of himself and what was important in life, who served his basest needs at the expense of so many.

The Russian agent, Janovitch, was walking around, smoking a cigarette outside, behind the house, with Jarvis guarding him. No need to make a run for it, Janovitch thought, and rubbed his sore knee. They seem a decent-enough crowd. Maybe we can all get out of here with our dignity intact somewhat, all but that philistine Henderson.

Luchesa was guarding Henderson in the house. Why didn't Anthony see that his emotions would overtake his professionalism just this once? Because Luchesa had never given him a sign in other high-pressure situations, that's why. They were a first-rate team. They had babysat some rich businessman's kid in the gay bars of Hamburg and stolen documents from prostitutes in Brussels. This was supposed to be a drug deal done by really bad people. They were upsetting the natural order of things. Anthony and his team were supposed to follow the money. It turned out to be not that at all. They literally stumbled into Henderson in the middle of it all, sweating profusely and nervously clutching some papers, as obvious as track marks on a junkie's arms. And Luchesa, a good man — whose father had emigrated to the U.S. with his wife and ten dollars to escape Stalin's pogroms and guaranteed death, the father who had walked over snow-covered mountains to freedom and worked hard for his wife and his wonderful son, and who took so much pride in the crisp dress uniform his wonderful son wore home every Christmas — just couldn't understand. And Henderson paid for that. They all did.

Anthony and Russell, his next in command, had come to an understanding with Janovitch. They each knew what they needed to do as they walked back to the house and felt the quiet. Too quiet. Anthony and Russell nodded to each other as they approached and pulled their service revolvers. Janovitch and Jarvis backed away to the cover of a tree. Russell called in to the house.

"Luchesa! Everything alright?"

Luchesa's voice sounded different when he answered, too relaxed, disengaged.

"Sure. Everything's fine now."

He came to the door and opened it slowly. Anthony and Russell were back and on either side, 45's drawn. Luchesa looked around and told them to come in. The first rays of a brilliant dawn sun were slicing through the trees. Anthony only wanted to sit against one of those trees and witness this beauty of nature. But he saw blood. Luchesa had gotten revenge on a traitor, for his country and for himself. Henderson sat in a wooden chair, his hands still handcuffed behind his back, blood oozing from the carotid artery in his neck, awaiting death with a dazed look on his face. They could have rushed to his aid, but they took their time, floating in the unreality of it all, wondering how to cover their tracks. They didn't even un-cuff him. Henderson had a good start on them. He was dead in under two minutes. Revenge. Anthony wondered how many more graves he would have to dig.

The phone rang him back to the present. He decided to answer it for the first time in a week. It was time.

Wisniewski was elated. He and Nicole had worked through their dominant-submissive games in exactly four days and emerged intact and together, for now, as he raced to save the life of the man who, when awake, would ruin him by reclaiming his woman. He would fight for her. That, in itself, was exciting to him, to face off for this woman, each pleading, raining presents on her, paying extra attention to each caress, each nibble, lick, and thrust, each scent and taste, the three of them swabbing at each other's canvases in their sensual triptych, arguing over representative sounds: Bach or Lareena McKinnett or Horace Silver; only because she wouldn't expect it, but would deserve it and be embarrassed by it, finally relent and revel in it, for the short time that it would remain civil, until she had to decide, or not.

He grew hard as soon as she entered the room, day or night, energized or exhausted. It was axiomatic, a given formula of life: room + Nicole + Wisniewski = erection. His erections were his new life, as her perfume wafted though his nostrils, attacking all of his senses, as blood flowed freely through his body, all systems go, as his hand would touch the small of her back, flow across her hips, over her ass, clothed or not, sending him into a delirium he hadn't known, but which, she told him, her other man, that Warner, expected. Constantly-expected delirium, he thought. What an impossibly high level of pleasure that must be. Enough. He had thought of a new approach to his cure.

Wisniewski felt that Paul would emerge from his rest (he no longer referred to it as a coma) when he was ready. But what was ready? He was obviously somewhere that was beyond what two weeks in Cozumel could cure. He would need to re-enter the atmosphere of reality in stages, and drift on gracious waves in his physiological space capsule before being retrieved, cramped and tired, to face the blaring lights of the physical world. It would take some detective work. He would ask Nicole.

They had dined simply, on crab-stuffed salmon and tortellini in West Chester, where she wouldn't see anyone she knew. As he explained his new approach, she was quiet and thoughtful, but generally, if guardedly, receptive.

"It's known as psychological forensics," he told her. "It's finding out what makes him tick and pushing the right buttons to get him to respond the way we want him to, which, in this case, is merely to wake up and be okay with it."

"Hmm. So you would want to come by the house and go through his things, his stuff?"

"Uh, yes."

She sipped her wine, her third glass. He hoped she would remember this in the morning. He loved her slightly drunk. She had her head cocked to one side with her legs crossed and a mysterious half-smile on her face. Her hair was perfect, her lipstick a maddening shade of molten lava. Her simple black dress hugged her breasts and hips just enough for every man in the room to forget who they were with for more than a moment as she sat down. Vivaldi was playing. I'm going to come! he told himself. He felt unworthy.

"Okay. Whatever you think is best. Let's go." She got up and began to walk toward the door, throwing her silk scarf over her shoulder as the other men in the room thought they were going to come, too. He scrambled up, threw too much money on the table, and rushed dutifully behind her.

He drove towards the turnpike. As they passed an office park, darkened for the night, huge parking lot visible, she told him to turn into the drive.

"Wha..."

"Shut up and find someplace to put your dick in my mouth."

He did. His Johnson barely felt air for forty-five minutes. Up and down, dry and wet. He couldn't believe that people walked around and lived this much pleasure, again the constantly-expected delirium.

Nicole was the slut she used to be with Paul, but hadn't been for a long time now. She was far away as she pleasured him to the brink of extinction. Wisniewski felt no connection. He began to feel used. She was acting out, working through something. Suddenly he knew that he didn't have a chance with her after tonight, that he never did, really. He sat back and came and cried and came. Then he took charge and threw her on the back seat and jumped into her from behind. She bucked and demanded that he fuck her harder and faster just as he came so hard and screamed so loud he felt as if he left his entrails in her, again. Spent in his *petite morte*, his little death, he had to watch her take herself to where he couldn't, fingers between her legs, her back arched, her whole body stiffening as her eyes opened wide, then closed before he witnessed the trace of a smile he hadn't seen before, of silly, sublime satisfaction, of release, his demise. He felt useless. He took her home without a word.

The next day, he knocked on her door, the door of the house she shared with Paul Warner, his former sworn enemy who posed to him two of the most difficult problems he'd ever faced, his wife and his coma. She opened the door in an open robe, her luscious body peeking out, tantalizing. Her hair was a mess. Her mascara from the night before was smeared, vampire-like, across her teary face.

Her breath reeked of alcohol, whiskey, as she led him into a media room without a word. She motioned to a beautiful, overstuffed chair. He sat down and she was on her knees. She unbuckled and deep-throated him before he could protest, before he could tell her how she had made him feel useless, how she had damaged his opinion of himself. It faded into a haze. He saw pastel swirls as he closed his eyes and registered that there was something about this house, there was a feeling here as he exploded in her mouth, but not exhausted after a day of intellectual exploring, stayed hard this time, turned her around, still on her knees, rammed his point home, not caring about her needs for once, and shot liquid fire into her, warmed her as she let go, really let go and cried and came and cried and came and collapsed with him and slept a really good sleep this time, and wondered how she could live a minute longer without her Paul.

When he awoke, he felt changed again. Forty-seven years old and all of a sudden he didn't know who he was. He was now a terrified man in a terrifying world of emotion and suicide bombers. He was too exposed. He tried to tell himself that he preferred comfortable love to passionate love, no love to painful love, quiet release to wrenching, draining, gut-busting sex.

He extracted his legs from under Nicole's inert form, her eyes still damp from crying, found a bathroom, cleaned himself up, and got dressed. He walked around the house as a blind man newly-sighted. It was amazing. Expensive, but not ridiculously so. Awash in color, bolds muted by touches of grey, a cornucopia of textures. Overwhelming, but just short of too much. And art, everywhere there was art. In a wall-size painting, an achingly beautiful life-sized sculpture that surely came from Rodin's studio, in furniture from Scandinavia and upstate New York and English drawing rooms and

China and Africa, in wall hangings from Morocco, in country accessories seemingly from Provence, in plates by Dali.

Wisniewski was not aware that any but the very rich could actually live in a house like this — a small-scale museum, library, theater, and restaurant — but Paul Warner apparently had a dream and wanted to live inside it all of the time.

Nicole woke up and looked around. Finally, she was drained, emotionally and physically. She was surprisingly clear-headed, as if she had emerged refreshed from her own coma. She got a whiff of herself and ran to clean up.

An hour later, showered and full of French toast, bacon, eggs, grits, coffee, orange juice, and vitamins, she looked up from the Times and looked over to Paul's number one bookcase, one of many, numbered, carefully arranged and catalogued. Number one, containing approximately one hundred fifty books, was labeled "Current Reading". She walked over and began looking at the titles and browsing, searching for clues. After fifteen minutes the bookshelf seemed to contain all the weight of the earth. My God! It gave her a headache. Jaques Barzun, Joseph Campbell, Rheinhold Niebuhr, Isaiah Berlin, Chekhov, D.H. Lawrence, Ralph Waldo Emerson, Henry James, George Orwell, Plato, and too many others. Then there was the music criticism, the film criticism, the Harlem Renaissance writing, the contemporary black intellectuals section, the history section, and, at the very end of the bottom shelf, tucked back a little behind the others, was what looked like a thin journal, with no writing on the spine. She pulled it out and looked inside. There were three CDs. It was a call for help.

THE REAL LIVES OF DREAMERS

Wisniewski was upstairs in the office. It was huge. One wall was lined with books with exotic-sounding titles: Awk, Gnu, the Zen of Java, Apache, UNIX. Along another wall were carefully-catalogued technical and business periodicals in binders. An entire wall was filled with framed photographs, digitally manipulated to render a distant fantasy world with big-breasted Amazons and exotic spaceships cruising through purple and orange canyons. A bay window looked out on to the back yard, a beautiful view. The desk was Scandinavian, teak, with a keyboard and flat-panel monitor and two huge computers, no, servers, on the floor on either side, the kind he would see in those high-powered computer magazines someone insisted on leaving in his waiting room. No surprises here so far.

He looked in a closet. In boxes. In plain brown paper bags, out of place in this environment of organizational efficiency. There was an old, yellowed photograph of a beautiful young black woman on what appeared to be a familiar college campus. She was wearing a blue hooded Swarthmore sweatshirt. Yes, it was the Swarthmore campus. She had an innocent, happy, dreamy look in her eyes, the look he wished he could inspire in Nicole.

He dug deeper into the bags. There were more photographs, all of them with explanations on the back, some of them quite good, of London, Paris, castles in Heidelberg and cathedrals in Cologne, Canterbury, and Strasburg. And more women who appeared to be European, in museums, in restaurants, and in parks. Most of them had the same dreamy look as that of the college student. There were pictures of soldiers in their barracks lying across bunks, exhausted, a younger Warner with a goofy look on his face, two very handsome men who appeared to be brothers standing in front of a sex club in Hamburg, hash smokers in a café in Amsterdam, jazz musicians outside a club in Hamburg, a blues guitarist in Berlin, Warner posing in a suit like a fashion model, a group of maybe twenty black men playing African drums in a small, smoky room. This guy lived. Wisniewski, who always felt that his life had been one to covet, felt pangs of envy.

He felt stiff. He looked at his watch. He had been in that office for three hours and he knew he hadn't skimmed the surface of what was there. He got up and wondered how what he had learned so far would help him treat his patient. He was lost in thought, looking out the window at the gardener planting rose bushes.

"These might help."

Wisniewski turned with a start. It was Nicole. She handed him three home-made CDs. They were labeled 'Ultimate Music I, II, and III.' She had showered and looked fresh and in control again.

"He was working on these just before the accident. He came in and screamed about how he could change people's lives with this music, the way he put it together. He worked on them for weeks. He had CDs and old albums and tapes out all over the place. I could barely walk in the room."

Wisniewski knew this was the answer. He almost screamed at her for not mentioning it before now, but then realized that this was the perfect time, that the course had needed to be run completely. It was up to him to bring Warner across the finish line. He thanked her and flew down the steps, then flew back up to kiss her lightly and rushed home for a few minutes, then nearly flew to the hospital. He had to do this just right. Then he remembered. He had forgotten to look on Warner's computers.

Edwidge Smith thought about the parade of people traipsing through Mr. Warner's room. There had been that good-looking

THE REAL LIVES OF DREAMERS

one who had just gotten back from Hawaii, the one who had paid for Mr. Warner's upgrade to a luxury suite. An extra fifteen hundred dollars a day and he didn't blink, just warned them that his accountants would go over the bill line-item by line-item. That hospital suite looked a whole lot better than her apartment. She'd a moved in there herself if she could.

He thought she was Jamaican until he guessed Haitian after hearing her speak. He even knew where Port-au-Prince was, had even been there once or twice, he said. Well, was it once or twice, or many times? Lawd, Lawd. What I wouldn't do to get a man like that, just for a night. An educated man. He probably liked white women, though. All the rich ones do. Look at that Mr. Warner. He was a little yella for her tastes. The rich one, though, he had a beautiful tan from Hawaii. Mmmm.

The wife. Hmm. There were rumors about her carryin' on with Dr. Wisniewski. She didn't believe it for a minute. Not that egghead. He was about as sexy as a dishrag, if you asked her, until he walked in there with that new suit yesterday, anyway. And had the biggest smile on his face, like he had just won the Powerball Lottery or somethin'. Hmm. Could be.

She sure knew how to dress with her pale self, though. Had a butt almost like a black woman, too. They used to talk about white women with their flat asses, but not any more. They must've found the butt machines at the gym or somethin'. More power to 'em.

Here comes the new doctor. Shaweena called her 'The bitch'. One of the uppity ones. Black folks got a little education and they thought they could give orders like white folks, she said. Not to her, they couldn't, she said. They wasn't white and never would be, she said. Edwidge couldn't believe it. Shaweena didn't listen to Edwidge warn her about her attitude. Of course, she was fired. Now she was suing the doctor and the hospital for wrongful termination. Had one of those lawyers who advertised on television while the soap operas were on. These black folks in America, she thought. They'll kill each other before letting each other succeed. Half of 'em tryin' to get away from the other half. The other half findin' any excuse not to work. No damn pride.

She looked at Mr. Hawaiian tan like he was fresh jerk chicken. He looked back, too. Maybe he did like black women, but only the stuck up ones. He seemed kinda friendly, though. I got an extra hundred right here to prove it. All I did was give him some directions.

Dr. Wisniewski. That man been actin' like he was crazy. Had her helpin' him prepare the room for somethin', actin' like it was a church or somethin'. Had us take out the catheter like he just knew Mr. Warner was goin' to come out of it. Next thing you know, they'd be bringin' in an exorcist. Nobody asked her, though. She coulda brought a priest from Haiti. He'd a had Mr. Warner running around Franklin Field like he was in the Penn Relays. She had seen it happen.

Everything had to be just right, even burning incense. In a hospital! That Mr. Warner was drivin' everybody crazy bein' in a coma.

Now, who is this coming? Don't even ask. I know who you came to see. That way, to your right. These were the highest livin' black folks she had ever seen. And they weren't even famous! Look at that suit! It had to be soft as butter!

Anthony emerged from the hospital elevator holding the arm of an older man, more for his own peace of mind than for usefulness. The older man, who had attracted attention everywhere he went that day, was lean and strong at eighty-four, and dark as coal.

His head was covered by a thin layer of nearly straight mixed grey hair, and he wore an exquisite, hand-made light grey suit. There was an air about him that commanded deference, but he was extremely gracious when spoken to and offered conversation easily. His eyes, though, were hard, almost looking through people, except when they softened when speaking to the younger man, whom he obviously adored. "This is my son," he said to all who would listen. "He just got his Ph.D". Jimmy Turner had come to America.

Anthony was standing at a window on the other side of Paul's hospital suite. Jimmy Turner sat by the bed in the very comfortable chair into which Terry had sunk. The doctor said he thought it would help if he talked to Paul. Jimmy didn't know about that. He wondered if everybody looked this healthy when they were in a coma. Paul looked like he could get up and run a race. He was somethin', that Paul. This chair doesn't look as comfortable as it is, he thought. He sat back and remembered the first time Anthony brought Paul to Eindhoven.

Paul shot into Jimmy Turner's house like a blast of wind. Anthony had gone into town. He heard Belinda was back, but that wasn't true. Where did that woman go? Anyway, Paul was staying with Anthony in the house that Belinda gave him, just over the way. He had the biggest smile Jimmy had ever seen, told him how happy he was to meet him, and he meant it, too. Yes, sir. Paul asked him about his time in Kansas City, made him tell him stories about the guys. He saw all the books and the Atlantic Monthly and the New Yorker and the International Herald Tribune and smiled an even bigger smile. Jimmy thought he was going to break his cheekbone. He laughed so hard. He treated Jimmy like he was a famous scientist or a scholar or something, called him an autodidact like himself. Jimmy joked and said he'd throw him out if he didn't stop cussin'. That Paul made him shine. He never thought he was anybody special, even though his children always told him he was, and some others did, too, but they were his children and his friends. Well, that was nice, but what was he supposed to do, stick his chest out and go on TV?

That Paul, though, he said it from the heart, from his own life. That was different. And then that buck had the nerve to run out to the car and bring back a Kansas City Monarchs baseball jersey, just like the original. That's when Jimmy Turner lost it for a minute, when he had to turn away and wipe his eyes. Yeah, those Negro National League ballplayers were somethin'. Yes, sir. Jimmy Turner saw Jackie Robinson play. And Satchell Paige. And the best hitter there ever was, even though he took too sick to make it to the majors after they opened up to Negroes after the war. That'd be Josh Gibson. Oh, yeah.

Yeah, we Negroes have a lot to be proud of, he thought. We didn't ask anybody for anything', just a little respect, that's all. What was it that James Brown sang? 'Don't want nobody to give me nothin'. Open up the door, I'll get it myself.' That pretty much said it, didn't it? We didn't go around cussin' and fussin' and callin' it culture like they do today. Paul sat there in a daze as he told his stories, like he was watching Moses bring down the Ten Commandments from the mountain or something.

That Paul could have been a jazz historian, too. He puffed up like a Thanksgiving turkey when he told Jimmy about all the musicians that came from Philly. The Heath brothers, Kenny Barron, McCoy Tyner, Jymie Merritt, Odean Pope, Grover Washington, Jr., Byard Lancaster, Bobby Timmons, and Benny Golson, one of his real favorites. The list went on and on. He brought some CDs with

THE REAL LIVES OF DREAMERS

him, good stuff, some of it a little too wild for Jimmy's taste, but good music. Boy, that Stanley Cowell. He was teaching, Paul told him. Paul told him that a lot of the guys were teaching in universities. Jackie McLean, Archie Shepp, Rufus Reid. Why, they even had an Institute of Jazz Studies at Rutgers University! Times sure had changed. It made him feel good. He always knew the music was something special. It just took white folks, Americans that is, too long to admit that black folks could be that smart.

Well, everybody knew Paul couldn't drink too much. After dinner and a couple of shots of Old Granddad, he got this faraway look in his eyes. Why, he even started crying like a baby. Told Jimmy that Anthony was the luckiest man in the world to have a father like him. That embarrassed Jimmy. He had to go over and hug him. Had to rock him in his arms like he was in a cradle, this big, strong man who looked like he could snap your neck with one hand while he was holding a book with the other. Had to apologize for his father, a black man who passed on some good genes, but didn't have a clue. He told him that a man was supposed to take care of his children. If you don't want to take care of children, don't have 'em. It was as simple as that. People made things too difficult. All this birth control technology and young girls were having more babies than ever. He didn't understand it. It was his opinion that that was the chief weakness of the species, the long maturation of children, that and the propensity to hate. Children need love and time. He knew as soon as he saw Anthony and Agnietje that he wanted them. That hadn't been his plan that day, but it turned out fine, more than fine. Yes, sir. They were his life, up to a point. A man had to live his own life, too. Had to have his secrets. Yes, sir.

BARRY NIX

Jimmy Turner opened his eyes, glad that he had broken his expatriate vow. Paul was helping him right now. He would offer what he could. Well, what should he say? He just started talking.

"Paul, this is Mr. Turner. What are you doin', son? You and I still have some things to talk about. Are things that bad? They tell me you're runnin' a con on all of us. Well, you can't con a con artist, so I think you should get on up. Let's go hear some jazz, son. You've got a lot of people who love you. Come on, now. You look too alive to me to be doing anything but resting. Snap to it, soldier. I'll be waiting for you."

Jimmy Turner got up and tenderly kissed the sad-looking man on the forehead. He straightened up with some effort. He knew he didn't have too much time left, maybe five or six years. That would be just right, as far as he was concerned. He just buried Heinz last year. That was hard. That man was looking for a favor and wound up changing his life in that bar after Helga's funeral. Helga. His wonderful Helga. He hadn't cared much for women and sex after Helga, not like these rabbits today, jumping into the lettuce patch with anybody. Sex was sacred to him. Oh, he had his women friends, but he just never cared for sex the same way ever again. To each his own, I guess. Tough Jimmy Turner wiped a tear from his eye.

Yes, his mission here was almost finished. It was his opinion that a man didn't need to live much past eighty, and he was already eighty-four. If you can't do some decent livin' in that time, shame on you. Yes, sir, shame on you. Time to go now.

L ena sat on the bed in her blue lingerie. She had never left, but Terry was the only one who could see her. Poor Paul. So unhappy. She had been unhappy, too, in spite of Terry's love, the best that any woman could ever ask for. What was wrong with her? She was never really of this world, even while making a fortune in real estate. That seemed easy. In the right place at the right time. Making the right man scream with pleasure. A secret strategy. The Seaman's Charity Association. What a story to tell. Forgive me, Terry. I didn't want to chase you away.

Terry deserved better, but she was already on her way out when they met. Her journey was set. She had made him happy, but had doomed him to a life of sadness. He had made such good use of the money. So many people he helped! What a good man. She looked at Paul.

"Dear Paul. Almost time to wake up. Prepare yourself, sweet man. You still have much to learn, and much to do. You are far from finished."

Arthur, the mad genius of North Philadelphia, unheard of for so many years, was beside her, his saxophone in his hands. He startled her. He was a raggedy man in a stained and tattered working musician's uniform, black sport jacket that was too small, black pants, white shirt open at the collar. He needed a shave. His short hair needed combing. She hadn't heard him. He was in her world and the other world at the same time. He must be a special musician, she thought.

He approached the bed like a caring doctor. She was in shock. He acknowledged her presence with a polite nod. Then he began to play.

The sheer beauty of his playing, like all great art, made Lena question the meaning of everything in the world and outside of it. She felt like she had a heart attack. She was happy and sad and seven million gradations in between. For someone to walk on this earth today with that energy was beyond even her understanding. Even the years of sordid behavior had not diminished his purity. She could do nothing but let herself be swept away by it, and sleep peacefully at last.

Arthur finished playing and looked at Lena sleeping peacefully beside Paul. Paul opened his eyes.

"Arthur."

"Paul, baby. Don't worry about a thing. You need a few more hours. Close your eyes, daddy. I haven't played like that in twenty years. I let you down. I should have let you produce my album like you wanted to."

"I begged you," Paul said weakly.

"I know, daddy, I know. This world wasn't made for cats like you and me. Lena either." He nodded to her prone figure, beautiful in the light of the setting sun." But you can't go yet. I'll look you up soon. Peace."

He was gone. Lena was gone. Paul closed his eyes again.

"Where are you? he called. He didn't answer himself. He had been there for seven days without music, when he woke up, anyway. Of course, his dreams had been full of music. A man could only take so much. He would be on his own soon. Just a little more sleep.

Wisniewski entered the room. Everything was set. He checked Paul's machinery, then his bed sheets. Still dry. Good. Everyone had their instructions. They weren't to be disturbed. He closed the curtains and lit some incense. He reached into his briefcase and, gingerly, as if handling a precious newborn, took out the journal and the CDs, and wondered if they held the answers for the two men in that suite. He put the three CDs in the changer that Anthony Turner had brought before Wisniewski had a chance to order one brought in himself. It was of an extremely high quality, he noted, as the music began. Nothing too special so far. He sat down on a floor pillow that he had also brought from Warner's house and opened the journal. He didn't make it past the middle of the second piece of music.

He heard an angel singing, backed by flutes and sitars, and an angel chorus echoing her pleas to take her with him on his journey, and guitars, clear and harmonious, raucous and distant. He felt rhythm, always rhythm, driving, sometimes gently, sometimes forcefully into his core. There was a didgeridoo and more sitars, Benedictine chants, questions asked in French and German, swirling strings, inner-city blues, soft parades and purple hazes; melodic, then wailing saxophones, street-corner vocalizing, directions stopped and changed on a dime, lush orchestrations and spare cries, weeping cellos alone in a church, drums of passion, acknowledgements and wails and descriptions of English gardens, tables and droning chants, stoned lovemaking and highway rides under a night sky, raindrops and thunder and expressions of love and hope amid sobbing poetry, and, finally, after he had cried and laughed and been swept along on a current of baroque violins riding on a wave of rhythm, of drums and tambourines and church hollers and cymbals and washboards......he awoke to a new self.

Paul looked around. Something was wrong. Well, maybe not wrong, but changed. No, not changed at all, just different. He was tired of change, the only constant, they say, these days. He didn't want different. He wanted peace. There, he said it. Unfortunately, no one was around to hear his simple, yet meaningful declaration. Funny thing coming from him, Paul, the complex one, the one who confounded people, simply unable to be sociable enough to let an idiot spout his opinion at a nice sociable gathering and leave it at that. Dangerous, he was, to a nice sociable gathering.

A shadow entered the room, if you could call this hazy place a room. He didn't introduce himself, just started talking. People were rude these days. Oh. Him again. No, someone else. Someone very cold.

"People don't care about politics anymore, fool. We know now that there's no hope for those people. There have been enough conversations, enough money spent, enough chances given. The best we can do is pluck the ones with some sense out of the miasma, the ones who will be socialized. I said socialized, fool, not brainwashed. Things like closing the bathroom door when they're doing their business, eating quietly in a restaurant, letting lawyers do the fighting. Handling the primitive impulses, the maleness, in decent ways like watching sports, playing video games, and jerking off to pornography, because men and women are past the point of getting along very well. The West has been won. The geeks are running things. The rugged individual is dead. All you have to do is look at newscasters to know that. But some, even some polite ones, don't know it yet. Put your Johnson in your wallet and in your hard drive (hard drive, get it?). Get drunk and crash your car with that girl of your dreams who doesn't go anywhere without her vibrator, but don't upset the damn apple cart, fool. Wait, I've got some extra superlatives in my car. Here are some exclamation points. Now you're set. Go tell somebody that something venal is important, charge a good price, and show some mindless idiot smiling. And don't forget the tits. Keep 'em occupied while I slip tactically around to the side. My lawyer and accountant are already in the car. And listen. Take some friendly advice and forget that spiritual slash happiness shit.

THE REAL LIVES OF DREAMERS

Your happiness can't support a planet full of hungry people. That's my job. Later."

He was gone in a haze, expensive engine rumbling but nothing visible. Paul just stood, no floated, no, sat. Damned if he knew what he was doing, or where he was. If he was where he thought he was he should be seeing some big-legged women in tight dresses, not listening to some objectionable self-styled philosopher. Where was the other guy, his other self, or part of himself? Damn!

He tried to go back to the previous phase. He started to sense that he was too late. Then, without warning, he heard waves. It seemed as if a river began to course its way through him and carry him along on a current that was at once purely physical in a systemic way — all pain and stiffness left his body in a flash of time; pleasurable — there were tingles on top of tingles, streams of pure energy and light, then stiffness again, and an unbearable tension in his gut, then a slow, twisting, achingly intense release; emotional— tears flowed from his eyes, unbidden and effortless, releasing hidden traumas and correcting malicious trespasses; spiritual — he felt unspeakable purity, more white lights; and intellectual — he summoned wisdom and knowledge locked away in deep chambers within him, the knowledge of revelations, of collective histories and cosmic cultures, of mathematics and the sun, of sufferings and conquests; he saw child farmers with bent-over backs, men enslaved, women raped, freedom regained, rituals celebrated, and hearts triumphant; but wordless, of an all-consuming and all-generating energy, a ball of illogical, painless fire racing through him, illuminating his creative desires in three-dimensional splashes of harmonious colors. He asked a wordless question and immediately, in a nanosecond, answered it with a silent realization. He had found it. He was in the middle of it. It had come from deep space, light years away, and overtaken him. It was sexual and non-sexual, but it was IT! He breathed deeply. He knew he would find it. He knew he would find it! He knew he would find it! He knew he would find it! Aaaaaaaagh! He basked in the glory of its perfection. His perfect orgasm.

D aylight announced itself quietly. Wisniewski was sitting against a wall with his head bowed. He didn't know where he was or what day it was. He was empty. He felt like he had no body. He didn't want to raise his head yet. Gradually, he was able to control the muscles in his neck and, slowly, look up. Sunlight streamed into the room. Reality returned to the new day. He smiled warmly to himself. Soft music played, a piano trio in space, no not in space, but just over the hill, just out of reach, to bring him along in his fragile state. He turned and saw the hospital bed, empty, the instruments of his trade quiet, no longer playing their beep beep music that signaled life, the tubes inert, no longer flowing with the lubricants of physical being, the lonely needle at the end of the I-V sticking no one. Paul. He panicked, but only for a millisecond, before he felt strong, reassuring hands on his shoulders. He turned his head again. Paul Warner had been sitting in a chair, the chair in which Terry had seen his past. He was looking rather well, wearing pants, a thin cashmere sweater with a collar, and a sport jacket, each in a varied shade of grey. His long legs were crossed at the ankles. He was bathed in sunlight. Wisniewski was relieved, but still couldn't get up. He had found peace and nothing could change that now. He seemed to feel all of his blood flowing through his body. He amazed himself. It was times like these that understatement worked best.

"Mr. Warner."

"Dr. Wizniewski."

"Nice of you to join us. You gave us a bit of a scare."

"Sorry about that. I had no evil intentions."

"I'm sure you didn't. I…your wife."

Paul already knew. He didn't question how.

"Shh. Let there be no ill-will between us. I really need a cup of coffee. What do you say you clean yourself up and we go get a steak? I'm a little hungry."

"I'd like that, but… what is this music?"

"It's *Elm* by Richard Beirach. A spirit. There is much I have to share with you. You have much to learn……..What's your first name?"

"Nigel."

"Mine's Paul."

"A pleasure, Paul."

"All mine."

They shook hands warmly.

Paul was pondering mental illness and how events could turn a sane, socialized, well-adjusted individual into someone who withdrew from life, and wondered why so many obviously mentally ill people were allowed to walk the streets and infect the sane with their viruses, the homeless and managers, housewives and administrators, junkies and dilletantes. He was in his backyard, turning over hamburgers, steaks, salmon fillets, hot dogs, and vegetables on a brick grill that he had built by a recent Italian immigrant, a talented man from Italy. Like an ancient shaman, he was sending aromatic smoke signals to the whole neighborhood, unofficially vying for best griller, the one who inspired generally well-fed passersby, strangers on foot or on wheels, to seriously consider pleading for a plate of heavenly food.

Terry, sitting in the garden, was happy about a lot of things. He had taken some heavy hits, but he was still rich. His friend was out of his coma and healthy, mentally and physically intact, so far. Paul had no desire to speak of his experience away, but it had obviously affected him profoundly. There were grey hairs that Nicole told him weren't there a few weeks before. And there was something in his eyes, a peace.

And he had found love with Cordelia after five years of going solo, of women wanting to get close and being pushed away, accusing him of fearing commitment, of dreaming whenever he wasn't working. Eight years together now, he thought. He wondered if she suspected that the dreams had returned.

He had come early that morning to help prepare for the cookout that Paul insisted on having for his friends. Anthony objected at first, but Terry felt that it would be perfect therapy. Surprisingly, Paul, always his own man who made all of his own decisions, allowed them to discuss his actions in his presence. He was grateful to take a back seat for a while. He was glad for their time together. They had talked and laughed about the old days. Cordelia would come later.

Paul had sent out a plea, whether or not his stubborn ass wanted to admit it, and they had responded as friends, were richer for it, and wondered, for the first time, how sane Paul really was, if he was letting himself stretch out or if he unrealistically expected himself to be too mentally fit, too emotionally flexible. He had always handled the pressures of his life with aplomb. Now he seemed to lack focus. He had been pushed back too many times, moving on relentlessly because he held himself to the standard that he believed he should, that of great men in difficult times, in times that were gone forever. It was time for Terry and Anthony to intervene, to save Paul from himself. With Terry's money Paul could do anything, and he could show the rest of them what to do. He remembered their conversation earlier that morning. Unbelievable.

"Nicole told me you thought you had money problems."

"Thought?"

"Paul, did you forget about your account with me, silly muh fuckah? You're my partner."

Paul laughed. Why, you! I'll bring Mulebone up in here if you don't watch yourself!"

"Oh, no, not Mulebone! Terry got serious again. "You didn't really forget, did you?"

Paul looked sheepish. He was almost mumbling, the way he did when he was guilty or, God forbid, wrong about something. "I didn't do anything. I just helped a friend. I didn't invest any money with you."

Terry's mouth dropped. "You didn't do anything? You didn't do anything?! Do you have any idea how much money I made because of your wild ravings that day you met me at the airport, the list of companies to look out for? Remember when you called and gave me tips from information you read in those technical journals of yours? I told you then that you always had money as long as I had money. Then you came in and consulted. Didn't I thank you enough? Why do you think I moved here instead of back to Minneapolis, or New York, or anywhere else. Because you were here, you damn fool! Then we both got busy, into our careers. I didn't tell you how well I was doing because I didn't want to scare you off, to think that money would change me that much. And you were flying off to your consulting appointments, doing really well. I told you that you always had a job with me, you never had to worry about anything. Then you stopped returning my calls. Me! My calls! Anthony and I love you more than anybody ever has!"

There, he said it. Terry was walking around, pacing and ranting. Damn fool! Paul looked sad, like a seven year-old about to cry. He began studying a tree limb. He started mumbling again, trying to convince himself that he had made the right decisions, swimming against the tide.

"You paid the rest of my way through school. You gave me money. That was enough. I made it on my own. It's just that those fucking thieves fucked it all up for all of us and I had a hard time dealing with it. I though technology would save us all for a while."

Terry calmed down. "And you thought that was enough, huh? Paul, let me put it this way. You don't have any money problems. How much do you think I'm worth, keeping in mind that my holdings are down 59.6%?"

"I don't know. Come on, Terry. It doesn't matter to me. I can let you have a few thousand if you need it."

At this, Terry was so upset his heart began to flutter. He began to get dizzy. He instinctively dropped to the ground and did ten push-ups to release his angry energy, to get his blood pumping hard through his veins, to try to make some sense of the moment, a technique he had used to great advantage several times in the last few years. He finished and got up, flushed and out of breath. That's better, much better.

"Okay, Paul. Just humor me and take a guess, okay? Wait. Before you guess, I want you to know that I already gave Nicole a million dollars and sent a letter to the Vatican recommending her for sainthood."

"Are you serious?!"

"Yes, but not about the sainthood, though God knows she would have my vote."

"Thank you, Ter. She can give it as well as take it. She's not the innocent she seems to be, but....alright."

Paul started figuring, trying to remember the companies he had recommended. Then it came to him. Terry bought Microsoft at eight dollars a share, before Windows. In the airport that day, Paul complained that people didn't understand what was happening yet, that almost every computer ran MS-DOS and the stock was selling at eight, that they had everything in place. That he read about this guy Gates in Fortune and he was the real deal. And EMC. And Cirrus Logic. If he got in those stocks early, he made money, no matter what they did later, unless he just didn't pay attention, and he knew that wasn't the case. He didn't keep up anymore, though, didn't huddle around Jamir's terminal every couple of hours with four or five others checking the market like they did in '99. He missed that bunch. He wished their company had offered him a decent permanent job. But the commute was unbearable. 202 was a mess. And he was already building his dream house. It wouldn't have worked out. Still…

"Thirty million?" He knew that was too high an estimate, but he would play his game. It might be worth a couple of laughs.

Terry told him. He didn't stutter. He didn't laugh. Paul fell back against the tree with the interesting limb. The verdict was in. He was a fool. Terry, with tears in his eyes, hugged him hard and handed him a check for ten million dollars and told him there was more and said something about there being no more excuses, that it was time for action. Emotionally exhausted, they sat down with their backs against the tree and said nothing, then fell asleep and dreamed of the old days in the late-morning sun.

Paul had dismissed high-priced, show-offy gas grills with no regrets. He was a charcoal man and probably always would be, and the steak and grilled potato that he put on Terry's plate discouraged all arguments to the contrary.

"You want to open a restaurant? You handle the menu. Anthony can design it. I'll put up the money. Do you think you can duplicate this in a restaurant? Oh, my God."

His taste buds were singing songs of joy. This was a soul food meal with light touches the likes of which Terry had never experienced anytime, anywhere. Paul, at the grill and sporting a NASA baseball cap, had just put a rib slathered in barbecue sauce on his NASA plate with a picture of one of the space shuttles. He drank beer, German, of course, from a NASA pilsner glass, and left a partially-smoked cigar in a NASA ashtray. That's what he got for leaving Paul alone in a gift shop. When Paul was strong enough, the Mars Brothers flew to Orlando on Terry's dime. Disney World and the Kennedy Space Center could bring anybody out of themselves. What a time they had.

He wanted to fill his mouth with more food, but savor little bites at the same time. The flavors came in waves; spice after spice, tender, marinated, charcoaled meat that made him want to holler 'Mama'! Creamy cole slaw, corn bread *and* buttery biscuits, grilled corn on the cob, too, that made him shake his head and moan 'Lord have mercy.' And red wine, too. And then more. Please make him stop. There was caramel-flavored cappuccino and rich chocolate layer cake with chocolate icing weighted down by chocolate ice cream and raspberry pieces that left him glad to be alive, on this day, with this man, who took advantage of his weakened state and beat him

THE REAL LIVES OF DREAMERS

in a game of chess, beat him so badly that Terry had to laugh a big, hearty laugh and throw up his hands with what little energy he had left. Then the finest nap a man could have, warmed by sunshine, music playing, floating away to Kenny Garrett and Sonny Fortune, yeah. She came back just as he faded away, defenseless after so long. Another meal. In Germany. Don't. Cordelia is coming. No use.

Terry and Lena sat at home, having dinner. Lena looked off into space, then sported a mischievous smile.

"I had a picture in my mind."

Terry smiled with his own mischief. "What kind of picture?"

"A very erotic picture."

"Can you paint this picture?"

"No, I cannot paint it. It must be lived."

"I see. Am I in this erotic picture?"

"No."

He sighed "Too bad." He paused and fixed her with his gaze, loving the game they were playing. "You are a terrible woman."

"Am I?"

"Yes. You are. The worst."

"The worst? The very worst?"

"Yes. The very worst. I am leaving you as soon as I finish this wonderful dinner."

She feigned a huff. "You may be mean, but you have good taste."

"Yes, I have good taste. And expensive tastes. Are you expensive?"

"I am very expensive."

"And do you taste good?"

BARRY NIX

"I am delicious. I have the best honey in the world." She thrust her nose in the air. "Hmph! You are leaving me. Why should you care?"

"I may be a fool, shautige, but I am not insane."

Lena opened her robe and exposed her otherwise nude body as she stood up with her wine glass and walked over to Terry. She looked in his eyes, pushed his chair to the side, and straddled him. She took a sip of wine and another one and let it dribble out of her mouth, down her neck and between her breasts, over her stomach, around her navel, and straight to her honeypot. She threw her head back and closed her eyes.

"Then taste me before you leave me, foolish man."

Terry kissed her neck and slowly licked at the wine, down her neck, over her shoulders, and toward her breasts. She threw her head back as her shoulders arched involuntarily.

"Oooh! Oooh! Taste me, baby. Taste me."

There was more to the dream, the memory. He had had it so many times. But it wouldn't come to him now.

He opened his eyes, pulled himself up, and reached over for his handheld computer on the table. In a few seconds Paul's poem was displayed on the tiny screen. He wrote it after it became obvious that Terry was in love and gave it to him. He didn't even have a copy. That's who Paul was, giving away things of value to himself, to be shared only with a few.

> Sated lovers lie
> Washed over by waves of joy
> Their breathing shallow, entwined

Sated lovers lie
their eyes closed
drifting to a cosmic beyond
their muscles, bone, and tissue
becoming one with the peace
for which their souls have searched
and found only with each other

Sated lovers lie
in the midst of forgotten crises
creating others with their love
knowing purity
dismissing the commonplace for now
aches and pains floating in a vapor above them
waiting to return until
sated lovers lie
no longer
sated

    While Terry was napping, Paul went inside to relieve himself. As he washed his hands, he looked in the mirror and saw himself smiling involuntarily. He hadn't been this happy in years. Terry was out cold. Anthony was on his way. He needed these men. He was through resisting help. He saw himself in many ways as a failure, but he could accept that now, joints perpetually stiff, muscles always sore, a head full of memories of unrequited love, dead compadres, and unfulfilled promises. He would find some measure of peace and go on. Ending life had suddenly lost its appeal, like Carolyn that day so many years ago. Why didn't he call her in South Carolina? She would have made a good wife. He remembered their last day together.

BARRY NIX

He wouldn't have thought about ending his life then, not while walking the hard streets with her, looking over his shoulder, wondering if he'd live through the day. He had lived so much life already and would be missed by only a few if he left it, but.....he would go on for now. He always had choices. That's why he had the little plastic bag full of almost-pure heroin in his nightstand drawer, so he could go out the right way, smiling and scratching, if he wanted to go.

And Helen, his love from the suburbs, before his family's fall from economic grace, before he was embarrassed to be found in an inner-city school by the father of yet another previous suburban girlfriend, Jacqueline, another beautiful, sweet, smart black girl. Her father was an English teacher who offered a warm, sympathetic smile and a pat on the shoulder, arranged to get him out of there to a public school a little farther out, where the kids at least could read near grade level. He who had been the only black child in his suburban Catholic school classes, and the smartest one in those classes from their integrated community, really the first of its kind in Bucks County, before the white girls approached puberty and the parents, almost apologetically, saw fit to move their families to more 'traditional' neighborhoods. But, yes, Helen, my Helen, so dark and alluring, beautiful with her glasses and her probing questions, her high standards. He tracked her down at Swarthmore years later, made love to her in her dorm room, came too fast, wanted more to prove he was a better lover than that, wanted to marry her, but had to go. There was a ride to catch. He was leaving town, on his way to somewhere, and had some deal, something to provide for his survival, but to leave her there crying, so sweet, God, it was more than he could take right now standing in front of a mirror with his stomach about to burst, and he sobbed for a long time, the tears as big as raindrops, but not hidden this time, because he felt he had been such a fool,

THE REAL LIVES OF DREAMERS

but had been powerless to be like everyone else and now he almost wanted to die again so he'd better clean himself up and get outside because his nightstand was only a few steps away.

He took some medication and felt better. This was hardly a day for depression. It was a glorious day, a dream cookout, a barbecue for dreamers. There was magic in his life.

Maybe he really had been lucky. One day, in deep thought after the day's classes, in his first college days, when he was about twenty, during his period of discovering bebop and progressive, Coltrane-influenced, spiritually uplifting jazz, he realized something important. This, of course, was before celebrity became an all-consuming passion for a nation weary of reality. He found that some of these musicians, in addition to Kant and Nietzche, Spinoza and DuBois, Martin and Malcolm, could articulate a philosophy by which he could live. He found affirmation, masculinity, intellectualism, eroticism, art, and deep humanity in their music. He was home. Wasn't that what had gotten him through it all?

Anthony arrived with Jennifer and Nancy, his former mother-in-law, and Mr. Turner. That old man could wear some clothes. He took to Nancy like a baby to a rattle. She blushed. Paul looked at Jennifer and at Anthony, laughed and teased Jennifer, good-naturedly, about her size.

"Damn, baby, you are plenty of woman! Wooh!" He looked at Anthony with that Paul look, that almost-Mulebone look.

"An-tho-ny! You know she must be jelly, 'cause jam don't shake like that!" Jennifer blushed while Anthony pretended to be offended, chased him around the yard as he celebrated to himself. Paul was back.

Jennifer playfully scolded Paul for making her violate her diet. She had already lost seven pounds. She had been looking forward to flying to Amsterdam with Anthony and Jimmy that night, but Anthony saw a look pass between her and Paul, a look beyond jelly and jam. Out of respect for him they avoided each other. It was a little too obvious. Anthony and his father looked at each other in silent conversation, pondering what to do. Jimmy Turner almost imperceptibly shook his head. Maybe it was just a powerful curiosity between those two, and maybe more. Who knew? Anthony thought of Belinda. During their time together, he dreamed of coming back to her as a mature man, unapologetic for his youth and lack of worldly experience. She had denied him that honor.

That Paul is some man, Jimmy Turner said to himself. And my son! That was right before he paid double for an extra ticket home. He was surprised. It didn't take much convincing for Nancy to join him. Yes, sir!

Nigel Wisniewski and Sharon, his administrator, whom he had brought, were caught messing around in one of the upstairs bedrooms.

Nicole didn't come. She had breathed a long sigh of relief and was packing her bags as Terry came to take her to the hospital following Paul's wake-up call. She said she was leaving, going away for a long time to clear her head. Terry hugged her hard and gave her a rather large check. She thanked him profusely and booked a flight to an exclusive resort on an island where Hollywood stars went to get away.

"Paul will understand," she said. Nigel breathed his own long sigh of relief.

Terry and Cordelia spent the night. By mid-afternoon of the next day, a Sunday, as they were preparing to leave, Terry walked around the house trying to make sense of all that had happened in the last few weeks. To further his confusion, Paul solicited his opinion on what must have been over a thousand pages of writing that he handed him in several wrinkled, stained, dog-eared manila folders and a large office records box. There were handwritten poems, wildly printed song lyrics, well-articulated essays, several rambling stories, even digital artworks and charcoal sketches. As far as he got through it in one morning, Terry found some of it amazingly insightful, some a bit obscure, almost all of it worthy of serious consideration. Twenty years of thinking. He was exhausted after a few hours. Could what he had read really be that good? He would get it to an editor friend the next morning. He didn't need any more surprises now, thank you.

Paul was in his bedroom wondering about the nightstand, thinking he couldn't stand to be alone with his thoughts again. He needed Nicole, but understood why she wasn't there. It was most likely over. He would find himself a black woman with shared cultural experiences. Yeah, sure. He panicked at the thought.

There were no more excuses for inaction. What should he do? What did he love? He sat down. Ruth Naomi Floyd's gospel jazz had transported him to another realm of thinking for a solid fifty minutes. Where was he? Yes, what to do now, what did he love? That was easy, music and art and film and photography and …….. whoa! Okay, music. And film? He had money now. He could open a jazz club, a chain of jazz clubs, and not care about making money, only about getting people to come and hear the music. Yeah. Yeah! He could produce shows by the artists who did so much for him. Yeah! Bring the music back to the people, down home, with plenty of rhythm and soul like in the sixties when cats like Stanley Turrentine and Grant Green and Herbie Mann were getting snubbed by the critics and receiving raves from the people. And the blues, of course. BB King and certain gospel, anything with real feeling. It was hip music, yeah! It had been done before, he knew, but maybe the technology could put a different slant on it. Of course it could. And films? How many good actors were out of work? Sheeeit! They'd die for a good script and a decent payday. All it took was organization and an eye for talent. Not having to worry about profits would be liberating. Maybe they could only sustain these ideas for a few years, but they would set the example, provide a new model, maybe. They could even play life-affirming hip-hop, hard as it was to find. Maybe, just maybe... Suddenly, there was a lot of work to do. Yeah! Terry would help him. He'd love to stretch out. The ideas came in waves. He felt like a surfer riding the big one, the best he'd felt in years. Yes, they had responsibilities. They could have fun, too, right? Yeah, baby! He heard the sportscaster Dick Vitale's voice, with a slight dialectical slant. 'Warm up the buses, mothafuckahs!'

Terry found Paul dancing around in a circle, listened to his ideas, and grew excited as hell. It was what he needed, Terry thought, a sense of purpose beyond making money, giving it away, and sitting on boards. They brainstormed excitedly. Hearing the commotion, Cordelia walked in with a big smile and hugged Paul. Terry called his assistant in from Jersey to help. Cordelia started a spread sheet, but she couldn't get the ideas down fast enough. Paul and Terry were like two fiends, whirling dervishes in another world, itching for Anthony to return, probably like the old days, she thought. They spent a couple of hours on the Internet conducting research and ordered several hundred dollars' worth of books and CD's. It would have to wait for a little while, though.

Paul caught his breath and went into the kitchen to grab some beers. He couldn't....well, yes, he could! They could! Terry's cell phone rang in the office as Paul threw some peppers, onions, and mushrooms in a frying pan with butter, minced garlic, and Worces-

THE REAL LIVES OF DREAMERS

tershire sauce. Terry walked into the kitchen as the vegetables lent the room their own fragrance. He looked serious, crisis-serious.

"That was Anthony. He needs our help. It's Luchesa. He's snapped."

Yet another reason to live a little longer, to not give up; a mission.

Paul stood up to his full height, his eyes clear, his mind instantly focused, looking and feeling in control again; yes, after so long, My God. He bellowed with authority, leaving no doubt as to his intentions. He was ready to go up that hill.

"Let's go!"